Holly ·

FOCUS

Professional photographer Dana Secrest has a secret and doesn't even know it. When she storms from her best friend's home on Christmas Eve—not the wisest decision she's ever made—security contractor Sam Galdicar follows her to save her from her own hot temper and impulsive action. Upon arriving home, Dana discovers her apartment has been ransacked. Then an attempt is made on her life. She doesn't know who's trying to kill her or why, but Sam is determined to protect the woman whose eyes don't need a camera to see the truth.

FOCUS

Published by
Hen House Publishing
Springfield, Ohio USA

ISBN: 9798639767388

To my husband, David, who believes in me.

Chapter 1

Dana

Dinnertime chatter about my photographic expedition to Palmisano Park faded into ritual gift-giving. White lights twinkled on the Christmas tree as I watched Sonya pull away the pretty wrapping paper, open the box, and pick up what at first glance resembled large, heavy chandelier earrings. They weren't earrings.

Fear flashed in her eyes, swiftly masked by a polite smile. I looked away and saw the lust glittering in her powerful, billionaire husband's eyes. He licked his lips in anticipation of using the bejeweled nipple clamps on his wife, who loved him too much to deny him anything, no matter how unreasonable, degrading, or humiliating. She loved him with a slavish devotion that brainwashed a normally intelligent woman into living a life as a sex slave. The red leather collar she wore testified to that.

And, just like that, I'd had enough.

"No," I growled as I half-rose and leaned across the dining room table to swipe the box from her hands. My tight grip crushed the sturdy cardboard. As I settled back into the chair, my voice strengthened and I focused my anger upon him. "No, you selfish prick. You will not use these on her."

He glared at me, surprise morphing into anger. I wanted to wince, but held my ground against the much bigger and imposing man.

"How dare you!" Bradley Vermont snarled, using the domineering voice that cowed his employees, colleagues, business associates, and Sonya. She ducked her head and cringed, waiting for the punishment he meted out regularly in their master-and-slave relationship. What little I'd witnessed of their hardcore BDSM lifestyle made my stomach churn, although Sonya swore that Brad loved her, took care of her, and gave her indescribable pleasure alongside the pain.

"I dare because your wife, the woman you vowed to care for and protect, wears bruises that never heal. Because your wife is pregnant and her body is extra-sensitive, and you care only for your own filthy pleasure!"

My chair screeched across the floor as I jumped to my feet. I threw the damaged box across the table at him and yelled, "If you cared as much for Sonya as you do for your designer shoes, you'd see that she's terrified of you! She hurts, damn it!" I reached over and grabbed my coat. "You disgust me. I hope she comes to her senses and divorces your ass."

Not going so far as to spit upon him—although the temptation beckoned—I swiveled on my heel and stomped out.

"Dana!" Sonya cried, her voice soft and filled with tears.

I stopped, but didn't turn to look at my oldest and dearest friend. "If you have any self-respect left, Sonya, you'll leave this jerk. He's done nothing but abuse and brainwash you and call it love. You deserve better than him."

I saw myself from the luxurious penthouse, wiping my eyes on my sleeves. The winter wind whipped around me as I buttoned my coat in mid-stride. I'd gone an entire block before realizing that I'd left without my purse and camera case.

Damned if I would go back to beg for it.

So, I walked, fingers curled inside my coat pockets, occasionally tapping the zippers to the interior pockets where I stashed recently exposed rolls of film. Yes, I used film. I *liked* film. Without money for a taxi, I was in for a long, cold, exhausting night. Luckily, the property owner of my apartment kept spare keys to each residence and would let me in. The catch was that I just had to cross half a city without being run over by a drunk driver or getting mugged.

Not for the first time, I regretted the choice to move to Chicago. I ruminated over my freelance business and thought that I'd managed to accumulate enough in savings to tide me over for a few lean months. I was earning enough to move back home to St. Paris, a minute speck of a village in southwest Ohio. I'd grown up in St. Paris, where the still-depressed economy hadn't recovered like most of the nation and property values were low. I could buy or rent a place for less than I paid for my cheap apartment in the big city.

And breathe clean air.

A hand landed on my shoulder and spun me around. I gasped, shrieked, and struck out with both fists. Unfortunately, I'd never learned how to fight properly, so my assailant had little trouble avoiding my wild blows and restraining me.

"Where in the hell do you think you're going?" Sam Galdicar growled as I struggled against his grip.

"Let me go, you goon," I growled back at the big, burly bodyguard to handsome, occasionally charming, and always domineering gazillionaire Bradley Vermont. His hands tightened and I sneered, "Or are you going to beat me like Brad beats Sonya?"

Either the words or the withering tone had the desired effect and he released me. I stumbled a step, turned around, and resumed walking.

"He doesn't beat her," Sam said as he fell into step beside me.

"Like hell, he doesn't," I retorted and muttered a profanity that insulted the man's parentage and character and would have resulted in my mouth being washed out with soap if Dad were around to hear the vile words.

"He doesn't isolate her from her friends and family," he added, trying to soften my harsh opinion without success. "If he did, you'd never see her."

We stopped at a crosswalk. I glanced at him. With his butter colored hair, square jaw, and cleft chin, he didn't offend a woman's eyes. His masculinity was rugged rather than pretty.

"No, he doesn't need iron bars and locked doors. He's sufficiently cowed her enough that she's afraid to do *anything* without his explicit approval. He's sucked the will from her. She doesn't think anything beyond what he wants her to think. She says no word he has not approved and given her permission to use. She eats nothing but what he feeds her with his own hands." I cast him a hot glare. "Does that sound like a healthy, consensual relationship between adults? I don't think so."

Sam sighed. "Dana, Brad needs control."

"Hah. Brad needs *therapy*, medication, and a swift kick in the ass," I retorted as the light turned and I stepped off the curb.

"Dana, where in the hell do you think you're going?"

"I'm going home."

"You live eight miles across town," he pointed out.

"So, go back home if you're too weak to walk," I sneered and wished I'd either not forgotten my purse and camera

case or that I'd worn footwear more appropriate to an evening hike across the city in winter. My feet in their kidskin
ballet flats and nylon tights were freezing. I would have
preferred a ride in a warm taxi.

He grabbed my arm again. I spun around on a patch of
ice and clutched at him to keep from falling. Sam steadied
me and I slapped at his arm.

"It'll take you four hours to get home if you don't freeze
to death by then or wind up a crime victim," he pointed
out.

I slapped his arm again. That time he released me.

"Look, dickwad—" city living had really downgraded
my vocabulary, another reason to move back to a rural village where manners tended toward that famed Midwestern civility "—if you want to escort me, I can't stop you.
But I am *not* going back there."

Sam sighed. I started walking again, albeit a little more
carefully due to the icy patches on the sidewalk. He fell
into step beside me. I pulled up the collar of my wool coat
and hunched my shoulders, shoving my hands as deeply as
possible in the pockets. Damn, I should have worn gloves.
And lined woolen pants with wool socks and boots. And a
hat. Oh, hell, I shouldn't have stormed out of there without
my belongings.

He held his silence for the next umpteen blocks, for
which I told myself I was grateful. My breath puffed in
white clouds as I hurried, despite knowing that a steady
pace would have been more prudent to cover the distance. The temperature sank like a stone and I shivered as
I walked. Although I clenched my jaw, I couldn't help the
chatter of my teeth. A taxi rolled by, its wheels crunching
on dirty snow and ice.

"Dana, you're freezing," he declared.

"I know," I managed without stuttering.

"You've got to stop and warm up."

Casting him a quick glance of intense dislike, I said, "Unless you've got a hot bath, a warm bed, a hot meal, and a fresh change of clothes tucked away in your pocket, I've got to keep going."

A few steps more and his hand again clamped around my arm and yanked me to a stop.

"This is getting old," I grumbled.

He pulled a key from his pocket and smiled at me. "Everything you demanded is right here."

"What?" Apparently, the cold had turned my brain into icy slush.

"I live three blocks over. You're coming home with me."

"No."

He grinned at me. I wanted to swat that grin off his face, but shivered too violently for decent aim. Of course, I told myself, his height—fully a foot taller than mine—had nothing to do with it.

"Bath, bed, food, and clothes are just three blocks over. Now keep your word."

My jaw would have dropped, but I was concentrating too hard on clenching.

"Damned, stubborn woman," he muttered and, with a grunt, scooped me up.

"Hey!"

"Quit squirming, Dana."

I bucked and squirmed, but he didn't put me down.

"I'll put you over my shoulder if you don't stop it right now," he threatened.

"Asshole," I muttered with resentment and a stunning lack of originality. But I stopped struggling.

"Shrew," he grumbled.

I leaned my head against him and said nothing. At least he hadn't called me a bitch. The use of "shrew" made me wonder if he'd ever read Shakespeare. I shook my head. Yep, my brain had obviously turned to slush if I had the lack of focus to contemplate Sam's literary preferences.

The three blocks passed beneath his long-legged, surefooted stride. The doorman to his apartment complex didn't blink an eye as Sam carried me through the door. I wondered if Sam carrying a woman through the door occurred regularly, or if the doorman just didn't care enough to inquire. Neither option reassured me, although the blast of warm air in the lobby felt altogether too wonderful.

Sam carried me into the elevator. I started squirming again.

"Put me down, Sam."

"No."

His arms tightened and I subsided.

"Okay, you've demonstrated that you're bigger and stronger than I. I'm properly impressed. Now, will you put me down?"

He huffed a sigh that bespoke long suffering. I didn't buy it.

"I promise to behave," I said as the elevator rose.

He chuckled in my ear and replied, "Don't make promises you can't or won't keep, Dana."

It was my turn to exhale a sigh.

The elevator gently slowed and stopped. The doors slid open and Sam carried me down a corridor. He stopped in front of a nondescript door and I thought he'd have to put me down to use his keys.

I thought wrong.

He carried me into his apartment and straight back to his bedroom. With a grunt, he settled me on the bed, rather than just dropping me.

"Stay put," he ordered, pulled off his gloves, and stuffed them in his coat pockets. He turned around to rummage through his dresser drawers.

Damned if I would. I scooted off the bed and stood. Or I tried to stand. But my frozen legs buckled and the rest of my body seized, toppling me to the carpeted floor in an ungraceful heap.

"Don't you ever do as you're told?" he demanded and hauled me up, settling me on the bed again.

"I don't follow orders blindly," I said.

"And I don't give them without reason." He bent down and began unbuttoning my coat.

"What do you think you're doing?"

"You wanted a hot bath, remember?"

"You are *not* going to undress me," I protested.

One corner of his mouth lifted in a knowing, superior, mocking smirk that I wanted to slap off his face. "Do you think your hands will work?"

"Give me a few minutes. They'll thaw out."

He shook his head as though bemused by my unreasonable behavior. "Dana, it'll be a miracle if your hands and feet aren't frostbitten. Let me take care of you."

With as much dignity as I could muster, which wasn't much, I replied, "I'm a big girl, Sam. I can undress and wash myself."

He sighed and straightened to his full, impressive height. "The tub takes five minutes to fill. If you're not in there within five minutes, then you'll let me take care of you."

So saying, he turned on his heel and disappeared into the *ensuite* bathroom without waiting for my consent. He emerged a moment later.

Over the sound of rushing water in the background I asked, "Why?"

His expression grew bleak, then sad. He sighed again and replied in a low voice, "Because you're right about them."

I clamped my jaws shut before I could blurt something rude and offensive. Samuel Galdicar didn't agree with me often, much less admit to my being right about anything. I needed to savor the moment, not crush it with a sarcastic remark. So, I nodded and brought my icy hands to the next button on my coat and held them there. He just looked at me for another few seconds, then left the room, shutting the door behind him with a soft *click*.

I silently cursed my useless, frozen hands. My fingers would not bend, much less manipulate buttons. The joints began to ache horribly and I realized that, yes, I had at least a case of frostnip, if not frostbite. The pain increased as my hands began to thaw, every knuckle feeling as though a hammer had been taken to the joint. Tears flowed unheeded down my cheeks as I struggled to undress. I managed to remove my coat, but then came the struggle to grip the zipper on my wool dress. In my exasperation, I didn't realize Sam came back until his large, warm hands settled over my still chilled ones, startling me.

"Let me," he said softly.

I slumped in defeat and let my arms drop. The quiet slide of the zipper competed with my sniffles of self-pity and pain. I heard a quick, sharp inhale as my dress slid off my shoulders and down my body to puddle on the floor. With deft efficiency, Sam removed my slip, bra, shoes, tights, and panties. My cheeks burned as I refused to meet his gaze, turning my head and closing my eyes because I did not want to see what he thought of me.

"Into the tub with you," he said softly and put his hand at the base of my back, adding guiding pressure to steer me forward. As I walked, pain bloomed in my feet as delicate joints protested the warming of the flesh there, too. A moment later, I stood dumbly beside the deep tub as he turned off the water.

"Can you get in by yourself?" he asked.

Tears streaming down my cheeks, I shook my head.

"It's okay, kitten. I'll help."

He scooped me up and slowly descended to his knees before lowering me into the hot water. My hands and feet screamed with agony upon immersion and I wept openly, the combined pain being more than anything I'd ever suffered.

"I know it hurts, honey," he soothed as he scooped water and poured it over my shoulders.

Helpless as a baby, I let him bathe me.

Chapter 2

Sam

Dana Secrest, best friend of billionaire Bradley Vermont's wife Sonya, never knew how much maintaining a clinical, professional demeanor cost me as I undressed and bathed her. With iron determination, I ignored the aching demand in my loins and the pain of the zipper imprinting itself on my dick as she shivered and wept from the pain of thawing hands and feet. I wanted this smart, talented woman badly—I had for years—but she was off-limits, and I refused to take advantage of her helplessness.

My employer, that same Bradley Vermont, called me cold-blooded after I neutralized a shooter in his office building before the disgruntled ex-employee could take down other coworkers. My former colleagues in the Marines called me the Iceman because I never lost my cool control, no matter how hot and fast the lead flew around us in whatever hellhole the government sought to set our boots. Nothing, really, had demonstrated any power to stir my blood, except this opinionated, pigheaded firecracker of a woman whose photographic art hung in my office. I'd praised her work more than once to my family.

It didn't help that she was right about Bradley and Sonya. My client was too rough with the woman, especially now that she was pregnant. He'd not learned the difference between dominant and domineering, and if he'd discovered the limits of his masochist, as a proper sadist should, he certainly did not heed them. I hadn't thought it too terrible until that night's explosion when I realized I needed to risk my job and have a candid discussion with Bradley about his wife's recurring injuries.

I knew he loved her. I knew she loved him. But what they had together was toxic. Dana was right, as much as I loathed to admit it. She'd seen what I had not wanted to see, and shone the harsh brilliance of truth upon it. In my years of service as Bradley Vermont's personal bodyguard and head of security, we'd become friends, which meant I spent a lot of time with Sonya and, therefore, Dana, her best and probably only friend. That woman and I butted heads more often than not.

I'd come to true manhood in service to my country, protecting the weak. My failure to protect Sonya shamed me, even though I was employed to protect her husband. Kissing the last three years of lucrative employment goodbye was going to hurt.

Speaking of kissing …

Dana slumped in the tub, leaning her forehead on her knees as I continued to lather and rinse the softest, silkiest skin my hands had ever touched. She sniffled, but at least those gut-wrenching sobs had ceased. She truly cared for her friend's well being.

"Do you think you can stand?" I asked, my voice husky with ruthlessly restrained lust.

She sighed and nodded.

"Let me help you."

She allowed me to take her hands and raise her to her feet. I put her wet hands on my shoulders to give her something to cling to while I pulled a towel off the towel bar and wrapped it around her. Without waiting for her to lift her leg, I swept her into my arms and lifted her from the tub. She gasped in surprise, but did not protest. She had apparently learned the futility of that.

I carried her into the bedroom and set her on the edge of the bed. "Stay put, Dana."

She sniffed, but stayed while I took out an old tee shirt from a drawer and plucked a comb from atop the bureau. The rustling of cloth told me she'd taken the initiative to dry off her body. Pity. I'd hoped to do that. I turned around and she held the towel up to hide her exquisite body from my gaze as though I hadn't already seen and touched everything.

I handed her the shirt, "Here, put this on."

She clamped the towel to her chest with one arm and reached with the other to take the shirt. "Turn around, Sam."

I stood there and grinned, enjoying her discomfiture. It wasn't nice of me.

"Please," she whispered.

I turned my back to her and wished I'd thought to install a mirror above the bureau.

"Okay," she said in a dull voice when she was ready.

I turned around and felt a possessive sort of satisfaction at seeing her wearing nothing but my shirt, clothed in only what I gave her. But her dull expression issued no invitation.

"You'll sleep here tonight," I said.

Her hazel eyes narrowed with suspicion. "And where will you sleep?"

"Here. It's my bed."

She struggled to her feet. "I can sleep on the sofa."

I shook my head. "You'll do no such thing. You're still chilled through."

"I don't trust you, Sam."

I blinked in surprise. Her distrust infuriated me, but I admired her forthright honesty. Looking into her eyes, however, I saw fear. That alone stayed any angry words. Putting a finger under her chin and tilting her face to meet my gaze, I said, "I've already seen and touched you and I didn't molest you, now did I? Trust me, Dana. I won't do anything you don't want."

"Hah."

I laughed, since we both knew I'd already done several things she hadn't wanted, all to protect her from the consequences of her impulsive decisions.

"I'm not having sex with you, Sam."

I enjoyed the fiery blush that spread up her neck and face. She continued to hold my gaze, even though fine tremors of fear rippled through her body. Uncertainty flashed across her face.

"I don't force women," I replied. We both knew I didn't have to force women into my bed. "I'll take care of you and make sure you get back home tomorrow, safe and sound and still untouched."

Her blush deepened.

Oh, shit, I'd hit a nerve.

"How old are you, Dana?"

"Er ... twenty-five."

"And you're still a virgin, aren't you?" I tried to whisper, but my voice rasped instead.

She averted her gaze, taking her chin from my light hold. I held my silence and placed my palm against her cheek, applying just enough pressure to compel her to meet my eye again. "Aren't you?"

"It's called self-respect," she whispered. "Sex is too ... too intimate to be casual about it."

Understanding dawned. "And you've yet to find a man worthy of giving yourself to?"

She nodded and wrenched her face away from my touch again. The old-fashioned—dared I say quaint?—attitude charmed me. I'd always favored experienced women, but the thought of being a woman's—*this* woman's—one and only lover ignited inside my brain and spread like wildfire through my body. I determined at that instant that I would be the man to whom she gave herself and I also decided that she'd never give herself to anyone else.

Dana Secrest was *mine*, even if she didn't know it yet.

Chapter 3

Dana

Tired of being manhandled, tired of butting heads with the stubborn man, and just *tired*, I let Sam install me into his bed. I shivered. The bath helped, but it hadn't thawed the bone-deep chill that made me wonder if I'd ever be warm again. I clenched my jaws to keep from moaning with pleasure when the mattress behind me dipped and Sam's burly arms pulled me into the heat of his body. The coarse hair of his muscular thighs cradling my bare thighs made me shiver again with unwanted awareness. He wasn't wearing pajamas and I wore nothing beneath the oversized tee shirt he'd loaned me for the night.

"Relax and go to sleep, Dana," he murmured into my hair, the moist heat of his breath stirring the strands. "You're safe."

The truth ringing in his voice reassured me. Safety was Sam's job: he wouldn't lie about that. Exhaustion pulled at me and with the last of my consciousness, I remembered my manners and whispered, "Thank you."

His low chuckle was the last thing I heard until morning.

I awoke to the rich fragrance of coffee and inhaled deeply of the beckoning scent. My stomach rumbled. Blinking against the allure of going back to sleep, I remembered that I wasn't sleeping in my bed. Feeling a distinct lack of trust and then guilt for lacking that trust, I took a quick inventory of my body as I lay alone in the big bed. My heartbeat calmed with the acknowledgment that my body sported no suspicious wetness, stickiness, or tenderness. Sitting up and brushing my hair back with my hands, I decided I owed the big lug an apology as well as a big dose of gratitude.

I headed to the adjoining master bathroom for the usual reasons and hissed at the messy tangle of curly hair. *I shouldn't have gone to bed with it wet.* Despite the enduring fashion of long, flowing locks, I kept my dark, curly hair at a manageable length, a short cut that proved easy to style and maintain with regular visits to the stylist. Past boyfriends said it complimented my cheekbones.

Unfortunately, brushing out the tangles simply wasn't an option. *Ah, a comb!* Taking an extra few minutes, I ducked my head under the spigot in the tub to drench my hair and used a hand towel to pat it dry. I picked up Sam's comb and began the tedious process of combing out the tangles. With short hair, it didn't take long. When my hair air-dried, I'd look a bit like an overgrown poodle, but at least the curls wouldn't be a frizzy mess.

I looked at yesterday's clothing with distaste. At some point Sam had folded the items neatly and left them on the bedside chair, but I wasn't particularly enthusiastic about putting on yesterday's underwear. However, neither was I all that happy to go commando. I sighed and adopted that stiff upper lip of stoic endurance the British use to face life's little hardships, because I knew I would have the opportunity to change into fresh clothing as soon as Sam took me home.

"Dana, do you want two or three eggs?" he called through the bathroom door.

Startled, I stammered, "I—uh—I—"

"Get dressed, woman," he ordered. "After breakfast, I'll take you home."

"Be there in a minute," I replied, unable to prevent the hot blush that spread across my face and neck. With a moue of distaste, I donned yesterday's clothing and left last night's tee shirt neatly folded on the chair.

Somehow he knew when I opened the bathroom door, because he called out at just the right second, "Kitchen. Now."

I followed the smell of coffee, fried eggs, and toast. My belly rumbled in anticipation. The apartment, not as extravagant as I might have expected, proved no difficulty to navigate. At my appearance, Sam set two plates on the kitchen table, a dark-stained vintage Hepplewhite. The old-fashioned, simple elegance of the style surprised me, smashing yet another preconception I had of him. Bradley Vermont's taste ran toward ornate Baroque. I belatedly noticed one more difference between their two domiciles: Sam's apartment wasn't decorated for the holiday.

He directed a quick glance at me, surely noting every detail, and said, "Take a seat. Coffee?"

"Please," I replied and obeyed. "And thank you. You're being very kind and I appreciate it."

A small smile touched the corners of his mouth at my careful politeness. I lifted the glass of orange juice to my mouth and sipped.

"Sorry I don't have grapefruit juice," he murmured as he settled a mug of coffee beside my plate then seated himself.

"This is lovely and beyond expectations," I replied and wondered how he knew I preferred grapefruit juice.

He lifted his fork and said, "Dig in."

I dug in and judged his cooking as competent, nowhere near the level of my dad's, but then *nobody's* cooking matched his. Mom's culinary skill didn't extend much further than following the instructions on a box of macaroni and cheese. The son of two celebrity chefs, Dad taught me everything I knew about a kitchen. Unfortunately, I lacked his creativity with food.

After shoveling a few bites down his gullet, he asked, "Okay?"

"Yes, it's fine," I replied.

He gave me another small smile. "Not as good as yours."

"How would you know that?"

"Sonya shares your cookies," he replied.

I sniffed. "Cooking and baking differ."

"Really?"

I frowned and pointed my fork at him. "Are you *trying* to start an argument with me?"

Sam leaned back and took a swallow of coffee. The mug didn't hide his grin. Setting the mug down, he replied, "You're easy to rile. It's fun."

I sighed. "I suppose you have a dossier on me and know pretty much everything about me."

"Of course," he replied. "I'm extremely good at what I do."

"And so am I," I retorted. For an insane second, I wished I had my camera so I could capture him: *The Arrogant Male at Breakfast.* With that square jaw, those twinkling eyes, and that proud expression, he would have made a fortune gracing the covers of romance novels. I could see him doing particularly well garbed in period costume.

"Do you have any tattoos?" I asked.

His eyebrows went up, a sign that my question had surprised him. I wanted to preen at the accomplishment. Then his small smile broadened and his gaze turned sultry.

"Wanna see them?"

I kept my cool demeanor and met his gaze without melting. "There's a studio in the city that specializes in custom cover art for a couple of the big publishers. If you're looking for a side gig, you'd do well as a cover model."

"You think I'm handsome?"

I huffed. "You *know* you're pretty."

"Pretty?" he echoed, looking offended.

"Pretty," I said with a curt nod, pleased to have disconcerted him. He wasn't the only one who could needle someone. I'd die before admitting that he made Henry Cavill look like a troll.

"I don't need a 'side gig,'" he muttered under his breath.

Having taken a glimpse of the apartment (modest, but in an expensive part of the city), his furnishings (simple elegance, high quality), and wardrobe (those bespoke suits I always saw him wearing), I knew he wasn't hurting for money. I did wonder what kind of car he drove, since anytime I saw him getting out of a vehicle, it was to precede Bradley's exit from a limousine. The reminder of Sam's closeness to my best friend's husband doused my small, wicked pleasure in having needled him.

With a sigh, I finished eating and carried my plate, juice glass, coffee mug, and silverware to the sink. "Where do you keep the dishwashing detergent?"

"You don't need to wash the dishes, Dana."

"Of course, I do. You cooked, now I'll clean."

"Just stick them in the dishwasher."

I shook my head. "Those don't clean as well as washing them by hand."

"Dana." His voice took on a warning note.

"Sam," I mimicked in the same tone. Then I took a deep breath. "Look, you did me a huge favor last night. I wasn't as grateful as I should have been and I want to make up for it, at least a little bit. Let me repay your kindness by washing the dishes."

"You're not in my debt, Dana."

"Of course, I am. I acted rashly, rushing outside because I lost control of my temper. I'd probably be frozen in a ditch somewhere or a victim of a mugging if you hadn't come after me. I'm not so proud that I can't admit I was stupid."

"You were impulsive," he agreed as he rose from the table and carried his breakfast dishes to the countertop. "But you lost your temper because you care. You had the balls to confront Bradley about the way he treats Sonya."

"Intestinal fortitude," I corrected under my breath.

He grinned at me. "Don't like dirty talk?"

I preferred not to answer that taunt and deflected his impertinent question, "The dishwashing liquid?"

He reached beneath the cabinet under the sink and brought out a bottle of Palmolive, the same brand my mother preferred.

"Washcloth? Dish towel?"

He extracted those from a nearby drawer and handed them to me.

"Shoo. I got this," I said and waved him away.

Instead of wandering to some other room, he returned to his chair at the kitchen table and watched me wash dishes, including the nonstick, ceramic-coated aluminum skillet in which he fried the eggs. I did my best to ignore him, but his steady regard stirred my blood and made my skin tingle. He rejoined me at the counter and, as I dried off each item, put them away, a place for each item and each item returned to its place. *Tidy. Organized.*

"You ready?" he asked as I dried my hands and folded the dish towel, setting it on the countertop.

"Yeah. You know where I live?"

He raised an eyebrow and reminded me, "Dossier, remember?"

Oh, yeah.

"Get your coat on. We'll take my car."

"If you lend me your phone, I'll call an Uber."

"You left your purse at Bradley's, remember."

I sighed. *Damn it.* "My camera case, too."

"I'll take you back to Bradley's to collect your things, then I'll drive you home." Seeing my discomfiture, he took pity on me. "You won't have to see them. I'll fetch your stuff."

"Thank you, Sam."

I meant it, too, because in the three years we'd known each other, I'd not realized that broad, muscled chest concealed a kind heart.

Chapter 4

Sonya

Every muscle hurt as I rolled over. The swollen tissues between my thighs throbbed with a delicious ache that reminded me of the extreme pleasure my husband routinely delivered. But even that ache couldn't drown the soreness of new bruises and the red welts striping my back, buttocks, and upper thighs. Putting one hand protectively over the baby bump thickening my formerly trim waistline, I stretched out my hand to feel cool silk, which meant that Bradley had already left for work.

The feeling of relief that washed through me made me cringe, which aggravated the aforementioned aches and pains. I wanted to take a couple of aspirin or ibuprofen, but dared not. Bradley had forbidden me access to any painkillers or alcohol or any number of things that non-pregnant women took for granted. Disobedience had consequences. I was never quite sure how he knew the things he knew, but suspected he had cameras spying upon me. I knew the household staff and security personnel reported to him.

I couldn't linger long in bed. Not only did my bladder demand relief, but a quick glance at the alarm clock on my husband's nightstand informed me that I needed to get moving if I were to make it to church on time. For all his restrictions, Bradley put none on my faith and even encouraged me to attend worship services. He'd decided which church I attended to ensure I associated with the correct congregation of the preferred socioeconomic stratum, but put no impediment on the actual practice of faith. I relished that small freedom.

After a shower, careful application of cosmetics, and styling my hair, I donned a conservative dress that cost more than the wages I'd earned in my entire first year of employment as a teenager working for a fast food restaurant. After four years with Bradley—three as his wife—I'd come to accept such outrageously expensive garments with accompanying jewelry as normal.

It made me wonder just how badly I'd lost touch with reality, especially when I saw my best—and only—friend, Dana, hustle for photography gigs to pay for rent, groceries, and film. I knew the lifestyle I lived wasn't normal, despite the reams of popular literature exploring the subculture of wealth and kink.

Slipping my feet into designer shoes to match my designer dress, I headed to the kitchen where Pierre, our French chef, bade me sit. I obeyed and waited for him to serve me whatever he'd decided to prepare for breakfast. I once had the audacity to request a simple breakfast of scrambled eggs and toast. That didn't end well, and my ass burned for the next two days after the paddling I received for having upset Bradley's expensive chef.

Cognizant of a pregnant woman's delicate stomach, Pierre took pity on me and served fresh croissants with melon balls and lightly sweetened tea. I had no idea where he acquired such lusciously ripe honeydew and cantaloupe in the middle of winter, but I greatly appreciated it.

After breakfast, one of Sam's cadre of bodyguards snapped into place beside me as I headed out.

"Good morning, Gordon."

"Good morning, ma'am." He flashed me a polite and empty smile as he escorted me to the lobby where a limousine waited just beyond tall glass doors framed in heavy brass. "Church this morning?"

"As usual," I replied and slid into the spacious back seat of the vehicle. He sat in front with the driver.

I left the partition down, again as usual. Long ago, I learned to assume that everything I did or said was either recorded or reported to Bradley, even within the confines of the limousine. The partition was merely fakery imparting a false sense of privacy. I let my gaze wander from the window separating me from the common folk outside, to my lap where my gloved hands rested in a loose grip, to Gordon's broad shoulders and the back of his head.

I dared not let my eyes rest too long on any one thing, especially any man. If I admired a thing for too long, Bradley bought it for me whether or not I actually wanted it. Somehow, I'd yet to convince him that just because I admired something didn't mean I wanted to possess it. Bradley obviously didn't comprehend the concept of window shopping. When I'd once allowed my gaze to linger a smidgen too long on a man, that man subsequently found himself unemployed, discredited, and utterly ruined for having done nothing more than receive a handsome combination of genetic material.

The limousine stopped in front of the church, a grandiose affair of soaring columns and marble to rival any Roman Catholic cathedral. Dana sometimes teased me about that. Regardless, I enjoyed looking at the stained glass illuminated by sunshine streaming through, the graceful lines of vaulted ceilings, and the golden accents of brass candlesticks. Although the church was plain and spare compared to papist construction, I found nothing to protest in this house of God. It all pleased my eye.

Gordon escorted me into the church and sat in the pew behind me, ever watchful. I slid in next to a prominent politician's wife and their two teenage daughters. She welcomed me with a friendly smile before shushing her children who gossiped about their classmates. Mean girls.

The processional hymn began with a stirring ripple of music from the band. The wealthy parish paid for professional musicians and singers rather than rely upon the vagaries of volunteers. I'd once enjoyed singing in the church choir; now that opportunity was forbidden. Discontent nibbled at the edges of my carefully composed serenity.

Reverend Howard J. Blankenship walked to the pulpit, singing with the choir. His bald brown pate gleamed beneath the chandeliers. His strong baritone, amplified by a discrete microphone, rose above the choir's song, complementing it. He faced the congregation and waited until the hymn ended before launching into that Sunday's service featuring a long reading from the Bible and a much longer sermon on what it meant and how it related to our lives. He always included a small history lesson, careful to put the Bible's words into the context of the contemporaries who wrote the books. This Sunday he spoke of spousal obligation, which I thought an odd topic for Christmas morning.

"The Roman church has done us a favor!" he shouted.

Audible gasps rose from the congregation.

"Yes, a *favor*! They undertook a word-for-word translation of the holy scriptures using the words as originally written. This impacts our understanding of Ephesians, chapter 5, verse 22, which says, 'For wives, this means submit to your husbands as to the Lord. For a husband is the head of his wife as Christ is the head of the church. He is the Savior of his body, the church. As the church submits to Christ, so you wives should submit to your husbands in everything.'

"Does this mean what we have been taught? No! Because the words we learned do not mean what the original authors intended. Instead of *submit*, the word should be *subordinate*. What that means is that husbands and wives should bow to the wisdom and need of the other. Where a woman has greater wisdom, her husband should recognize and acknowledge his lack and follow her guidance and example. Where a man has greater wisdom, his wife should recognize and acknowledge her lack and obey him."

Rev. Blakenship paused to take a drink of water.

"This is the most misconstrued and abused passage in the Bible!" he thundered, emphasizing the point by pounding his fist on the railing. Sitting in the front pew, I saw the gentle sway of his wife's and mother's hats as they nodded in agreement. "The Bible does not order men to *make* their wives obey! The Bible instructs men to love and respect their wives. The Bible gives no man the authority to oppress, punish, or retaliate against his wife for her disobedience. Men, in fact, are directed to greater obedience than are women: men, 'Love your wives as Christ loved the church.'"

I swallowed as his words struck me to the core. The debacle of Christmas Eve dinner flashed through my mind, as did Dana's exhortations to save myself. I bit the inside of my cheek and tasted blood. Intent swelled within me, a sudden and desperate need to escape. But how could I escape my bodyguard? How could I get free of Bradley's control? Doubts assailed me. I looked down to find my hands clasped tightly together, the knuckles white. I forced myself to relax them. Irony flooded me at the realization that Bradley had indeed taught me control. There was no way that Gordon or anyone else could detect the storm of emotion and new determination flooding through me.

The pastor's oratory wandered into examples of foolish husbands who suffered the consequences of denying their wives' wisdom and more examples of women who suffered greatly from their husbands' oppression of them. Some of the examples were taken from history, others from current news headlines. In each case, he made the point that husbands and wives ought to seek each other's joy and well being.

My mind raced. I thought of the lavish and often exquisite gifts Bradley gave me when all I wanted was his time, time spent in places other than the bedroom or the dungeon where he kept the equipment he enjoyed using on me with or without my consent. As the reverend continued, I reflected on how I'd quickly learned to consent from a position of fear rather than from a position of pleasure.

Oh, my husband could and usually did deliver exquisite, blinding, toe-curling pleasure. But it came with pain and humiliation. I fingered the thin white collar around my throat. It felt far too tight.

The politician's wife next to me caught sight of my small movement with a mother's eagle eye and reached over to clasp my other hand. I glanced at her and she returned a look of sympathy and understanding. She knew what that collar meant and seemed to suspect that I no longer accepted my position as submissive slave to my husband's dominance. *You are not alone*, her eyes seemed to say.

I dared not look back at Gordon. He'd never looked upon me with anything other than stoic professionalism even on the occasion when he'd wordlessly offered me a jar of arnica cream to help soothe my bruises. I'd used up the small jar's contents two months ago.

The service finally concluded with another rousing hymn. Rev. Blankenship took his usual winter position inside the vestibule where he didn't have to bear the full brunt of the cold weather as he greeted congregation members on their way out. He shook hands with all, hugged some, engaged in brief conversations with many. Obediently, I rose and took my place in the line of worshippers leaving the church. Gordon went ahead to wait for me just outside the front doors where I was expected to walk down the marble steps and slide into the waiting limousine just as I did every other Sunday morning.

When my turn came to greet the pastor, I squeezed his hand and whispered, "Help me. *Please.*"

Eyes narrowing, Rev. Blakenship did not release my hand. His smile faded and he whispered. "Is your choker too tight?"

I nodded as tears welled in my eyes and overflowed.

"Suzanne," he called out in a low, urgent tone. His wife snapped to his side and he transferred my hand to hers. "This lamb requires shelter."

"Sanctuary," I murmured, knowing that while many churches still practiced sanctuary, it held no legal force.

Suzanne Blankenship, pastor's wife and southern transplant, responded with a wide smile and an invitation to join her in the kitchen.

"Why, I remember when I was pregnant with my fourth child. Nothing but tomato juice would curb my nausea. Today, I can't tolerate the taste!" she babbled as she led me back through the church and into the adjoining parsonage.

I wondered how long Gordon would wait before he started searching for me. I wondered how persistent he would be before dragging me back to Bradley.

Suzanne sat me down in her cozy kitchen and poured me a glass of milk. "Y'all need calcium."

I found my finger again running underneath the edge of the collar.

"You want me to unfasten that vile thing?"

I nodded, unable to speak, unable to bring myself to remove it. She moved behind me and her warm fingers quickly unfastened the clasp that my clumsy fingers dared not touch. Bradley allowed me to put on a collar to coordinate with my outfits, but never allowed me to take one off. Suzanne dropped the collar on the table.

"Would you like to talk about it, woman to woman?"

I opened my mouth, but the words wouldn't come. A door slammed open and I flinched. Heavy footsteps resounded on the wooden floors until they stopped on the kitchen tile. Gordon's gaze flickered to the collar lying on the table.

"Mrs. Vermont, you're to come with me."

Suzanne looked at me, her expression steady and giving nothing away. I understood that going or staying was my choice. She would not interfere with my decision.

I averted my gaze and whispered, "No."

"I'm under orders, Mrs. Vermont."

Suzanne's hand settled over mine, warm over my cold flesh. Her touch gave me strength. I repeated my answer in a hoarse voice, "No."

"Mr. Vermont will not be pleased."

I shuddered, knowing that the punishment he'd mete out would be beyond anything I'd ever suffered for prior defiance. Slowly, I stood and raised my skirt, exposing the dark bruises and welts on my upper thighs as well as haute couture silk panties. I heard the hiss of indrawn breath behind me. The reverend had come home, followed by his mother.

"Brutality offends the Lord!" Reverend Blankenship shouted. He glowered at Gordon and pointed one thick finger at him. "Begone, minion of Satan! Begone from God's house!"

Gordon's cold eyes flared with some strong emotion—or perhaps it was just annoyance. He nodded, turned on his heel, and departed. I released my skirt and let the heavy fabric fall back into place.

Rev. Blankenship held my gaze as he seated himself at the table and his wife brought him a slice of pie and a glass of cold milk. He took a bite then said, "Your husband's a powerful man, Mrs. Vermont."

I nodded.

"This won't be easy."

I nodded again.

"Howard, you could lose your position over this," his mother hissed.

Struck by the consequences the reverend and his family were likely to suffer for supporting my bid for freedom, I turned to leave.

"A shepherd cares for his flock and rescues those that are lost," he intoned. "As Jesus Christ saved the world, I can do nothing less than save one of my flock."

I trembled, unsure whether to stay or go. A pair of warm hands settled on my shoulders and gently turned me around. I looked into the soft smile of Suzanne Blankenship's kindness.

"No woman should bear marks like that. You're staying with us."

My fragile control shattered and I collapsed into her arms, weeping as though my heart had broken. As though something else had broken inside me, I felt liquid warmth soak my panties and run down my legs. Suzanne gasped. I looked down. Blood trickled over the expensive leather of my shoe.

Chapter 5

Sam

My body hummed with awareness of the woman seated beside me inside the dark red Volvo. I berated myself for envying the belt buckle that wrapped around her and secured her to the seat. Rising early that morning, it took a great deal of discipline to roll away from her warm body and let her continue sleeping rather than rouse her with kisses and sublime pleasure. I hoped she did not intercept the many covert glances I shot at her.

"Why do you keep looking at me?" she asked with growing suspicion.

Of course, I had no such luck. My usual luck with women deserted me when it came to this prickly representative of the female of our species.

"Just trying to figure out why you are so determined to dislike me," I answered.

Her mouth opened, but no sound came out. I felt justified in confronting her with her unreasonable prejudice.

"You go out of your way to antagonize me," she blurted after a moment's thought.

"Until last night, I would have said we'd hardly spoken." I kept my tone mild and reasonable, knowing that would irritate her.

She shrugged and looked out the passenger window instead of responding to that comment. With her face turned away, I felt free to let my gaze roam over her. Even in the wool coat, she was slender, her curves subtle, a distinct contrast to the voluptuous eye candy I normally indulged in. Holding her against my body the night before, I'd felt the lithe strength of her long limbs toned from exercise. I watched her left leg jiggle, a sign of impatience or anxiety, maybe both.

"Nervous?" I inquired.

"Hm?" she replied and, looking down, realized she'd been fidgeting. She forced her leg to be still. Her hazel eyes flickered to mine, then away. "I'm not nervous."

"Sure," I said with obvious disbelief.

She flashed me a look of dislike.

"I just call 'em as I see 'em," I quipped.

She huffed. "Look, just drop me off. I'll get my things and you can be on your way. There's no need to drive me home."

"I said I'd collect your belongings and drive you home, and I will," I said. "I'm not going to take the chance that you'll do something stupid again."

Dana gasped and clenched her small fists, obviously exerting strong control not to punch me. Flags of red streaked her high, prominent cheekbones and her hazel eyes blazed like emerald fire. Figuring she wouldn't endanger the both of us by striking the driver, I added, "You're beautiful when you're angry."

Of course, I smiled when I said that. My smile widened when her nostrils flared and an inarticulate sound of pure rage erupted from her throat. She turned away from me again to glare through the passenger window.

I pulled the SUV into the luxury condominium's underground parking garage and parked in my usual spot.

"Stay put," I ordered. "I'll get your things."

She pressed her lips together for an instant, then spoke, "Would you please check on Sonya while you're up there? Make sure she's all right?"

Her obvious care and worry for her best friend softened my heart, made me wonder what having that compassion directed toward me would feel like. "Yeah, sure. I'll check on her."

Before exiting the car, I informed her that the vehicle was modified so that, when locked, the doors would not open from the inside or the outside. I warned her, "I'll know if you do as you're told."

I pocketed the car key and locked the doors, expecting her to test my word, and she did. Before I reached the elevator, my cell phone chirped a warning. I pulled the device from my pocket, activated the voice app, and said, "Relax, Dana. I'll be back in a few minutes."

The app transmitted my voice to the onboard speakers. I heard her gasp in surprise.

"Who the hell are you, James Bond?"

"Yes."

I chuckled, closed the app, and dropped the cell phone back into my coat pocket as I rode the elevator to the penthouse. Bradley met me at the door.

"Merry Christmas," he said, exerting himself to be polite. His eyes glittered with high emotion, though he acted calmly as he ushered me in. "You do realize you have the day off?"

"Merry Christmas, Bradley," I replied, then explained my presence. "I'm here to collect Dana's things."

His nostrils flared. "Did you catch the little bitch?"

My own ire rose at his words, but that was not the time to take him to task. "I found her. She's safe."

"Pity," came the dismissive answer.

Anger sparked. Perhaps it *was* time to confront my employer about his treatment of his wife. Bradley directed me to a small table where Dana's belongings had been neatly stacked. Sonya's doing, no doubt. I heard a muffled moan as I picked them up. I looked up, met my employer's gaze, and held it for a few long seconds without flinching.

Glancing toward the master suite, I said, "I'd like to see Sonya, wish her a merry Christmas."

"No."

I felt my eyes narrow. "Bradley, don't force my hand."

"Sonya is resting," he said and folded his arms across his chest.

"I'd still like to check up on her."

His eyes narrowed. "Don't you trust me with my own wife, Sam?"

That soft tone carried a wealth of menace. Bradley's billionaire status conferred a great deal of social and economic power that he did not hesitate to wield with brutal and calculated efficacy. Like a mafia *capo*, he owned politicians, judges, and more than a few cops. If he terminated my contract and spoke of his dissatisfaction with my service, I'd have a difficult time finding another employer. The circles in which Bradley Vermont traveled were small and fairly incestuous.

Knowing I edged perilously close to being fired, I still did not back down. "I've seen the bruises on her, Bradley. A good dom doesn't leave bruises like that, an abuser does."

"She's my *wife* and she loves it when I mark her," he growled, his pale blue eyes intense.

I tried again, drawing on an association that had begun before this man became my most lucrative client. "Bradley, I introduced you to the lifestyle, remember? I used to dabble in it, and I know what distinguishes a good dom from a not-so-good one. Get some training before you really hurt Sonya and lose her."

"This doesn't concern you, Sam."

"She's *pregnant*."

"She's *mine*."

I backed down before the exchange could devolve even further. With a slow nod, I headed toward the door and said, "Wish Sonya a happy holiday from me."

He nodded, a curt gesture that showed no forgiveness. "Sam?"

"Yes?" I paused in the doorway.

"Challenge me again about how I treat my wife and I'll crush you."

"Understood," I replied, then added, "sir."

The door closed behind me.

I doubted I'd see Sonya again, except from a distance. I'd always thought Bradley protective of her, but now I wondered if he was, instead, overly possessive of her. Did he see her as a person? Or did he see her as some*thing* that belonged to him, a possession? I wanted to kick myself for not recognizing his controlling nature earlier when Dana had obviously seen it ... and called him out on it.

That thought led to wondering whether Bradley would crush her as he threatened to do to me if I stepped out of bounds again. Perhaps, I thought, she was too small and insignificant for him to bother with. I certainly hoped so.

The elevator doors opened and I headed for my car where Sonya's good friend waited and worried. Unlocking the vehicle, I set her purse, camera case, gloves, and hat on the back seat.

"Did you see her? How is she?" she asked, her expression worried.

I hated having to admit that Bradley wouldn't allow me to see her, but didn't want to lie. The small muscle at the base of her jaw clenched and she pressed her lips together in a thin line of angry disapproval at my negative answer, but she didn't hand me my balls on a platter. Her restraint surprised me, because I expected her to shoot the messenger.

"Perhaps I should go up there," she muttered.

"I don't think you should do that," I cautioned. The SUV hummed to life and I backed it out of the parking space.

"Why not?"

"Bradley's livid," I explained, navigating through the parking garage, slowing down to let some idiot in an over-priced Ferrari whip around a corner too fast. Tires skidded on the smooth concrete as the driver hit the brakes to avoid crashing. I waved him on. "You'd be lucky if he doesn't have you forcibly removed from the premises and then charge you with harassment."

"It wouldn't stick," she protested, knowing that, ordinarily, she was right.

I raised an eyebrow in silent denial. She correctly interpreted the expression and huffed.

"Oh, all right, it would stick, but only because he's got gazillions."

"Money talks, sweetheart."

"I'll call her," she stated as she reached back to collect her purse.

"If she still has her cell phone," I said and eased the vehicle into traffic. "But go ahead. It can't hurt to try." I paused, then suggested, "Maybe begin with an apology."

"Apologize?" Her voice hit the higher register of human hearing.

"Apologize," I repeated. "Unless you want to alienate Sonya entirely and ensure that Brad cuts off all outside access to her."

She opened her mouth, then closed it again. I was sure it hurt her to admit that I had a good point and might even be right.

"You're right," she admitted with a pained sigh. "I know Bradley checks her phone. He probably has every text and email and call either recorded or copied to his phone."

I said nothing, because it was true. He did. My firm had set it up, despite the invasion of Sonya's privacy. I had since regretted doing so. I turned onto Broadmoor and the SUV rolled through the city's main shopping district. On Christmas, the district was a ghost town, so we encountered no traffic delays.

From the corner of my eye, I watched as Dana quickly typed a message. I said, "Mind if I see that before you send it?"

"Why?"

"I know Bradley better than you. Let's make sure that nothing in that message makes the situation worse."

She blinked at me, then agreed with a sullen nod.

"I'm not trying to monitor what you're doing," I said to reassure her nasty suspicions. "I want to help."

"Why?"

"Why?" I echoed.

"Yeah, why do you want to help? Sonya isn't your friend. You're loyal to Bradley Vermont." She spat his name.

"I went to war to protect those who couldn't protect themselves," I said in a quiet tone that gave no indication of the horrors I'd encountered in three tours of duty overseas and multiple assignments in other ugly hotspots. "I don't like seeing any woman being abused."

Her cheeks flushed red with embarrassment. "Oh."

She met my gaze, then lowered hers. I saw curiosity in her eyes and knew she wanted to learn why I no longer served in the military. She opened her mouth and I wanted to wince at the question I assumed would come.

"My biological father was killed in Iraq a month before I was born," she said, her voice quiet and solemn. "Mom remarried when I was six. She died when I was seventeen. Cancer."

I nodded, seeing no reason to remind her that I already knew that from her dossier.

"My stepdad's a good guy, you know. Mom used to say that she'd sworn off soldiers, but she married another one anyway, well, an Airman. Dad's Air Force."

I nodded. The man she called "Dad" had been formerly employed at Wright-Patterson Air Force Base in his twenties and early thirties. What he did was classified; Dana probably didn't even know. I'd informed Bradley that there was no reason to dig more deeply into the man's background. For once, Bradley had taken my advice. Or maybe he'd hired a less scrupulous investigator. I didn't know and, frankly, preferred not knowing.

I turned a corner and parked along the curb of the stately Victorian where Dana lived. She unbuckled her seatbelt and gathered her gloves and hat.

"Stay put," I said. "I'll walk you to your door."

"You don't have to do that," she protested.

I gave her a small smile and said, "My parents raised me to be a gentleman. I know you don't think too highly of me, but I *will* see you safely to your door."

Chapter 6

Dana

I accepted the inevitable with less grace than was warranted. It was badly behaved of me, but I wanted to retreat to the comfort of my own home and snuggle with my cat who was surely convinced he would wither away if I didn't feed him *right now*. Sly never believed me when I told him he could stand to lose a few pounds.

Sam followed me up two flights of stairs to the third floor of the gigantic old house that had been split up by a former owner into three apartments. The third floor apartment was the smallest and, by virtue of no elevator, the least accessible and, therefore, the least expensive. Still, it boasted soaring ceilings, interesting nooks and crannies, and a much larger space than I would have otherwise been able to afford. The current property owner had also approved of me converting a small anteroom into a dark room, because I preferred to work with film when pursuing my artistic endeavors.

"Meow?" came Sly's inquiry as we approached the door.

"You have a cat?" he asked.

"Yeah. I got him a little over a year ago."

He nodded, probably adding that tidbit of information to the mental dossier he kept on me. I pulled out my keys and moved to unlock the door, but he stayed my hand.

"Those scratches are recent," he observed, pointing out fresh gouges in the door frame that I hadn't noticed. "Your cat didn't make those, unless you let him run loose."

I shook my head. "No, I don't let him outside, except on a leash."

Worried, I bent down to examine them. My heart sank. "*Shit.* Someone broke into my apartment."

Sam probably raised an eyebrow at my vulgar language, but I wasn't concerned about his reaction to my unusual use of profanity. He grasped my upper arm and pulled me back.

"Stay put. I'll go in first."

His bossiness annoyed me, but I saw the sense in it. He was better equipped to deal with an intruder than either Sly or I. I nodded, letting him know that I had no desire to prove myself any more stupid than I already had in the last twenty-four hours. He grasped the doorknob and turned it.

Great, something to replace. The doorknob and latch are broken.

On the upside, few people ever ventured to the third floor, so I probably had some time to get the locksmith out to make that fix before someone else burgled my home.

While I occupied myself with those thoughts, Sam entered my apartment. The door swung open on silent hinges. Sly hissed and retreated at top speed to the farthest reaches of the third floor. Obeying Sam's direction to wait, yet unable to resist the impulse of curiosity, I leaned sideways to catch sight of the interior of my apartment.

I gasped in horror. "Oh, no!"

Sam rejoined me a few minutes later and declared the apartment cleared. "Call the police."

I felt my chin tremble as I again obeyed one of his sensible orders. My hands shook as I pulled out my cell phone and dialed 911.

"What is your emergency?" came the dispassionate inquiry. "Police, fire, or medical?"

"I-I've b-b-been robbed," I stammered.

"Is there an intruder in your place now?"

"Er ... no."

"I'll alert law enforcement," the woman said. "What's your address?"

I gave it to her, belatedly realizing that Sam had wrapped an arm around my shoulders and held me close to his solid bulk. I appreciated the support and wondered if my knees would buckle if he withdrew that support. The call terminated so the line would be open for someone who had a real emergency.

Shoulders hunched in a gesture I acknowledged as self-protective, I said, "I need to go inside, see what's missing."

"All right," he murmured. "I'll stay with you."

"Thank you," I said, and meant it.

Sam stepped over the threshold with me and I gasped again at the wanton destruction and the strong odors of excrement, spoiled food, and spilled perfume. My furniture had been overturned, the cushions ripped open. The small Christmas tree lay in pieces on the floor, the glass ornaments smashed and the garland torn to pieces. Drawers were pulled from their moorings, their contents scattered. I advanced to the kitchen. The refrigerator door had been left open, and the dairy and meat dumped out and left to spoil. Cupboard doors were yanked off their hinges, glasses and ceramic plates broken, the shards strewn across countertops and the floor. Sly's food and water bowls and litter box had been overturned, too.

"I'm surprised your neighbors didn't call the cops," Sam commented. "Destruction like that makes a lot of noise."

"They're out of town for the holidays," I explained the absence of the married couple who lived on the second floor. Absent, too, was my landlord who lived on the first floor. "They asked me to water their plants while they're gone."

Wary, I navigated the wreckage to my bedroom and couldn't help the whimper that erupted from my throat at the potent reek of a shattered perfume bottle. Again, the contents of emptied drawers were strewn about, torn, and soiled. A quick glance through the gaping door of my closet showed my clothing there had suffered a similar fate. I felt the warm softness of a furry body wind around my calves. Looking down, I saw my big, black and white cat. I stooped down to pick him up and cuddled him in my arms as I surveyed the utter destruction of my bedroom. My eyes widened.

"Is that—?"

"Yeah, someone got mad and shit on your bed."

The size of the feces clearly indicated that Sly had not been so uncivilized. I wrinkled my nose against the strong odors.

"Check your jewelry box," Sam said.

I checked. "My jewelry's gone."

Everything was missing. The only jewelry of real value that I owned was my mother's pearl necklace, bracelet, and earrings which I'd worn the night before. I'd inherited a couple other really nice pieces, but those remained back in St. Paris in the house where Dad lived.

"Do you have pictures? Receipts?"

I shook my head. "Except for what I wore to last night's dinner, everything else is costume jewelry. Even new, it wasn't worth more than a few hundred dollars."

He frowned at that, but said nothing.

I continued to look around my ruined apartment. My laptop computer was gone, which really made me angry. I heaved a sigh of relief remembering that all my client information and photos had been saved to the cloud. I wept over the ruined negatives in my dark room, the photos that would never be developed, the ones which had been developed and now lay in torn shreds on the floor amid a toxic slurry of photo developing chemicals. I ignored Sam's murmured comment that he hadn't thought anyone used real film anymore, much less developed it. My bathroom, too, suffered the same rage of destruction.

The cops finally arrived. They took down my name, snapped pictures, asked a bunch of questions, and somehow managed to insinuate that the wreckage had been my fault. When they left, I buried my face in Sly's soft fur and cried some more. The overwhelming task of cleaning the disaster defeated me.

"You're coming home with me," Sam said, settling a hand over my shoulder. "You can't stay here."

I sniffled. "What about Sly?"

"Walmart's open today. We'll stop there, pick up some clean clothes for you and some stuff for him. I expect you'll be my guests for at least a week."

I didn't want to accept, but didn't see any better alternative. With a shaky exhale, I accepted his generous offer, followed up by, "I've got to call Dad."

He nodded. I transferred Sly to his arms, which surprised them both. However, Sly endured it without grumbling, although I couldn't say as much for Sam. I called my stepfather.

"Hey, Dad."

"What is it, pumpkin?" The concern in his voice indicated to me that he knew right away something was wrong. My stepfather was a good man. "What's wrong?"

"My ... uh ... my apartment was burglarized." I took a deep breath and lost the fragile hold on my composure. "It's ruined. Everything's ruined!"

"Calm down, pumpkin," he urged and gave me a moment to get myself back under control. "Are you alone?"

"N-no."

"Then let me talk to whoever's there with you."

Wordlessly, I handed the phone to Sam, exchanging the device for Sly.

"Sir," Sam said and identified himself. They conducted a conversation in low tones and clipped syllables. It ended with Sam saying, "I'll take care of her, sir."

"Just ... just a couple of days," I mumbled, reluctant to impose upon his generosity more than I already had.

He focused his blue eyes on me and nodded. I didn't make the mistake of thinking he agreed with me; I knew he merely acknowledged that I'd spoken. *Arrogant man.*

"Yes, sir, I'll see that she's brought home. She can use the break," Sam said and ended the call. He held my gaze with his and said, "You'll stay at my place tonight. Tomorrow, I'll accompany you back to St. Paris."

"It's a five-hour drive. One way."

"And you don't have a car," he pointed out. "It's too much of a hassle to fly you and that furball to Dayton. I'll drive you."

My arms tightened around said furball. Sly sank the tips of his claws into my shoulder in warning. I eased my grip and he rewarded me with a whiskery nuzzle.

"Dad doesn't like cats. He's allergic."

"He'll deal with it," Sam said. "He asked me to bring you home and that's what I'm going to do. Now, let's get your sweet ass back into my car so we can salvage what's left of Christmas."

My lower lip trembled as I realized that his holiday had been ruined, too. I felt terribly guilty, even though the burglary hadn't been my fault.

"I'm sorry," I whispered as we headed down the stairs. Mind racing, I mumbled, "I have to call insurance."

"So am I," he replied. "I'll call a cleaning service and schedule them in as soon as they have availability. We'll call the insurance company when we get home."

"That's very kind of you. You'll have to let me know how much I owe you."

He grunted softly. "You don't owe me anything."

"Of course, I do. I've absolutely ruined your Christmas holiday."

"No, you didn't."

"How can you say that?"

He sent me a small smile, although he looked askance at my cat. "I was going to spend the holiday alone, probably in the building's fitness center, and dine on a TV dinner. I was going to be bored out of my mind. You aren't boring."

"Glad I can keep you entertained," I replied in a dry tone, not bothering to mention that I, too, had planned to spend the holiday alone, drinking hot cocoa, and watching sappy Christmas movies while curled up on my second hand sofa with Sly. So much for plans.

I put Sly in the back seat of the SUV and climbed into the front passenger seat. Buckling myself in, I wriggled my cold toes inside the flimsy protection of my leather ballet flats while Sam crossed in front of the vehicle and took his place in the driver's seat. Disliking vehicular travel, Sly soon started yowling. I winced. Sam threw me an annoyed glance, but said nothing, apparently knowing that cats didn't respond well to orders to shut up. In a moment, we were on our way to the nearest Walmart where, as he predicted, the store was open for business as usual.

I could not believe the number of customers, but remembered to say a small prayer of thanks that the store was open. I had no desire to return to my apartment and sort through the wreckage of my clothing to find something that hadn't been utterly destroyed. I sighed, realizing I was probably going to get rid of everything. And probably move. I didn't feel safe in my third floor apartment anymore.

Inside the big box store, I purchased some basics: panties, bras, jeans, shirts, socks, and sneakers. I bought a new leash and harness for Sly, a litter box, bowls, cat food, and cat litter. I got the bare necessities in toiletries. Sam said nothing when I whipped out my credit card to pay for it all.

We drove back to his apartment, Sly yowling all the way until I lugged him from underneath the seat to wrestle him into his harness. The doorman raised his eyebrows in surprise and not a little disapproval when he saw my cat, although he did nothing but greet the building's tenant and guest as we passed through carrying our baggage. Harnessed and on his leash, Sly slunk behind me, sticking close to my heels.

"I've never seen a cat do that," Sam commented as we rode the elevator to his floor.

Sly sent him a flat look of feline dislike. I shrugged. "I've had him on a leash since he was just a little kitten. He's used to it."

Sam snorted as though amused and led the way when the elevator stopped and the doors opened. In short order, we were in his apartment. I scouted out an unobtrusive place to put Sly's things and quickly got him taken care of. The rotund kitty attacked his kibble as though he were starving. I couldn't blame him for being hungry.

My host carried my new wardrobe and other belongings to the guest bedroom, which, to be honest, wasn't much to talk about. There were no pictures on the eggshell white walls, no curtains over the windows. The double bed was covered in a boring gray bedspread. Plain wood furniture added a touch of neutral color: a nightstand and bureau. The ensuite bathroom was similarly bland and uninspired. The obvious quality of the furnishings could not disguise the lack of personality: this condominium was where Sam lived, it was not a home. However, I was in no position to complain. I put my stuff away and rejoined Sam in the living room.

"Um, Sam?" I blinked at him, surprised to see him ensconced on the sofa with Sly in his lap as he used a remote control to flip through the channels. He stroked the cat with his other hand.

"Hm?"

"Do you mind if I use your computer?"

"I'll get you something tomorrow morning."

"But—"

"Sweetheart, you've had a pretty awful twenty-four hours. Give it a rest. We'll deal with it tomorrow."

I ignored the "sweetheart" and plopped down beside him on the sofa before remembering that I needed to call my insurance provider, glad I'd followed Dad's advice and gotten renter's insurance. I couldn't refute what Sam said, nor could I demand he allow me the use of his computer— which he obviously did not want me to touch. Manners forbade me abuse his hospitality by attempting to use it anyway. I dug out my cell phone and noted the low charge. *Great, another thing to buy—a charger.* I scrolled through my contacts, selected the insurance representative's number, and reported the burglary. I set the phone aside and rubbed my temples and wondered what else I needed to do.

Sam transferred the remote control to his other hand and wrapped a muscled arm around my shoulders. He pulled me against him and murmured, "Relax, honey."

Again, I obeyed him and marveled at my unwonted acquiescence. But he was right: the last twenty-four hours of melodrama had wiped me out. Sly shifted to my lap and stretched his considerable bulk over me, a warm, purring, nearly boneless weight. The comfort quickly lulled me to sleep.

Chapter 7

Sam

The cat slithered off Dana to explore its new, temporary digs. From the corner of my eye, I watched her oversized, overweight cat slink through my apartment, then return and drape himself over her body, insinuating himself under her hand as he snuggled into position. She'd slumped against me, her even breathing indicating her withdrawal from stress. I occupied a few seconds watching her graceful hand flex in the big cat's fur and felt the rumble of its loud purr. The poor woman had endured a lousy Christmas and it wasn't yet noon. I supposed I ought to be grateful that she and the furball took quiet comfort in one another, rather than either of them indulging in caterwauling. I glanced at the cat again and annoyed myself by recognizing that I felt a spurt of jealousy. I wanted Dana Secrest to seek comfort from me.

I set aside the remote control and eased away from her, gently lowering her so that she lay on the sofa. I lifted her legs up and she curled into a more comfortable position, the cat conforming his body to the curl of hers. While she slept, I made some phone calls which meant leaving messages with a professional cleaning service and a couple of my agents. I didn't ask them to devote their family time to watching an already burglarized apartment because I doubted the perpetrator would return that same day. What hadn't been shattered, shredded, or smashed, had been soiled. I left a message instructing them to salvage what they could. It wouldn't be much.

My agents responded to my request in cool, clipped tones until I told them to wait until the next day. Then I heard relief and gratitude, which reminded me that most folks *liked* spending time with their families. That, of course, reminded me to make the obligatory phone call to my own family. I went into the third bedroom which I used as a home office and shut the door.

"Merry Christmas, Conrad," I said to the clipped, cut-glass diction that greeted me on the first ring.

"Mr. Samuel, it's a pleasure to hear your voice," replied my parent's butler, the man who'd been more of a father to me than my own. That didn't mean he affected a warm and fuzzy demeanor, but he extended a kindness and compassion to me that both my parents lacked.

"How are you doing, Conrad?" I asked. "Did you take that vacation to Cancún?"

"I did, thank you for asking. I even managed to acquire a bit of a sunburn."

I chuckled, finding the mental image of our butler sunbathing on the beach in his three-piece suit and shiny shoes ludicrous. I dared not allow myself to imagine him wearing a Speedo. "I'm glad you enjoyed it."

"Thank you. I'm sure you didn't call to speak with me, Mr. Samuel, so I'll hand you over to your father."

I sighed. "Thank you, Conrad."

A moment later, my father's Texan drawl oozed across the connection. "You still playin' with those yankees, or are you ready to come back and do a real man's work?"

"Merry Christmas to you, too, Dad," I replied. "I hope all's well."

"If you'd get your ass out of Chicago, you'd know the answer to that," Samuel Macintyre Galdicar III snapped. "I'm gettin' near to retirement and it's past time you took over the business."

If only the business were just the ranch, I would have considered it. But the business also included oil and gas and a level of dirty politics that made my blood run cold. I found it ironic that I'd met my most lucrative client, Bradley Vermont, through my father's connections. Dad might not have approved of my chosen career, but he'd eat glass before witnessing my failure. Over the last few years I'd acquired more than one contract through his helpful referral.

"Dad, Toby's better suited to the business than I am," I replied with perfect truth. My younger brother was the spitting image of our father in both looks and personality. "Even better, put Toby in charge of the oil and gas and Elaine in charge of the ranch."

"Your sister can't handle the ranch."

I swallowed a sigh. My sister could handle the ranch better than any of us, but our old-fashioned father considered the presence of her uterus as evidence of an utter lack of capability. Women, he expounded, were good for two or three things, only two of which were mentionable in polite company. None of those things included ranching or business. I often wondered how my mother managed to swallow that line of thought, but her own chilly demeanor forbade such intimate chat. She'd learned her place and duty as a senator's daughter.

"You'll come back and fulfill your obligations to the family," he insisted as he did every time we spoke.

"I like what I'm doing, Dad. Pass me on to Mama, please."

With a harrumph, my disgruntled father passed the phone to my mother, who answered it in her usual well-modulated, cool tone, "Merry Christmas, darling."

"Merry Christmas, Mama. How are you doing?"

She launched into a litany of trivia. She'd changed personal trainers, because the last one had the gall to suggest that she was no longer 29 years old with a youthful metabolism. She spoke with disappointment that Elaine had turned down yet another dutiful proposal by one of the hand-picked bachelors whose wealth, pedigree, and social standing met my parents' exacting approval. She lamented that Elaine was apparently besotted with the *most* unsuitable man—a bull rider, for heaven's sake—who had the vulgar audacity to call her *sugar* or his *sweet little heifer*. I choked back a laugh, turning it into a cough.

Damn, but I loved my sister. I wondered if she truly liked the bull rider or if she dated him just to spite our parents. Either was likely.

"What's his name?" I asked. "How did they meet?"

"Peter Redclaw," came the icy response. "He's an *Indian*."

I held my silence as I jotted the name on a Post-It® note for future reference and thought, *Well, that's interesting.* I scribbled a note below the name to run a background check. The bull rider's heritage didn't concern me, but protecting my sister did.

"They met at ... oh, it breaks my heart to admit it, a *rodeo*."

"Is Elaine still barrel racing?"

"Yes." Mama's voice hissed that last letter, always a sign she was fit to be tied. "Your sister needs to grow up, Samuel. She needs a good influence and she's always looked up to you. Your word—"

"Oh, no," I interrupted. "Elaine's an adult. She'll make her own choices."

Cold, disapproving silence met my declaration which flouted the parental opinion that no female was an adult until she married and became her husband's problem to manage.

"Is Toby there?" I asked, changing the subject.

"Tobias has gone to the office."

"He's working on Christmas?"

"December 25th means little in other countries," Mama replied with haughty disapproval. "Your father insisted, as two important teleconferences were scheduled for today and he felt it imperative that he spend some time with family, unlike others I could mention."

Well, that wasn't subtle at all.

"And just what are you doing today, darling?"

"Working, I suppose," I answered. "You remember Bradley Vermont?"

"Such a nice boy, and handsome, too."

Grinning at my mother's description of my client and imagining his pained reaction to it, I explained, "His wife's best friend got herself into a bit of difficulty last night and needed some help."

"Oh?" Mom prompted. "Who's her family?"

"No one you'd know," I assured her. "She's a photographer, quite a good one."

"You mean that artistic photographer you've mentioned before—whose work you admire? She's a *career* girl? From where?" I heard a note of interest in her disapproval. Her life had pounded into her that proper ladies did not have careers; however, artistic hobbies were perfectly acceptable.

"St. Paris, Ohio."

"Never heard of it. Ohio, you say? I don't know anyone important in Ohio."

I chuckled at her flat tone of disapproving snobbery. "No, I don't think you have. It's barely a dot on the map."

I heard the clinking of china and cutlery in the background, indicating that the household staff was setting the formal dining room for a holiday banquet during which schmoozing would reign as the most coveted gift. Everyone who was anyone wanted Dad's favor. It made him insufferable.

"Well, tell Toby and Elaine I called and wished them a happy holiday," I said. Then I lied, "I've got to go. Just wanted to call and let y'all know I missed you."

"You *must* come home, darling. Your father's at a loss without you."

I repressed a sigh. Again. "Mom, let Elaine run the ranch. If nothing else, the work will keep her occupied with less time for that bull rider."

"I hadn't considered that," Mama admitted. "But running the ranch isn't suitable."

I clamped my jaw against argument, forcing myself to be satisfied with having planted the seed. Perhaps it would grow and earn my sister a modicum of respect as well as freedom. I bade my mother good-bye and she did not offer to hand the phone back to Dad or to Elaine, which meant that Dad had nothing else to say to me and that Elaine was probably out riding. I envied her that escape and missed it. Of all the advantages and privileges we had growing up, I missed the horses and miles of open range most.

Dana still slept when I emerged from the office. She did not stir while I fixed myself a sandwich and ate it. I glanced at the clock on the wall; it was too early yet to put the whole chicken I'd intended to roast for Christmas dinner into the oven. At least I had enough food in the kitchen to feed her a decent meal. I made a mental note to add a bonus and a thank-you to my housekeeper for her thoughtfulness and willingness to perform those extra duties for her bachelor client. With a glimmering of a holiday menu in mind, I pulled out an old copy of *The Complete Cook's Country TV Show Cookbook* and flipped through the pages. I didn't consider myself an adept cook, but I could follow a recipe.

In the military, one learned how to follow directions.

Chapter 8

Dana

I awoke to the mouthwatering aroma of roasting chicken and the soft press of Sly's furry head under my jaw. With a sneeze, I dislodged his furry bulk and sat up, realizing as I did so that Sam had draped a blanket over me. The thoughtfulness of the gesture warmed my heart. Obeying the demand of my bladder, I headed for the bathroom.

"Nice nap?" he asked when I came out. He settled the lid on a pot of boiling potatoes.

"Yes, thank you. I didn't know you cooked."

He shrugged. "I can follow a recipe."

I inhaled and gave him a smile. "Well, it smells wonderful. Thanks for letting me sleep. The blanket was a nice touch, very thoughtful."

A tinge of pink flagged his cheekbones. So, the big, badass bodyguard blushed at compliments? That was a secret I'd have to put to good use.

With a vague gesture toward the kitchen, I asked, "Is there anything I can do to help?"

"No, I've got it. I'm not doing anything too complicated."

"I'll have to return the favor sometime. I'm a decent cook. Dad taught me."

He cocked one eyebrow upwards. "Not your mother?"

I chuckled. "Mom could burn water. No, Dad's the chef in the family." And, in truth, my stepfather owned a diner and did most of the cooking there, too. But, of course, Sam probably knew that already from his dossier on me. His client, Bradley Vermont, would want background information on everyone.

"So, tomorrow ..." I began as I slid onto a stool.

"Yes?"

"I've got to get a new laptop computer."

"I'll take you."

I shook my head. I should have known he'd jump to that conclusion. "No, you don't have to interrupt your schedule any more than you already have. I was hoping you'd lend me a house key."

He turned to face me, leaning against the counter. "No."

"No?"

"Have you forgotten the state of your apartment?"

"No, of course not."

"That was malice, Dana. The average, garden variety burglar doesn't leave behind destruction of that magnitude."

I blinked rapidly. "I suppose you're familiar with 'average, garden variety' burglars?"

"I am."

"How?"

He shook his head and the corners of his mouth curled just a little bit. "You're not going to distract me that way."

"Look, Sam," I huffed, "it's probably likely that whoever burgled my home and destroyed it did so in a fit of pique because there wasn't much of anything worth stealing."

"I disagree."

"You plan on keeping me a prisoner here?"

He gestured toward the entrance. "You can leave anytime. You just can't get back in."

I couldn't leave Sly behind and he knew that.

"Besides, I'm driving you home tomorrow," he added.

"All right," I relented with a huff. I really didn't want to wait until returning to Ohio before buying another computer, but decided against arguing further. It wasn't worth the hassle. Once Sam dropped me off in St. Paris, I'd borrow Dad's car and head into Springfield or Urbana.

I wondered if the local colleges still had dark room facilities. I needed to develop the rolls of film I'd taken several days ago, part of a gig for the Chicago Chamber of Commerce. They hired me to take pictures of the city's parks for their annual parks and recreation fundraising drive. The recent snowfall on a quiet day at Matthiessen State Park made it look like a winter wonderland, a fairy-tale setting that made for great photos. I'd taken great care not to capture any footprints or trash left behind by other park visitors, so the blanket of snow appeared pristine, untouched and unsullied by human or animal presence. I'd half-expected to see one of Robert Vavra's unicorns flit through the enchanting forest.

At yesterday's ill-fated dinner party with Bradley and Sonya, I hadn't had the chance to say much more than I'd been to Jackson, Matthiessen, and Palmisano Parks over the past week and taken some lovely photographs. Sonya had once been my photography companion and, often, her beautifully photogenic face and figure served as my model. She once told me it was a photo I'd taken of her that had caught Bradley Vermont's eye and initiated his pursuit of her.

The poor woman hadn't stood a chance. I felt guilty about that, especially as he systematically isolated her from her friends and family.

"What time are we leaving?"

"Mid-morning," he replied. "I've got to notify my team and my clients, then we'll run a few last errands and be on our way."

I nodded, understanding the demands of professional courtesy. I wanted to notify my clients, too, but couldn't without computer access.

"Then may I use your computer for a little bit this afternoon? I just need to email my clients as to what happened and let them know I'll either have to reschedule appointments or delay delivery of their projects."

"What's your email client?"

"I use Gmail."

He frowned.

"It's convenient and free," I said.

"Not the most secure system."

"It's not like I work on top secret stuff."

"Come on, then," he said and led me to his office. "Contact your clients."

I took a seat in the black task chair in front of his desktop machine and scooted aside as he bent down to unlock the system and grant me limited access.

"I've logged you on as a guest. You have thirty minutes."

"Thirty minutes!" *Well, that doesn't leave any time to examine the décor or snoop.*

"Supper will be ready then."

With a snort, I logged in my username and password and opened my email account. I exercised brutal efficiency, letting every client know what happened and offering them a graceful out to either cancel or reschedule. I promised to be back online within two days. I did not look forward to the aggravation of reinstalling the necessary software and re-establishing the other settings necessary to do my work. *Damn it.*

I hit "send" on the last email a few seconds before the monitor went black and posted a message that the guest session had timed out.

"Supper's ready," Sam called.

Feeling disgruntled, yet knowing that I owed him gratitude, I joined him at the table which he'd attempted to make pretty with a tablecloth and coordinating napkins. I tried to conceal my sour mood and said, "This looks really nice. Thank you."

He gave me a small smile that let me know he saw right through me. "You're welcome."

We tucked into a simple meal that was nonetheless tasty and satisfying and accompanied by a crisp white wine. I didn't recognize the brand, since it wasn't something my local supermarket carried. Once again, I cleared the table and washed the dishes, the domestic tasks somehow settling my thoughts. I supposed there was a lot to be said for the therapy of mindless, menial work.

"Sam, do you mind if I use your computer again?"

He looked up, annoyed. "It's Christmas, Dana. Give it a rest."

I shook my head. "I can't. I feel restless, antsy, I guess."

He sighed and rose from the sofa where he'd been skimming through the viewing options on Netflix. I watched as he disappeared into his bedroom and returned with a pair of shorts, a tee shirt, and two towels. He tossed the clothing to me.

"Put those on," he said. "We'll burn some energy in the fitness room."

I shrugged and, again, did as he ordered. I had nothing better to do. The shorts had a drawstring inside the waistband which I cinched tightly to make them fit. The tee shirt hung on me. Were I a less modest sort, I could have used it for a minidress. I put on socks and sneakers and followed him to the ground floor where a handful of other residents made use of the equipment.

"Have you ever been in a gym before?" he asked in a low tone.

"Um, no," I answered, looking around at complicated looking equipment. "Not like this, not since high school."

I rather thought I got enough exercise hiking through the city and its many parks in the pursuit of photographs. My work often required me to put in ten miles or more of walking daily. Besides, I liked hiking in the outdoors.

Sam escorted me to a treadmill and showed me how to use it. The fitness center had television monitors positioned above and in front of the treadmills so those folks using them had something to watch. I spent half an hour on the machine and worked up a light sweat, then moved to a bench press and wondered how to adjust the weights. A man around my age jumped up to offer assistance.

"I got her," Sam's deep voice interjected. I felt him move behind me, surprising me when his hand settled on the flare of my hip.

The man raised his hands and backed away. "Sorry, man, I didn't realize she was yours."

Now, I realized. Turning to face Sam, I hissed, "What do you think you're doing? He was just being nice."

"He was being more than *nice*," Sam muttered. "You didn't see him stare at your butt."

I let loose a sigh, then grumbled, "Well, why don't you just whip 'em out and compare? Or maybe just pee on me?"

Bending his head so that his mouth was close to my ear, he replied, "When you're ready for my naked cock, it won't be peeing on you."

Heated embarrassment burned my skin. I raised my chin and stiffened my upper lip and said, "Just show me how the damned thing works. Please."

Sam chuckled, forbore to sling an innuendo or six at me about how his naked cock worked, and set the weights to 25 pounds, showing me how to increase the weight. Then he helped me position myself correctly beneath the handlebars. Assured I could operate the device without injury, he meandered to a bank of free weights. I lay down on the bench, worked through a few reps, and felt the oversized shirt work its way up my body. The lump of fabric was uncomfortable, so I sat up and gathered it neatly, then knotted the fabric around my midriff to keep it more or less in place.

The young man Sam had chased away returned and stood where I could admire his muscled thighs. "I could count reps for you if you like."

"Huh?"

"Count reps," he replied, eyes glancing toward the wide swath of bared skin where the shorts had slipped down and the shirt had ridden up even further. "That way you get an even workout."

"Sure."

He squatted beside me and smiled, showing dimples beneath a fashionable 3-day scruff of beard and straight white teeth. I pumped iron and he counted. When he reached 50, he suggested I change positions and adjust the machine for a different upper body workout. I glanced at Sam who lay on a bench and hefted formidable looking barbells.

The sight of his sweaty, bulging muscles made my mouth water and I swallowed, unwilling to admit I found him attractive ... er ... *yummy*. I lied to myself that I admired him as I admired a particularly beautiful sculpture.

My helper put his hands on me to help me with the correct position. He touched nothing inappropriate, but I felt his thumb swipe the soft inside of my arm a few times.

"I'm Jason, by the way," he said as I resumed pumping iron again.

"Dana."

"You a new resident?"

"No. Just visiting."

"Is he—" he jerked his chin toward Sam who'd realized I was no longer alone and glowered at us "—your boyfriend?"

I snickered. "Hardly."

"Then you're—"

"Mine," Sam snapped as he approached on my other side.

Jason grinned at him. "That's not what she says."

"She seems to be confused about whose bed she slept in last night."

My cheeks burned again at the implication of his words. "Sam!"

He smiled at me, but fury blazed in his eyes. "Sweetheart, don't mislead the boy."

I released my hold on the handlebars and the weights fell with a loud clatter. Leaning forward, I hissed, "Don't even go there."

"Hot, hot, hot," Jason commented under his breath. "She's a wild one, dude. When you're finished with her or if you want to share, let me know."

"Share?" I squeaked in outrage. "*Finished* with me?"

"I don't share," Sam replied, his voice cool.

Jason shrugged. "Your loss, man. A threesome can be awesome."

I rolled off the bench and squirmed out from between them. Getting to my feet, I stomped away, muttering under my breath. I didn't hear the rustle of cloth until a towel snapped around my waist like an unfurled whip. A hard jerk whirled me around into the bend of Sam's burly arm which held my body in place even as his other hand speared through my short, sweat-dampened curls and held my head where he wanted it. The fire in his eyes flared again and his mouth crashed against mine. I brought up my hands to push against a hard chest that didn't yield so much as an inch. His arm clamped me tightly against his body and I felt the hardening bulge of his erection against my belly as he tilted my head back to accept the hot tongue that plunged into my mouth.

An inarticulate sound of protest erupted from my throat and settled into a moan as I felt my bones melt.

Chapter 9

Sam

My cock went from interested to rock hard the instant Dana softened in my arms and submitted. I didn't bother to swallow the groan of rich, heated desire that surged through my body, because I had better things to do. Like explore her mouth with my tongue and slide one hand down the sweaty slope of her back to palm a firm, round buttock. She gasped when I squeezed her ass. Her soft lips molded to mine, her inexperience obvious. I wanted to pound my fists against my chest at having found the last innocent woman in the entire city. Oh, the dirty things I wanted to do to her!

In a tiny corner of my mind, I wondered if the men in this city were all fucking idiots.

"Hey," said the douche canoe who'd suggested a threesome. I tore my mouth away from heaven and glared at him. He grinned at me, but I couldn't punch him without letting Dana go—and that I was simply not doing. "Take it to the bedroom, not here."

An inarticulate sound of distress and embarrassment erupted from Dana's throat. My gaze flickered down. She'd turned her head away, although I saw the red flush of embarrassment color what skin remained within my field of vision. I wanted nothing more than to follow through on that bone-melting kiss, but the stiffening woman still imprisoned within my hands had lost the mood. I had no doubt I could arouse her again: the chemistry between us was explosive. However, she wouldn't thank me for causing her further embarrassment.

I pressed a kiss to her sweat-dampened curls and inhaled the warm scent of her. Exhaling, I willed my hard-on to subside.

"Sorry, kitten, I got carried away there," I murmured.

The fitness room's door opened, stirring the air and admitting a small group of men joking and laughing among themselves. For some reason, the lack of women in the fitness room on Christmas Day didn't surprise me. I'd have to analyze that later. The douche canoe hailed them, exchanging high-fives and friendly insults.

"Let's go," I whispered.

She nodded. I assumed she didn't trust her voice. I hoped she still felt buzzed from our kiss and hadn't yet regained the ability to form coherent words.

"I think I've had enough for one day," she muttered a moment later as we collected our towels and left the room. I made sure to position her closely in front of me to hide the erection that just would not go down.

We returned to my condo and she headed straight for the guest bedroom. Less than two minutes later, I heard the shower run. Satisfied she'd be occupied for a little while, I, too, availed myself of a shower to wash off the sweat of exercise and stroke my determined cock until my balls released their burden. I gasped in the steamy air and abruptly switched the water to cold. The shock of the icy spray damned near turned my slowly wilting outie into an innie. I shuddered as the last drops of my seed swirled down the drain, and then rinsed my heated body. When I emerged from the bedroom dressed in jeans and a soft cotton henley, Dana was sitting on the sofa. I felt her awkwardness from there. Sly snoozed in an armchair and ignored my approach, although he did twitch an ear.

"Hey," I said in a soft voice as I walked toward the sofa.

She looked up and her cheeks turned pink. However, she met my gaze without flinching.

"What just happened down there?" she finally asked.

I felt my mouth curve in a smirk. "We kissed."

Her full lips pressed together in a thin line before she replied, "I figured that one out, thank you."

"Then you're as smart as Sonya says you are," I quipped.

She made a sound and I could not quite tell if it was annoyance or humor. "No, really, Sam. I mean we've known each other for, what, three years? You've never been attracted to me. Why now?"

"I've always been attracted to you," I countered. "I simply never acted upon it."

Her eyes widened with surprise at my candor. Tilting her head, she blurted, "Why not?"

"Because you weren't my type."

"Your type?" Her eyes narrowed, probably imagining some bottle blonde bimbo with big hair and boobs and very little brain.

"Temporary," I explained. My gaze ran over her lean form and subtle curves. "You're anything but a one night stand."

"Oh." She swallowed. Audibly.

My words made her uneasy, maybe a little nervous. I liked it. I reached out to clasp her hand in mine. My big hand dwarfed her long elegant fingers and narrow palm, an artist's hand. I could imagine those fingers stroking piano keys or wielding a paintbrush or expressing silent emotion in graceful dance.

"Dana, I don't want to hurt you," I said, knowing her incapable of casual intimacy.

Her eyes closed, then opened again, wide with shock. I saw the questions she dared not ask for fear of answers better left unvoiced.

"I respect your decision not to give yourself lightly, but I won't deny that I want you."

She exhaled forcefully.

"I also won't deny that I've never considered marriage with any woman."

She averted her gaze. I didn't bother to explain my avoidance of the marital state, the debutantes who'd pursued me until I escaped my father's sphere of influence, the women who wanted to snag a man in military uniform just for bragging rights and government benefits, the cold and often acrimonious examples of marriage that characterized the social stratum in which I had grown up. I considered my own parents, an overbearing father and ice queen mother. How they'd managed to generate enough passion to produce three children was beyond me, especially since they loathed one another.

It never failed to amaze me that I'd never seen a great example of matrimony until I visited with a fellow service member's family. Paolo's blue collar family made me yearn for the kind of loud, boisterous warmth and affection that mine would have found vulgar and appalling. I could still remember the heavenly fragrance of his mother's cooking filling the too-small house with its noisy plumbing and drafty windows.

It broke my heart to see them at Paolo's funeral and I never understood why his mother didn't blame me for his death. Instead, she'd hugged me tightly against that pillowy body and promised me a home if ever I needed one. My teammate's father had wept openly on my uniformed shoulder and told me how proud he'd been of his oldest son.

"Sam?"

Dana's voice recalled me from bittersweet reminiscence. I blinked to realize that my eyes were wet.

"Sam, are you all right?"

The concern in her voice warmed my heart.

Voice thick, I answered, "Yeah, kitten, I'm fine."

I picked up the remote control and wrapped my arm around her shoulders to snuggle her against my side. She resisted, then relaxed and allowed her body to rest against mine. The cat jumped down from the chair and crept onto the sofa to occupy Dana's lap. Apparently, Sly felt as possessive of her as I did.

"Do you want to talk about it?" she asked.

"No." I pressed the power button and the 65-inch monstrosity of a television flared to life.

"All right."

She asked no more questions. She didn't pry. I didn't know whether to be grateful for that or to suspect she simply didn't care.

Chapter 10

Dana

The emotions flitting across Sam's usually inscrutable face indicated he was lost in old memories, unpleasant ones for the most part, if I were to guess. As I had enough bad memories of my own, I hesitated to pry. Talk therapy didn't necessarily do anything more than emphasize and intensify pain and hurt. Misery shared was not necessarily misery halved. That glimpse, however, gave me an insight into his character that showed me he had reasons for his insistence on casual relationships. I could not envision how taking someone into one's own body could be anything other than intimate.

That didn't mean I failed to recognize my viewpoint as a minority one, especially among my generation who hopped from bed to bed, yet needed safe spaces to cry if someone said something that offended them. I was glad Dad made sure I was made of sterner stuff than that. I sighed and felt the muscles of my face twist into a small frown. I disliked having to go home under a cloud of secrecy and humiliation, although why having my apartment burgled factored into either of those eluded me. Regardless, I couldn't shake the feeling that I'd done something wrong, something that had dire consequences. I only wish I knew what it was.

Sam and I sat through three half-hour television shows before I yawned.

"It's been a stressful day, Dana. I won't think less of you if you go to bed."

I accepted the graceful exit and made mine, heading for the guest bedroom.

"My bed," he called out.

I stopped in my tracks. Without turning to look at him, I replied, "I'm neither frostbitten nor chilled. I'll sleep by myself, thank you."

His expression probably darkened, perhaps turned sour, but he merely grunted, "Have it your way."

I did. I lay on the extra firm and uncomfortable mattress and pulled the covers over myself. I left the bedroom door open so Sly could come or go into the room as he pleased. He hopped onto the bed and curled himself by my ankles.

My mind raced for I didn't know how long before sleep claimed me and I awoke with a start, sweating, and quivering with fear, my body twisted around the warm, furry lump that was Sly. A whimper oozed from my mouth as the lingering wisps of whatever nightmare had gripped me in its icy claws scratched at my mind. I gulped great lungsful of air and pressed the heel of one hand against my racing heart. My blurry vision slowly began to clear. At that point I realized a dark presence lurked in the doorway, limned by faint light. I whimpered again and felt every sphincter clench. Sly snored.

"My bed," came the husky order.

The shadow moved from the doorway and an unseen arm wrapped itself around me, hoisting me to my feet. I stumbled, my feet cold and nearly numb. The solid shadow settled me on another mattress, softer than the one I'd occupied earlier. It dipped behind me as it climbed in and that big, strong arm once again wrapped around me. Heat seeped through the fabric of the oversized shirt I wore—Sam's shirt, I remembered—and soaked into my clammy skin.

"Go back to sleep," he whispered. "You're safe."

I went back to sleep and awoke alone with Sly curled into the small of my back.

Again, Sam cooked breakfast: instant grits, pancakes, eggs, and sausage links. It smelled wonderful, but I ate more from pragmatic determination than from any sense of hunger. I knew my body needed the fuel, though the food could have been ashes on my tongue. Still, I murmured polite thanks for the meal and the night's companionship that held the nightmares at bay.

After breakfast, I climbed into Sam's vehicle. We had errands to run before heading to southwest Ohio, not the least of which included replacing my laptop computer and replacing key wardrobe items and toiletries. That took longer than I anticipated. When we were finally on our way, my new laptop computer remained in its box, unopened, and snow had already begun to fall. I plugged the new phone charger into the USB port in the SUV's console. I was glad I still had my beloved camera. Finding a professional camera that used film wasn't all that easy, and never cheap. Most professional photographers used digital cameras. Only hobbyists and weird artist types like me preferred film. I looked at the leaden sky overhead and prayed we wouldn't run into truly nasty winter weather, always a possibility in the Midwest's unpredictable climate.

Before long, the constant hum of road noise and my cat's disgruntled protests filled the vehicle. Neither Sam nor I felt much like holding a conversation, so we didn't, beyond short questions as to whether the radio station selection was acceptable, did I need to use the facilities at the next rest stop, and to let him know when I was hungry.

I wasn't surprised when fat snowflakes splatted against the windshield. Mixed with rain, the wintry mix soon turned into an ugly mess of freezing rain and snow. Stop-and-start traffic progressed at a halting crawl as drivers navigated slick highways. Sam muttered under his breath about being able to walk faster than the speed of traffic.

Flashing lights and wailing sirens in the distance alerted everyone that even careful driving in such conditions did not guarantee a successful arrival at one's destination. I glanced at Sam. Black leather gloves hid what I guessed were whitened knuckles, judging from the way he clenched the steering wheel. A small muscle bulged at the back of his jaw, showing that he clenched that, too. The car in front of us slid. The Volvo's antilock braking system activated as Sam stomped on the brake, bringing the vehicle to a smooth halt. He waited without a single word of impatience as the driver of the car in front of us slowly rolled back onto the pavement. I thought the gritty shoulder probably offered that car a little extra traction.

"Do you think we should stop?" I asked as we slowly and carefully maneuvered around a jackknifed tractor trailer in line with the rest of traffic edging around the disabled hauler.

"We'll hit Warsaw in another ten miles or so," he said and rolled his shoulders to ease the tension. "It'll be dark in less than an hour and I'd prefer not to drive through this at night."

I didn't offer to drive instead. First, I didn't want to drive in that nasty weather. Second, I doubted he'd let me drive his vehicle. I'd driven trucks before; one could hardly grow up in a small, agricultural community without having done so. But Sam's conveyance probably cost as much or more than Dad's house, and I had no desire to wreck it because stubborn pride insisted me and my lady brain could operate that vehicle as well as any man.

I sighed and thrust the unnecessarily belligerent thoughts aside. Feminism was all well and good, but not when it got in the way of common sense and the practical matters of survival. I picked up my phone, still plugged into the console. "Let me check for hotels in Warsaw and see what's available."

"Thanks," came the terse reply.

After striking out with four hotels, I found a chain hotel a few miles northwest of Warsaw and booked the last available room there, entering in my credit card information to hold the reservation.

"Got a place," I announced.

"Good. Navigate for me?"

"Sure." I plugged the address into the phone's GPS and directed him to a parking lot packed with vehicles surrounding a worn hotel that had seen better days a long time ago. The excruciatingly slow pace of those slippery, treacherous miles placed us at our destination in full darkness.

"I'll get us checked in," I offered as he parked under the *porte cochere.*

He nodded and simply said, "Be careful. Pavement's slick."

I unplugged my phone and dropped it into my purse, climbed out of the vehicle, closed the car door behind me before Sly could make a break for freedom, and headed into the lobby where I took my place at the end of the line and waited. And waited. And waited some more. Finally, the harried looking front desk clerk beckoned me to approach. With a tired smile, she checked me in, instructed me to sign the agreement to pay for accommodations and refrain from smoking in the room, and handed me the keycards.

"You're lucky," the clerk said. "That was our last vacant room."

I glanced outside. The SUV no longer waited beneath the *porte cochere*. I assumed that Sam parked it somewhere. I looked back at her and met her gaze. "Yeah, I checked four other places before this one: they were all booked solid."

"I heard there's a really nasty accident at the western edge of town," she said. "Traffic's backed up for *miles*."

I nodded, unsurprised. "Lots of people will be trying to find overnight lodging rather than continue on through this mess."

She gave me another tired smile. "Hotel staff will be bunking down in offices and break rooms tonight. The general manager put the kibosh on anyone trying to drive home, says he doesn't want anyone's injury or death on his hands."

"I can understand that."

"Well, some of us have kids, little kids. I'm lucky my babysitter agreed to keep my boy overnight."

"There is that," I agreed. "I hope you and everyone else will get a bonus for going above and beyond duty tonight."

She shook her head in obvious doubt that such generosity would occur. "Wouldn't that be nice?"

I thanked her and headed outside. When I stood under the *porte cochere*, headlights flashed. I peered into darkness only dimly lit by parking lot lighting and streaked by falling snow and sleet. I considered sleet only slightly better than freezing rain. Knowing where the vehicle was parked, I minced a path to it to help carry in our belongings.

"I've got our bags, you take the cat," Sam ordered.

"Okay," I replied and snagged the leash attached to Sly's harness before he could shoot outside. His claws dug through the wool of my coat and he growled. "There's a side entrance we can use that's closer to the room."

He nodded and kicked the car door shut. The locks automatically engaged. Bending his head against the icy precipitation, he said, "Lead on, Macduff."

He followed me as Sly grumbled and growled and flexed his claws in warning.

"You don't want to walk in this, buddy," I whispered into his furry neck.

Careful, mincing steps carried us to the low stoop at the side entrance. I dug into my pocket to extract the key-card.

"You don't need it," Sam said. "The door's not locked."

"Well, that's real secure," I griped and pulled the door open. "We're on the second floor."

We stepped inside and trekked up a flight of stairs covered in filthy carpet. Sly squirmed, but I didn't want to let him down on that nasty surface. Who knew what nasty vermin would find a home in his fur?

A right turn and a long walk down the corridor brought us to the last room at the end of the building. I unlocked the door and we entered. Flipping the light switch revealed beige walls, cheap looking furniture, and bland décor that hadn't been chic even in the 1970s when it was originally installed. The scent of bleach lingered in the room.

"It could be worse," I said.

"Really?" Sam looked around with distaste.

I grinned at him and let Sly off his leash. "I don't see cockroaches or fleas."

Sam shuddered. "I think Afghanistan might have been better than this."

"Oh, come on," I cajoled, "we have hot and cold running water and indoor plumbing and there's an onsite restaurant."

He grunted and rolled his shoulders. "I'll see if there's a closer parking spot and get the rest of our things."

"You want me to help?" I handed him a keycard.

"No, you stay here. Don't open the door for anyone."

I nodded. He left. I slid the safety chain into the slot and made sure the deadbolt was secured. I still didn't feel terribly safe knowing that the side entrance was unlocked. Why, anybody could come in and wreak havoc.

I set up Sly's temporary litter box which he used as soon as it was available, then filled his bowls with dry kibble and water. He ate, drank, and curled up in the room's one armchair. I unpacked my toiletries and dithered, wondering if I ought to do the same for Sam. Deciding that it would be the considerate thing to do, I opened his overnight bag and reached in. My hand touched cold metal. I squeaked and snatched my hand back. I recognized that ominous shape even if I'd never held a real firearm before. Gingerly, as though the weapon might go off any second, I zipped the bag shut and gently deposited it on the luggage rack.

My stomach rumbled. I made coffee which, predictably, wasn't very good. But it was hot and had flavor, even if bitter. Sipping it gave me something to do while I waited for Sam to return.

Chapter 11

Sam

I stepped outside and hunched my shoulders against the inclement weather and sneezed. I blamed the sneeze on Dana's oversized cat, certain I'd be cleaning stray cat hairs from my vehicle's interior for the next six months. Lifting the collar of my coat, I trudged—carefully—across the slick asphalt, veering around potholes, in the general direction of my SUV. The hulking vehicle's still warm hood gleamed beneath the orange-tinged light from the sodium lamps arching high above. Blinking against the driving sleet and snow, I saw a shift of darkness, a mere flicker of movement where there should not have been any. I slowed my already deliberate, careful pace and veered again as though avoiding another liquid-filled pothole.

I hoped the hotel was slated for demolition soon, because the property desperately needed upgrading.

Peering through the precipitation, I caught another tiny flutter of movement and my hackles rose. I knew that kind of furtive shift in stance. It came from stiffening muscles screaming to be eased. It came from an unconscious adjustment for comfort. It meant danger, because someone lurked near my vehicle. I didn't know the reason for such behavior, but I did know it meant nothing good.

It was time to take control of this clusterfuck. George Washington was right when he opined that the best defense was a good offense.

I let my foot slide on a patch of ice and went down in a controlled fall. The ruse worked, which meant whoever waited for me wasn't a trained professional. A rush of darkness, scleras gleaming beneath a balaclava, the pale color—probably gray—of a hoodie beneath a heavy leather jacket, and the flash of expensive white athletic shoes crashed into me. I rolled and grappled with a fist brandishing a knife which left me open to several punishing blows from his other fist, including one to the back of my skull. Head ringing, I brought my knee up in a sharp movement that most men never expect another man to make, an assumption of professional courtesy, I suppose.

My assailant gasped and grunted and managed to shift his hips away from the crushing blow of my knee, which connected with his inner thigh instead of his genitals. However, his avoidance enabled me to wrap an arm around his throat and squeeze. I clenched my arm, and my assailant abruptly switched from lethal assault to fighting for his life. I delivered a few rapid punches to his kidneys. If he lived, he'd piss blood for a few days.

We rolled across the wet parking lot, slammed up against tires and vehicles. With a last-ditch, twisting buck, he broke free of my hold and rolled under another SUV. Gasping, he scuttled away, leaving behind his knife, which I appropriated for my own use. I hefted it, automatically noting its light weight and poor balance. *Cheap.*

In the darkness, I could not see his movements, but I, too, used the sense God gave me and the training pounded into me by the U.S. Marine Corps and scrambled behind another vehicle. My chest heaved, cold, wet air filled my lungs as I wiped water from my face. A spurt of orange and a muffled blast informed me that whoever wanted me dead had a firearm equipped with a silencer.

Training drilled into my mind and body took over. I ducked behind another vehicle for cover, then tracked the man who wanted me dead before advancing on him, moving in unpredictable bursts of speed and not always in the expected direction. Another sputter of sound and burst of orange helped me refine his direction. I crept closer. Three more shots hit the cars behind and beside me. The metal rang loudly as bullets penetrated their bodies. I ducked again, slipped, felt asphalt dig into my head, and rolled aside.

"Fuck! Shit!" The voice had a higher pitch than did the baritone grunts of my first assailant.

The knife wielding guy had a buddy with a gun. My chest heaved with deep draws of cold air as I tried to suss out whether there was a third.

"Goddammit!" The hissed profanity reached my ears as did the slap of soles hitting wet pavement.

I waited, then crept with all deliberate stealth toward my vehicle despite the instinct to pursue and kill. When I reached it, I noticed the scratches in the paint and the cracks in the window. Money couldn't buy everything, but it could purchase custom reinforcement and protection on a vehicle. Whoever had attempted to kill me had also attempted to break into the SUV.

I smiled. Whoever it was had failed on both accounts.

I dug into the pocket of my coat, which was sopping wet and probably ruined from rolling across wet pavement. My head throbbed and I gingerly touched the worst point of pain. Warm wetness met my cold fingers and mingled with the cold sweat and wet that coated my body. I realized my extremities were beginning to go numb. It was time to get a move-on. I dropped the knife into my coat pocket.

Collecting the remainder of our belongings, I hurried back to the door, deciding against moving the car at that time. I simply had no desire to ruin my upholstery. When I entered the hotel and reached the second floor, I tapped the toe of my shoe against the door.

"It's me, kitten," I dared not say her name aloud where anyone could hear it.

The slide of the safety chain and the click of the dead-bolt reassured me that Dana had taken prudent precautions. She opened the door. Her eyes went wide.

"Sam! What happened?"

The door flew wide open and I stumbled through, aware that my entire body shivered.

"My God, you're soaked through," she fussed and let the door close and latch on its own as she took the items from my arms and set them aside. Looking at me, she said, "Get undressed. You need a hot shower. *Now.*"

I knew she was right and a weak chuckle dribbled past my lips as I considered the reversal of a similar situation just two nights ago. I lurched as she tugged off my coat and reached for the wall to steady myself.

"Oh! Oh, my God!" she cried out again.

I followed the direction of her gaze. Apparently the wetness inside my coat wasn't entirely from puddles and wet weather. I grunted as I pulled off my shirt.

"It's not that deep," I said through gritted teeth, the numbing effect of adrenaline wearing off to ensure I felt the pain of lacerated skin. I wished I'd managed to crush the first guy's balls.

"You need stitches."

"I am not going out to the car to get the first aid kit, and neither are you."

Frowning, Dana ducked into the bathroom and turned on the water. "Can you clean yourself?"

I nodded.

She met my gaze, held it. Coming to the decision that I wasn't entirely debilitated, she helped me finish undressing and guided me to the bathtub where hot water steamed.

"Leave the door open. I'm going down to the front desk for a first aid kit," she said.

"Ask for self-adhesive bandages and scissors," I instructed. "I'll make do with butterfly bandages. You know what those are?"

She nodded.

I lowered my aching, shivering body into the water and gasped at the heat. It *hurt*. However, I forced myself to lean back and let the water warm my flesh. At least, my muzzy brain supplied, I hadn't popped a cockstand while she was undressing me.

Ignoring the pain of movement, I made a diligent effort to use the saltine cracker sized bar of soap to wash myself. More red stained the water when I washed and rinsed my hair. Palpating that wound, I decided it was small and shallow enough to heal on its own. I just wanted to be sure that it was free of parking lot grit.

By the time I levered myself from the tub and dried off my body, Dana had returned. She closed the lid on the toilet, pointed to it, and said, "Sit."

I gestured toward the countertop and said, "Wouldn't it be easi—"

"*Sit,*" she repeated.

I sat. She kneeled beside me and opened the first aid kit. "I told the front desk clerk that you cut yourself with your pocket knife."

She peeled the paper wrapping off a generic brand of bandage and cut the adhesive tab into a butterfly shape. She looked up at me.

"Can you hold the edges of your skin together or does that hurt too much?"

I grunted and pinched the edges together with one hand, giving her barely enough room to stick the bandage in place. We repeated the process, using all sixteen bandages in the kit.

"Where else?" she asked.

I bowed my head.

"Good Lord," she breathed and grabbed a washcloth. She soaked it beneath a cold stream of water from the faucet, wrung it out, and dabbed it at the still oozing cut. She rinsed the cloth, dabbed, rinsed, dabbed, until she was satisfied it was as clean as she could get it.

"I can't bandage that," she said.

"Just dab at it now and then. It'll scab over," I told her. Scalp wounds bled like a bitch.

She nodded. "You think you can make it to the bed?"

"Yeah."

I leaned on her, let her support me with her slender strength as she helped me walk to the king sized bed. She drew back the covers and helped me ease onto the mattress.

"Can you sit?"

"Yeah."

"Okay. I'm going to make you some coffee. Decaf."

"Okay."

She handed me the remote control for the television and busied herself with cleaning the mess in the bathroom and brewing a cup of coffee. She held the cup to my lips and helped me sip it, exclaiming over the bruises decorating the right side of my torso. We conducted a terse conversation between sips of the scalding liquid.

"What happened, Sam?"

"Attacked."

"A mugger? Out in this weather?"

"No. Target."

"Target?" Awareness dawned in her expression. "You mean you were targeted?"

"Yeah."

She considered that and made some other mental connection. "You or me?"

"Dunno."

She obviously realized that my coherence was fading fast. She set aside the half-empty cup. "You lie down. I'll help you. There you go, left side. Good boy."

"Woof," I muttered with a weak chuckle. The poor wit only confirmed that I needed to rest and recuperate.

She drew the covers over me. My vision blurred, then my eyes drifted shut. I heard the rustle of cloth, felt the mattress dip behind me, and then the heat of her body plastered itself against my still chilled skin. She draped an arm and a leg over me, covering me with her heat as much as she was able. I sighed, relishing both the closeness of her soft flesh and the heat of her against my body.

With a soft grunt, Dana's cat leaped onto the bed and landed on my pillow. I might have murmured something. I don't know. Some time later I awoke to a pounding headache and found that damned cat curled against my belly. The heat that furry little furnace exuded surprised me.

Chapter 12

Dana

Sam's gray pallor returned to normal by morning, for which I was grateful. I left him hugging Sly—although he'd never admit to having done so—as I used the hotel's complimentary tea bags to fix ourselves some morning caffeine. I showered, dressed, and checked my phone while Sam continued to sleep. When he roused himself, I averted my eyes to the masculine beauty of his muscled body as he disentangled himself from Sly and headed for the bathroom. He emerged, face a bit reddened from where he'd splashed cold water. I noticed he hadn't shaved and supposed he probably still felt the effects of whatever had happened the night before.

Sly hopped down from the bed and made a beeline for the litter box.

Sam sat. I picked up his overnight bag and set it on the bed, saying, "You might want to get dressed."

He grunted and rubbed his scruffy jaw. "Thanks."

I retreated to the armchair and asked, "So, what happened last night?"

"I was attacked."

"A mugger?" I asked for a second time.

"No. Muggers usually prefer not to get the shit beat out of them."

I blinked and wondered what the other guy looked like, because Sam looked like someone had beaten the stuffing out of *him*.

"He tried to break into my car," Sam continued as he pulled clothes from the bag, the words coming slowly as he thought over the previous night's events.

"Tried?" I prompted.

"Bullet resistant windows, tamper resistant locks." He pulled on a pair of boxers and grunted.

"Ah," I said as though I understood when, really, I didn't understand at all.

"It wasn't random. If it were, he would have run when I came toward the vehicle." He slid his arms into the long sleeves of another henley, grimacing as the skin stretched around the cut along his ribs. That shirt was dark green. He sure did like that type of shirt.

I nodded more to keep him talking than anything else.

"Which means we were targeted."

"We?" I blurted. "I don't have any enemies." I found that concept ludicrous. "Probably you, someone you thwarted working security."

He tugged on a pair of jeans. "No, whoever it was had to have been following us, tracking us somehow."

"How?" I asked as my phone buzzed. I picked it up. "Hi, Dad. ... Yeah, we're stuck in Warsaw. Nasty weather. ... Sure, if the roads are clear, we'll head out. If not, we'll stay put for another night. ... Love you, too, Dad."

"Your phone," Sam said and held out his hand. I glanced down. He'd put on socks and shoes during my short phone call. "Give it to me."

"Why?" I asked even as I handed it to him.

He looked it over, popped the cover to the SIM card, and removed the card. Then he set the phone on the window sill and extracted a big knife from his coat pocket. He hefted it.

"Sam?"

With a heavy blow, he smashed the knife's hilt into my phone.

"Sam! What are you doing?"

"It's bugged," he growled. "It's got to be."

"Are you crazy?" I demanded as he slammed the hilt into the device three more times in quick succession. "That's my phone!"

"And that's how *you* were tracked." He dug through the smashed pieces and pulled out a small button-looking thing with a thin wire dangling from it.

"Me?"

"That's a bug," he said. He carried it into the bathroom. The toilet flushed. I guessed what he did to the incriminating bit of technology. "Why would someone track you?"

"I haven't any idea," I whispered.

"Well, we can't stay here," he said. "Pack up. We're leaving."

I didn't argue, my mind stunned by the idea that someone had bugged my phone. I couldn't think why. Or who? Who would do something like that. It wasn't as though I had access to state secrets or anything like that.

Sam fetched his car and illegally parked it outside the side entrance. We loaded it up, Sly protesting at having to go back inside it. We drove around to the front and he accompanied me inside to the front desk where we checked out.

"The roads are still icy," I complained as the vehicle skidded to a slow stop.

"Let's get breakfast."

I glared at him, finding the lack of explanation exasperating. However, my stomach growled in approval of the plan to eat, so I didn't object. Protest probably wouldn't have done any good anyway.

We stopped a few miles down the road at a Bob Evans Restaurant. We left Sly in the car with a bowl of kibble. The hostess showed us to a secluded booth and took our orders for coffee (for Sam) and hot tea (for me).

"What the hell is going on, Sam?" I hissed.

Chapter 13

Dana

"When was the last time your phone was not in your possession?" Sam asked.

"When … the night I spent at your place," I spluttered. "So what? Sonya wouldn't have tampered with my phone and Bradley certainly doesn't need to."

"What about your camera?" he asked. "The card in your camera?"

I glanced through the window at the vehicle. "That camera doesn't have a card. I work in film."

"Film?" His eyes widened in surprise. "I thought that was a hobby, that you used film for the artistic stuff, not for the freelance gigs."

I sighed. "It started that way, but I realized that the photos I took with film were so much better than those I took with a digital camera. So, I work almost exclusively with film. I don't even own a digital camera anymore. If I want to take digital photos, I use—*used*—my phone."

"I'll buy you another phone—"

"Damn right you will."

He glared at me just as the waitress returned to take our orders.

"What does this have to do with anything?"

"It ties into the burglary," he said. "I know it does. They destroyed everything. Someone wasn't there just to steal something, they were searching for something, and I don't think they found it?"

"Who is *they*?"

"I don't know, not yet."

"Well, I don't have whatever it is *they* want. Next time, I'll explain that if I happen to catch them in the act."

The look he gave me left no doubt as to the idiocy of that statement. "Next time, they'll make a better effort to kill you."

"What? Why would they want to kill me when I don't know anything?"

"Either they believe you know something, or they don't believe that you don't know anything."

"That makes no sense, Sam."

His gaze sharpened. "Do you have the last rolls of film you took?"

My hand went to my coat folded beside me on the bench. "Yes, they're in my coat. I make it a habit to always remove the film from the camera as soon as the roll ends or I'm finished shooting. Why?"

"We have to get those pictures developed."

I shook my head, not wanting to believe that I had that kind of enemy, not wanting to admit that he had some valid points. "Sam, this is ridiculous. Someone broke into my apartment looking for loot. Remember, my jewelry and laptop were stolen. Someone saw your big, expensive SUV in the parking lot and my computer in the back seat and thought it, too, would make good pickings. You just surprised a thief and he retaliated."

He shook his head. "No, I don't think so." He raised his eyes and said, "Dana, you're being targeted and I'm going to protect you."

Chapter 14

Sam

"And in breaking news, the wife of Chicago tech mogul Bradley Vermont has been hospitalized. Medical profession-als cite HIPAA regulations prohibit disclosure of what ails one of the world's luckiest women. Other sources have de-clined to comment."

Hearing that on the radio broadcast as we traveled the last miles of a grueling drive to St. Paris, Dana gasped.

"Oh, my God!" she cried. "I hope she's not hurt. I hope Bradley didn't hurt her. She needs to dump his carcass."

I agreed. "He won't make it easy."

"He doesn't own the legal system."

I snorted, because Bradley Vermont did indeed own many of the politicians, lawyers, and judges who ensured litigation favored his interests. She glanced at me, her ex-pression worried. She knew what that snort meant.

"Dana, he's a powerful man with practically unlimited resources. If he can't prevent a divorce, he'll do everything he can to ensure that Sonya's ruined socially and financially. She won't be able to support herself, much less a child. He'll at least force her to turn over custody of their baby."

She frowned, not liking that all too likely possibility. What judge would choose to allow a child to be raised in poverty rather than given the myriad advantages Bradley Vermont could bestow? Her expression solidified into mulish determination.

"Dad would hire her. And she can live with us. I'll help support her and raise the baby."

"You'd volunteer your stepfather without his consent?"

She grinned. "Dad has always said Sonya was welcome to move in. He likes her."

I wondered if Larry Secrest more than just *liked* Sonya Vermont, but said nothing of the sort because I assumed that kind of May-December relationship of an older man and his trophy wife happened more commonly among my parents' social circles than in small rural towns like St. Paris. Dismissing the nasty, suspicious thought, I turned the corner onto Ohio State Route 235 and headed south. We passed a gently rolling landscape of mostly brown dirt and white snow, dotted with barns, farm houses, cattle, and the occasional horse. I thought I saw a llama, too. I had never ventured into southwest Ohio and nothing about what I saw made me regret the lack.

"Dreary, isn't it?" Dana commented with a sigh. "It's pretty here in summer and in fall when the leaves turn. Otherwise, it's just mud or mud and snow. Dad likes to tell me about when he was a kid and winter was always snowy with the occasional ice storm."

"Climate change," I said with a shrug.

"Dad thinks climate change is hogwash. I'm not so sure," she admitted and looked out the window.

We turned east on State Route 36. The small town of St. Paris soon appeared on the horizon.

"Where do you want to stop?" I asked. "Your father's house or the diner?"

"Let's hit the diner. I'm hungry."

The Hot Spot was on the small town's main drag. I parked the SUV along the curb and waited for Dana to make sure her unhappy cat had food and water before accompanying me inside the diner.

A middle-aged waitress wearing a sleeve of tattoos on her left arm and a red apron over her tee shirt and jeans looked up as the door opened, caught sight of who entered, and called out, "Dana, you're finally here! Your daddy's been expecting you. He's in the back."

"Still manning the grill?" she quipped as we stepped inside an homage to the 1950s. Pictures of Marilyn Monroe, James Dean, Elizabeth Taylor, Rock Hudson, and other big name movie stars decorated the walls.

"As always," the waitress replied and returned her attention to the table filled with patrons waiting to place their orders.

I followed Dana past the front counter and through a door marked "Employees Only." Standing at the grill and wielding a metal spatula with impressive skill, a tall, lanky man sensed the presence of someone behind him and went still. He turned around, shoulders tightening in readiness to fight. They relaxed when his gaze lighted upon his step-daughter.

"Pumpkin! You hold on just a minute while I plate these orders."

"Sure, Dad."

Larry Secrest deftly filled two plates which were grabbed by another waitress who carried them out, calling, "Welcome back, kiddo!"

"Business is good?" Dana asked as the cook enveloped her in a hug and kissed the top of her head.

"Busy as ever," he replied. Holding her at arm's length, he said, "Let's get a look at you."

She grinned at him.

"You're too thin. I'm gonna have to feed you before putting you to work."

"Dad, you always say that."

"And I'm always right," he retorted with a grin. He raised his eyes and met my gaze. "Pumpkin, is this the man who's been taking care of you?"

Dana's cheeks colored. "Yeah, Dad, this is Sam Galdicar. Sam, my dad, Larry."

Larry extended his hand toward me and I shook it. He played no dominance games trying to crush mine, but the strength of his grip made it clear that he tolerated no disrespect toward his adopted daughter.

"Thanks for bringing my little girl home, Sam."

"It was my pleasure, sir."

He looked at Dana. "You bring that cat, too?"

"Yes, Dad, we brought Sly."

The man snorted as a waitress brought in an order slip. "You'll have to confine him to your room, pumpkin. My allergies ain't getting any better."

She nodded. "Sure thing, Dad. I'll start looking for an apartment."

He turned back toward the grill and paused mid-way. "I'm not kicking you out."

"I know, Dad." She sighed and paused, something obviously on her mind. Then she blurted, "Dad, I'm concerned about Sonya."

His eyebrows shot up. "She finally leave that asshole?"

I wondered how diner owner and operator Larry Secrest had met technology billionaire Bradley Vermont. *Perhaps while they were dating?* Larry, obviously, had taken Bradley's measure and found it lacking.

Dana shook her head. "I heard she's in the hospital and I'd bet anything Bradley put her there. He's ... he's *mean* to her. Anyway, I want to help her, help her get her away from him."

Larry ruffled her hair and replied, "You know Sonya's always welcome here, pumpkin. You two were practically sisters growing up."

"Yeah, so, don't you mind if I invite her to stay in your house? She has nowhere else to go."

"'Course not," he reassured her. "Now get out of my kitchen. I gotta get cookin'."

We returned to the dining room and slid into a booth upholstered in bright red vinyl. It contrasted sharply with the black and white patterned tile and shiny chrome of the 1950s style diner.

"Dad always liked Steak 'n Shake," she explained the familiar décor. "But there's no local franchise and he didn't want to pay the franchise fees. There's one in Springfield if you get the hankering."

I shook my head and gestured for her to continue speaking.

"Anyway, he wanted to open his own hamburger palace. When he retired from the Air Force, he went to Sam and Ethel's in Tipp City and K's in Troy and Mundy's in Springfield for tips and tricks on an independent diner. The folks there were really nice, welcomed his questions, and helped him with suggestions. As you can see, he's made quite a go of it." She shifted in the booth. "The red, black, and white décor gets a little clichéd, though." She giggled. "It almost makes me want to come in one night with buckets of yellow and green paint."

"And what would you do?"

"I'd paint all the white tiles on the floor yellow and all the white areas on the wall green." She sighed. "Boy, that would piss Dad off something fierce, so I'd never do it."

I couldn't help but smile at her offended sense of artistry. My woman liked color and probably detested the monochromatic scheme of my condo. I blinked at the thought and wondered where the hell *my woman* came from.

The tattooed waitress approached our table and asked, "What do y'all want, honey?"

Dana rattled off an order without looking at the menu which I'd ignored. The waitress looked at me in expectation.

"I'll have the same," I said.

"You didn't even look at the menu," Dana remarked as the waitress promised our food would be ready shortly.

"I figured you knew what was the best here, so why order anything else?"

"But you might not even like what I ordered," she reasoned.

"I'm not picky."

She snorted. "I looked inside your refrigerator. There's nothing in there but leafy green stuff and boneless, skinless chicken breasts. Don't give me that."

I shrugged. "Just because I commit myself to a healthy diet doesn't mean I don't enjoy junk food once in a while."

She chuckled and shook her head. "A closet burger junkie. Don't let Dad hear you call his food junk food. He'll shoot you on sight."

"Quality ingredients, hm?"

"The best," she replied. "He gets pretty much everything from local farmers, except maybe the ketchup, salt, and pepper."

"That's impressive, a local business supporting local businesses."

Her smile took on a wry twist. "Yeah, the slow food movement has reached even hick towns like St. Paris."

"I didn't mean it like that and you know it," I chided.

She sighed. "No, and I'm sorry. I know you didn't. I get defensive sometimes. Where did you grow up?"

"Texas," I replied. "On a cattle ranch."

"Really?" Her eyes brightened with interest as she began to understand that I had some familiarity with farming types. "Why'd you go into security?"

"I enlisted," I replied. She made a rolling motion in a silent bid for details. "I wanted to get away from home" *There, that was true.* "And I found military life offered the opportunities I wanted." *True again.* "I did a few tours, worked my way up a few steps, then left." *Also true, if vague.* "I liked the security field and went into business for myself without the bureaucratic red tape and hassle of working for the government."

"That's impressive. You must be really good, otherwise Bradley wouldn't have hired you."

"I like to think so," I replied modestly.

She snorted again and chuckled.

"How'd you get into photography?" I asked, deciding it was my turn to play twenty questions.

"Dad gave me an old camera when he and Mom were dating, said it belonged to him when he was a boy. He showed me how to load the film and taught me how to take pictures. I fell in love with it, and he never let me regret following my passion."

I felt a sad smile tug at my lips. "He sounds like a great father."

"Yeah, he is."

Our food arrived and conversation ceased while we dug into the best hamburgers and french fries I'd ever tasted. The chocolate milkshake wasn't bad either.

Chapter 15

Sam

After we finished our meal, we drove through thickly falling snow to the Secrest home, a modest ranch style sided with red brick on a generously sized lot just beyond the town's edge. Two trips to the SUV and everything was inside. Sly made himself comfortable on the purple velvet bedspread on the twin bed in Dana's childhood bedroom still decorated with unicorn posters and pink patterned wallpaper. A freestanding clothing rack was positioned beside what looked like a closet door. A hand-lettered cardboard sign had been tacked onto the door and read in large, glitter-covered letters: DANA'S DARK ROOM. STAY OUT.

"Wow, this I would never have guessed," I commented, staring at the display of a young girl's sense of decor.

"Yeah, I've grown up," she murmured. "Mom hung the wallpaper. We didn't know she was sick then. I loved unicorns—hey, most twelve-year-old girls do, you know." She sighed. "Neither Dad nor I had the heart to ever remodel it."

I wrapped my arm around her and held her against me, a silent offer of strength and support. I hadn't known that type of familial closeness, but I definitely envied it.

Gathering her composure, Dana took a deep breath and said, "Let me show you to the guest bedroom. You'll stay there tonight."

"I'll find a hotel," I offered, not wanting to impose.

She chuckled, then said, "There aren't any hotels within ten miles of here, probably more. Look, Sam, you've done me a huge favor—and you don't even like me. Let me at least reciprocate with family hospitality."

I felt my lips press together in an effort not to blurt that she was wrong about my not liking her. The more time I spent in her company, the more I did like her. Actually, what I felt for her had only a little to do with *like* and a whole lot to do with *lust*. Instead, I asked, "Won't your father mind?"

"He'd be disappointed if I didn't offer and you didn't accept."

The drive from Warsaw, which should have taken maybe three hours, had stretched more than twice as long due to poor road conditions and myriad delays along the way. I didn't look forward to the drive back. A glance out the window boded ill for anyone's travel plans. Snow fell thick and fast.

"Then I accept," I said.

"I'll show you to the guest bedroom," she offered again and pointed to a door across the short corridor. She then pointed to a doorway at the end of the hallway. "That's the bathroom. No unicorns in there."

I laughed at her dry tone and left to fetch my overnight bag.

When I returned, she held the receiver end of an old-fashioned corded phone. I shamelessly eavesdropped on the conversation.

"Yeah, Shirley, I'm back for a bit. My place in Chicago was broken into, everything pretty much destroyed. ... Anyway, I've got to go shopping and replace my wardrobe and get a few other things. ... You still have Nate's old clunker? Mind if I borrow it? ... Oh, his stepson is using it? Okay, well, I'll stop by in a day or two to say hello and visit. Thanks, Shirley."

"You need me to hang around for a day or two?" I asked, offering myself as chauffeur and wondering just what the hell had come over me.

"No, that's okay, Sam," she replied. "I know you've got to get back to work. I'll wait until Dad's got a few hours off and borrow his car."

"How about Uber or Lyft?"

She snorted. "Here? In St. Paris? You have got to be kidding me. We're lucky to have high-speed internet."

I nodded and wondered how people functioned like that, which made me realize just how terribly spoiled I was. As I carried my bag to the guest bedroom, my phone buzzed. I recognized the caller and accepted the call.

"Yeah, Gordon, what is it?"

"Boss, you're not gonna believe this."

"Get to the point, Gordon."

"She left him."

"Be more specific. I want details," I demanded as I shut the bedroom door behind me.

Handsome, commanding, and obscenely wealthy, Bradley Vermont couldn't sneeze without media panic that he'd contracted some deadly disease. He attracted media attention like flies to shit and considered it his due.

Gordon relayed the essential details. That morning's usual—meaning *approved*—excursion to church where many of Bradley Vermont's social and business acquaintances attended more for the opportunity to see and be seen rather than for any truly spiritual benefit had yielded unexpected consequences. My phone beeped.

"Hold on, Gordon, Mr. Vermont's on the phone. I'll take his call and get back to you." I ended that call and accepted my client's hail.

"Sam, you fucked up again."

"Sir?" Now did not seem like the time to remind him that we were old friends.

"My wife refuses to return home—*my* wife! You have to bring her back."

"I'll be happy to speak with her—"

"I didn't ask you to *speak* with her, I told you *to bring her back*."

"Mr. Vermont, if she refuses to accept our escort, then we cannot force her to go anywhere."

"I don't care what she wants," my client spat. "You will retrieve my wife."

"Forcible retrieval is considered abduction," I reminded him. "I won't order my staff to commit a felony."

"Then do it yourself."

"I will talk with her and try to persuade her that returning to you is in her best interests," I said, not believing the last part of that sentence even as I spoke the words. Deep down, I cheered for Sonya Vermont and wished her success in holding on to her new resolve.

"I will *ruin* that interfering pastor," Bradley growled. "And if you don't retrieve my wife, I'll ruin *you*."

Nothing like incentive.

"Mr. Vermont, our contract is hereby terminated," I replied, my tone icy with fury at the threat. I disconnected the call and sent out a group text ordering all staff to withdraw from that assignment immediately.

Gordon called back. "What about Sonya? She needs protection from that asshole."

I raised my eyebrows at the switch from "Mrs. Vermont" to "Sonya" and wondered if Gordon fancied her. "Gordon, you may offer your service *pro bono* to Mrs. Vermont if you wish, but let me know so I don't reassign you."

"She needs someone in her corner, Sam."

"I know. She can't do any better than you." I paused, then added, "Make sure you get her a new phone. Hers is bugged."

"Gotcha. I'll keep you posted," he promised and terminated the call.

I set the phone down and rubbed my temples. A headache pounded beneath my skull. This shitshow was just getting worse and I sensed that it was all somehow connected. I just didn't know how.

I wondered whether I ought to inform Dana that her best friend had left her husband and decided against it. I preferred not to open that particular can of worms. I figured Sonya would contact Dana herself if she needed her friend's help.

Chapter 16

Dana

The house phone rang about 4:00 p.m. the next afternoon. Dad was due home in a couple of hours, so I answered it rather than let the call go to voicemail. Dad hated voicemail, alway saying that if the call was important, then whoever it was would call back. He was right more often than wrong, but I was home to answer it and saw no purpose in not doing so. I picked up the mechanical pencil he kept near the phone and held it poised over the tattered, spiral bound notepad placed there for taking down messages.

"Hello?"

"Dana? I thought I'd be talking to your dad."

"Sonya, is that you?"

"Yes. Um … your old home phone is the only number I could remember."

"Sonya, why are you calling my dad? Are you in trouble?"

She gulped a sob and the words poured out, practically incoherent. What I did learn was that she'd left the son of a bitch who tortured her and called it love. Trying to calm her down, I shushed her and asked, "Where are you now?"

"The parsonage," she whispered.

"The parsonage?" I echoed in confusion.

"You ... you know where I go to church?"

"Yeah."

"I'm with Pastor Blankenship and his wife. They're allowing me to stay with them in the parsonage for a little bit."

Reminded of my own compromised cell phone, I suspected that hers, too, was bugged. "Sonya, are you calling me from your cell phone?"

"Um ... no. Pastor Blankenship suggested I use the parsonage phone."

Good man. "That's good, Sonya. Your cell phone's probably bugged." At that point I floundered. I didn't know what to do for her, or if there was anything I could do for her other than provide an open ear and a virtual shoulder to cry upon. "Um ... do you have a lawyer?"

She wept, "No, I only have you."

Well, I'm no good for legal matters. "Sonya, you need to get an attorney, someone whom Bradley doesn't own." Privately, I doubted she'd find any lawyer in all of Illinois whom her husband either didn't own or couldn't intimidate. An idea struck me. "Look, Sam's still here—" I didn't explain about the fourteen inches of snow topped with a fresh glaze of ice that Mother Nature dumped on us overnight and this morning, preventing Sam from heading back to Chicago "—I'll ask him for a referral. Maybe he knows someone."

"Dana, I can't pay. Bradley's cut off my credit cards. I can't get into my bank account—"

I interrupted, "He's a co-signer on your bank accounts, isn't he?"

She sighed. "Yes. His name is on *everything*. I don't even have a driver's license anymore."

What a jerk. I took a deep breath to calm my own temper before it boiled over and I said something hurtful, like how my best friend had become a spineless puppet, a rag doll who let her husband do anything he wanted to her without protest. I'd said it before, although in much softer terms: a woman needs her own money.

"What about clothes? Jewelry?"

"Everything's at the condo." She sniffled, then her voice turned sharp, "I didn't think to bring a packed suitcase with me to church Christmas morning."

"Damn." I let her snappish tone roll off my back, even though it stung. She could have pawned the oodles of jewelry Bradley draped around her neck and wrists. She could sell the haute couture wardrobe on consignment. "Can you pawn your wedding rings?"

"My wedding rings?" came the faint echo of horror.

"I assume you intend to divorce him?"

"Um ..."

I took a deep breath, hearing her waver. Uncertainty and fear would shred her fragile resolve. In a slow, measured voice, I said, "Sonya, ask Pastor Blankenship to pawn your wedding rings and any other jewelry you're wearing. That 10-carat diamond on your hand will get you some ready cash."

"Dana, I loved him so much," she rasped. "How—how could it have all gone so wrong?"

"I don't know," I lied. I'd always thought Bradley Vermont controlling, arrogant, and mean, but my friend didn't need to hear that right then. "But you need to do what's right for you and the baby. You need to stay safe."

"Yes. Yes, you're right. Safe." Then she dissolved into hard, wracking sobs again and my sense of foreboding swelled.

"What is it, Sonya? What's wrong?"

"Th-there is no baby," she wailed.

"What do you mean? I've seen that baby bump."

"I lost the baby!"

"Oh, Sonya," I murmured, knowing that nothing I could say would soothe her distress. *That explains the announcement on the radio.* "Oh, Sonya, I'm so, so sorry."

A new voice came on the line. "To whom am I speaking?"

"Dana Secrest," I replied. "Is this Pastor Blakenship?"

"It is," came the simple reply voiced in deep, mellifluous tones that Barry White might have envied. Sonya's agonized weeping filled the background. "I'm going to hang up the phone now. Sonya needs to rest."

"All right," I said. "Pastor Blankenship?"

"Yes, Ms. Secrest?"

"Thank you for taking care of Sonya. She's my best friend."

"We'll do what we can for her," he promised, "but she cannot stay here indefinitely."

"No, no, of course not. Look, we're snowed under and no one's going anywhere right now; but, as soon as I can, I'll come for her. I'll bring her home. My dad and I will take care of her."

"Your loyalty to your friend does you credit, young woman. Call me before you come."

"I will. Thanks."

I hung up the phone and plopped onto the sofa next to Sam who somehow managed not to fidget from the enforced inactivity.

"What is it?" he asked.

"Sonya had a miscarriage."

His eyes turned bleak, although not a muscle in his face or body moved. "Poor woman."

"Bradley will blame it on her," I said, my tone dull with worry.

He didn't answer.

"If she lands in his clutches again, he'll take it out on her."

Again, he said nothing. The lack of response irritated me.

"Look, Sam, I know he's your buddy and you don't want to admit that he's an abuser, but—"

Sam stood and turned toward me, towering over me, *looming*. His fists were clenched. "Don't take your temper out on me, Dana."

I heaved myself back to my feet and stepped to the side so I could glower up at him. He still loomed, but not by quite so much as when I was slumped on the couch. I poked his chest with a stiff index finger.

"Look, you, you were around her much more than I ever was. You saw more than I ever did. You should have called the authorities to report—"

He grabbed my shoulders in his big hands. "Report what? That a husband and wife enjoyed *consensual sex* that got rough? Do you not understand their relationship at all?"

"I understand he beats her and calls it love."

"It's a special kind of relationship between a dom and a sub—"

"Yeah, yeah, I've read all about it." I could feel my upper lip curling in a sneer.

His hands tightened on my shoulders. "*Don't* interrupt me, kitten."

I blinked, mouth going slack at the commanding quality his voice assumed, a deeper, resonant tone that demanded obedience, *my* obedience. After a second's pause, I lifted my lip in a sneer. "I'm not a trained dog you can command."

He pulled me against his body, one hand sliding down to anchor me against his solid bulk. I tilted my head back so I could continue to glare at him. His other hand skimmed upwards, fingers running through my short curls to palm the back of my head and hold it where he wanted it. Dipping his face close to mine, he whispered, "You like it when I take charge."

I opened my mouth to protest, but he crushed his lips to mine. Sam's tongue plunged into my mouth, tangling with my tongue. He *ate* at my mouth, his hands holding me immobile against the sensual assault. I felt his arousal harden against my belly and the answering moisture gather between my thighs. Although I considered myself the Midwest's oldest virgin, I'd read enough romance novels to understand what that meant, to recognize the wet fire of lust that made my heart pound and my knees turn to jelly. I heard a low moan and realized it came from my throat. Then I realized I was kissing him back, that I pressed my body to his willingly, that I *rubbed* against him.

One big hand moved downward, cupping my ass, then kneading the pliant flesh. Fingers firmly pressed at the seam of my jeans and followed it between my legs where they stroked. If the crotches of my panties and jeans hadn't already turned damp, then his touch certainly elicited a release of moisture from my body that created a visible wet spot in the fabric. I moaned again, hands scrabbling at his muscled chest then angling upward to lock around his neck and hold him, encourage him, never let him go.

With a harsh inhale, Sam wrenched his mouth away from mine. I felt his heart thunder, saw his chest heave with each deep, harshly drawn breath. With deliberate control, he removed his hands from my body and took two steps back. I gaped open-mouthed, blood humming, dazzled with passion, and bewildered.

God help me, I did like it when he took charge.

"I won't take your virginity in your dad's house," he rasped, running a hand through that thick, wavy blond hair. "You'll come to my bed."

He turned on his heel, and stomped to the guest bedroom. My jaw dropped and I nearly shouted that he couldn't have it, that I'd never give him that gift. But the words wouldn't come, because my heart wouldn't allow the lie. I knew that if Sam had lowered me to the couch or marched me to a bed, I would have surrendered with a smile. I didn't know how I managed not to follow him and beg him to finish what he'd started.

After standing like a great looby for a long minute, I shook my head and put myself to work cleaning the house. I needed to keep busy. After I'd scrubbed, swept, vacuumed, and polished everything to within an inch of its life, I started on supper.

The phone rang. I answered it.

"Hey, pumpkin."

"Hi, Dad. What's up?"

"I'm closing the diner early."

That didn't surprise me. I glanced out the window. The county's snowplows hadn't yet gone beyond the main thoroughfares in their effort to keep up with the "white death."

"Pull out a chuck roast from the freezer and set it to thaw in the fridge. We'll have that tomorrow. I'll bring home supper from the diner for tonight."

"Sure, Dad," I replied, knowing that he'd bring home enough to feed an army just so he didn't have to throw away good food. The health department frowned upon serving leftovers to customers.

I did as he bade me and retired to my dark room where I occupied the time by developing the rolls of film taken in the days before Christmas.

Chapter 17

Sam

Dana was right. I *should* have realized that the rela-tionship between Sonya and Bradley had turned corrosive and uneven. I *should* have done something. But damn, I hated that she was right. The woman drove me nuts and made me want to bury myself balls deep inside her.

Lying on the bed, I unbuckled my belt and unzipped my jeans. I swallowed a groan at the relief of confinement and licked my lips, tasting that kiss again. I stroked my erection even as I hardly dared to hope that Dana would follow me into the guest room and bend to my will. The thought of her rosy lips wrapped around my cock made my eyes roll back and my balls draw tightly against my body. A few more strokes accompanied by graphic imagi-nation had me gasping. I covered the tip of my cock with a wad of tissues as it erupted.

After carefully wiping myself clean, I stuffed my dick back into my pants and confined it again. I draped a fore-arm across my forehead and found it damp with perspiration. With a grunt, I admitted that I wanted Dana Secrest like I'd never wanted any other woman. Surely, a few nights of passion would cure that uncharacteristic fascination.

Unfortunately for my libido, I could not force myself to ignore her firm intention to give herself to someone who deserved that gift. I admired that determination, that strong sense of self-respect. Too few women resisted the societal pressure to treat themselves cheaply, to reward promiscuity, and ridicule those who held themselves to a higher moral standard.

My phone rang.

"What now?" I muttered as I pulled it out and looked at the caller ID. Levering myself into a sitting position, I answered, "Hello, Mr. Vermont."

"Why aren't you here?" he demanded without the courtesy of a greeting.

"Because there's a foot of snow on the ground and it's still falling fast," I replied. *Does he not remember that I quit, or does he simply refuse to accept it?* The latter was more likely: the world bent to Bradley Vermont's preferences, not the other way around. "No one with two brain cells to rub together is driving in these weather conditions."

"That's not acceptable."

I decided not to antagonize him by reminding him that I no longer worked for him. *Perhaps I can use this opportunity to help Sonya out? Dana would like that.* "Mr. Vermont, neither of us controls the weather. I am not going to kill myself driving to Chicago."

"I want my wife back where she belongs."

"I'm sure you do, but you'll have to be patient." I paused, weighed the pros and cons, then forged ahead with my question regardless: "Have you heard from her?"

"No," he spat. "She won't accept my calls. I either have to speak with that damned preacher or with the lawyer he found for her."

I raised my eyebrows. Rev. Blankenship worked quickly. "Who's her lawyer?"

"Rita Zorokowski," he replied. "The bitch is a *shark*."

I knew the lawyer by reputation—*shark* described her perfectly—and wondered how Sonya could afford her. Instead of blurting that, I asked, "I assume you've cut off Mrs. Vermont's funds?"

"Damn straight. If the bitch won't come to heel—."

I winced and interrupted, "Mr. Vermont, it's unkind to speak of your wife in such terms."

"She's *my* wife and I'll speak of her as I please." He paused, then snarled, "And don't you dare presume to chastise me again."

I'd had enough. "Not to worry, Mr. Vermont. I quit, remember?"

"*You* quit?"

"As of our last conversation, my firm's service to you was terminated. Thank you for your past business. We will not be seeking a reference from you."

"I'll *ruin* you, Sam!"

"Goodbye, sir."

I ended the call, feeling immeasurably relieved, and shot off a group text recalling all my staff from service to Bradley Vermont, just in case the first had gone unnoticed or ignored. Gordon called a moment later.

"Boss?"

"What is it, Gordon?"

"I'm going to continue watching over Sonya."

"You think she needs it?"

"Yeah, I do."

I trusted his instincts. Gordon had saved lives on more than one occasion due to those protective instincts. "Can you speak with her?"

"The Blankenships won't let me near her, say she's refusing to see me. But I can talk to them, maybe persuade them that I'm no longer working for Mr. Vermont. Maybe then she'll see me."

I heard the distress in his voice. *The man's smitten.* "Do it, Gordon. Keep her safe."

"Yes, sir."

Finally, I felt good about something. I wasn't sure what was going on with Bradley Vermont, but it wasn't good and I didn't want Sonya to suffer any more than she already had.

I saw the gleam of headlights and heard the crank of the automatic door opener raising the garage door. Peering through the window, I saw a snow-covered car creep into the garage. Time to play nice for my host.

I left the room and meandered out to the living room. Dana wasn't there. I checked the kitchen. No Dana. I looked into the rest of the house. No lights under bathroom doors indicated the bathrooms were being used. Clenching my jaw, I ventured into her room, the shrine to unicorns and glitter. I didn't see her in there, either. I backed out, then wondered if she was hiding in the dark room. I walked back inside her bedroom and knocked lightly on the door.

"What is it?" she called out. "Dad?"

"No, it's Sam. Your father's home."

"Okay," came the reply. "Thanks for letting me know. Tell him I'll be out in a couple of minutes."

"Sure."

I backed away from the door and headed to the kitchen where I met Larry carrying several plastic bags. After relieving him of some of them and setting them on the table, I asked if there were more in the car to be fetched.

"No, thanks anyway. Where's Dana?" he asked as he opened a cabinet and brought out three plates.

"In her dark room."

He chuckled and grinned. "Tell her to get her ass in gear and come out for supper. If she's not reminded, she'll lose track of time and stay in there for days."

I glanced at the extruded polystyrene foam containers he pulled from the bags. Wonderful odors wafed from them and my mouth watered. With a nod, I left the promise of delicious food to fetch Larry's troublesome step-daughter.

"Food's here," I said, knocking on the door.

"I'm coming," she replied.

"I'll wait right here."

"Oh, damn it, Dad told you to, didn't he?"

I grinned, although she couldn't see through the wood. I heard the faint sounds of sloshing liquid and other things being moved around. After a few minutes, she emerged, looking disgruntled.

"I have to wash my hands."

"Sure." I stood aside to let her pass, but she gestured at me to precede her. "Ladies first."

"Really, Sam?"

"Yes, really. My mama raised me to be a gentleman."

She snorted, then sighed. With a longing glance at her dark room, she submitted to the inevitable and headed toward the bathroom. I followed her out of the room and waited at the bathroom door.

"Why are you still here?"

"Just making sure you don't forget to eat supper."

She grunted and threw another longing look at her bedroom door. "Damn it, I've got some really terrific photos in that roll."

"And they'll wait to be developed until after you eat," I said.

"I know Dad put you up to this."

"He warned me you tend to be single-minded when it comes to your photography."

"Hah. That's probably not the word he used."

I stopped her before we turned the corner to enter the kitchen. She glanced at my hand wrapped around her upper arm. "He only wants what's best for you, Dana." *So do I.*

She shook her head and sighed. "Yeah, I know. Sorry. I'm being a bitch."

I shrugged, released her arm, and followed her into the kitchen. She took in a lungful of the aromas rising from the kitchen table. "Smells wonderful, Dad."

He looked up from his cell phone and stuffed it in his pocket. "Sheriff's office declared a level three emergency. Everything's shut down. Good thing school's out for winter break, or students and faculty would be spending the night there. God, it's a mess out there."

"Any chance Sam can leave tomorrow?" she asked.

Larry shrugged. "Don't know, but not likely. I haven't seen snow like this in ages."

She looked at the table. "Well, it's a good thing you didn't cook your usual quantity today."

He nodded and invited us all to sit. We complied and after a quick bow of our heads and recitation of grace, dug into the bounty he brought home. Somewhere outside, a dog barked. As we ate, conversation turned to mundane topics, the weather, and the latest school shooting—that time in New Mexico by another bullied student who'd finally snapped.

"Larry, do you mind if I do my laundry here tonight?" I asked, remembering that I had nothing clean to wear the next day.

"No, go right ahead," he replied with a speaking stare at his step-daughter.

She got the message. "Sam, just set your dirty laundry outside and I'll do it. I'm out of clean clothes myself and it doesn't look like I'll be going shopping tomorrow or probably the next day, either."

"Thank you."

She nodded. "Looks like I'll have to scrounge around and try to find my old clothes from high school."

"Do you think they'll still fit?" Larry asked with a frown.

She shrugged. "I expect they'll be too tight. When I moved to Chicago, I took everything with me that fit."

"Get some sweatpants and a shirt from my bureau," he said, leveling a look at me that I met and held, one man to another acknowledging the presence of a lovely, nubile, young woman in our midst.

His glare warned me to keep my hands to myself. I desperately wanted to offer her my shirt to wear because the idea of her wearing another man's shirt—even her stepfather's—made something inside me roar with outrage and possessive jealousy.

Chapter 18

Sonya

"I don't want to see him," I muttered when Suzanne Blankenship informed me that Gordon Pasqualle asked to meet with me.

She nodded and left to relay the negative response, only to return a moment later.

"Honey, he says he's no longer employed by your husband and he won't attempt to return you to Mr. Vermont's keeping."

My eyebrows shot upward in surprise, then angled downward in suspicion. "Really?"

She nodded. "I'm a good judge of character. He's not lying."

I sighed and relented. "All right, I'll see him."

She nodded and disappeared again, returning less than a minute later leading him into the parsonage's old-fashioned front parlor. I looked up at Gordon and waved my hand in a vague gesture of silent invitation to take a seat.

He did with a quiet murmur of thanks to Suzanne who gave him a small smile.

"I'll be right outside if you need me, Sonya."

"Thank you," I replied, relieved that she wasn't abandoning me entirely to the bodyguard.

I took his measure as he sat quietly and endured my hostile scrutiny. He leaned forward, elbows resting on denim-clad knees. He wore hiking style boots, suitable for the recent inclement weather that practically immobilized the entire Midwest. The white of a cotton undershirt peeked from beneath the collar of a dark red crew neck sweater that had the effect of making burly shoulders appear even broader. Threads of silver glinted at his temples and I noticed the little crinkles at the outside corners of his eyes. For the first time, I wondered how old he was.

"What do you want, Gordon?" I asked, knowing my cold tone and blunt question were rude. I simply didn't care.

"I came by to see how you're doing, Sonya," he replied, mossy green eyes dark with honest concern.

"I lost my baby. How do you think I'm doing?"

He winced and his expression emanated sorrow. He extended a hand toward me. I ignored it. Withdrawing it, he said, "I'm sorry, Sonya. Truly, I am."

I averted my gaze. The hours spent in the emergency room and recovering from the dilation and curettage the physician performed to ensure no tissue remained within my womb remained a horrible memory.

"I don't even know if it was a girl or a boy," I blurted, my voice hoarse.

"Mr. Vermont knows about the miscarriage," he said.

I flinched in automatic expectation of punishment. Doubtless he'd get out the flogger and use it with vicious precision. Then, when my flesh screamed in pain, he'd fuck me senseless. And, somehow, he'd make me enjoy it and beg for more.

In a dull voice, I asked, "Who told him?"

"I assume the hospital did."

"What about HIPAA?"

"Most rules don't apply to Bradley Vermont. You know that."

I sighed, because I knew that billionaires received preferential treatment from everybody. Bradley certainly enjoyed it and took advantage of it.

"I've been in contact with Sam," he volunteered.

I shrugged.

"Mr. Vermont is no longer our client."

Good. I thought it, but didn't say it. Instead, I asked, "Is Dana all right?"

"Sam says she's fine. They're snowed in at her father's house."

"Ah," I replied and thought, *She's not coming back.* "You know I grew up with her?"

He shook his head. "I know you've been friends with her for a long time."

Gordon's quiet, undemanding presence seemed to loosen something within me so I could let down my guard. It made me babble.

"I grew up on a farm not far from her father's house. She rode with me—horses. We did the 4-H thing together in high school. We worked together in her father's diner after school. Then we went to college."

I didn't tell Gordon that was when my life went off the rails. As a freshman, I met a driven doctoral student who worked as a teaching assistant in one of my classes. He took a fancy to me. The first time Dana met him she didn't like him, but she held her tongue and simply warned me to be careful. He finished his degree; I didn't.

I wish I'd listened to her.

We lapsed into silence. It wasn't comfortable, but I didn't know what to say to break it.

After an eternity that was probably only a couple of minutes, Gordon said, "I'd like to help you."

Stunned, I blurted, "Why?"

"Because when your marriage is finally dissolved, I can do what I've wanted to do for the last three years."

I blinked. "Which is what?"

"Ask you out on a date."

I blinked again. "You're not serious."

"Of course, I am. Do you think I'd be here talking with you if I weren't?"

"You might be here trying to get back into my good graces, to get me to trust you so you can drag me back to my husband." I pressed my lips together, rolling them between my teeth before saying, "Besides, you never gave any indication of being attracted to me. How would I ever have known you wanted to date me?"

Gordon favored me with a small smile. "I'm very good at my job and I don't poach other men's wives, but rest assured that you're gorgeous and sexy, and that I want to get to know you on a personal basis."

I felt heat creep across my neck and face.

He held out his hand again. I looked at it, but did not take it. He withdrew his hand and rose to his feet.

"I'll talk to the household staff and see if they can liberate some of your clothes, at least, so you won't have to borrow something to wear."

I snorted, a quiet, ladylike, delicate snort. "Hah. Bradley won't let a single thing go."

"Maybe not, but it won't hurt to try." He crossed the short distance between us and brushed a lock of my hair over my shoulder. "Sonya, I know you're skittish and I understand why. I don't blame you. But know this, I'm a patient man and I won't hurt you."

Looking at my hands twisted together on my lap, I blinked away sudden tears. I was accustomed to the predatory patience of a stalker, the same lethal, edged, manipulative patience that characterized my husband when he was on the hunt for the next big deal or when he wanted to do something to me.

I felt the light stroke of his hand over my hair and heard him whisper, "I want to show you how gentle a man can be."

Teardrops fell to my lap as he walked away.

Chapter 19

Dana

The next day, for the first time that I could remember, Dad didn't open the diner. Confined to the house and waiting for the county's snowplows to clear the roads, we tried to keep ourselves occupied without getting on each other's nerves. My body practically hummed whenever Sam was near. I didn't quite know what to make of it, but the few times I caught his pale blue eyes focused on me made my blood heat and something low in my belly flutter with anticipation.

Dad drew Sam into the kitchen where they sat at the table and played cards.

"You want to play, honey?"

"No, thanks, Dad. I'm going to read."

Only paying partial attention to the book I'd read before, an old favorite, I eavesdropped on their conversation, learning a little more about Sam's family and discovering he preferred single malt scotch to Kentucky bourbon. None of the details he revealed told me much about who he really was as a person. That lack annoyed me even as I remonstrated with myself that I didn't want to know, that it wasn't any of my business, that I didn't even like him.

Liar, liar, pants on fire!

Exasperated with myself, I retreated to my dark room where the chemical magic of developing photographs commanded my attention. I frowned at many of the pictures which had seemed so magical when I took them and now looked merely pedestrian. A few, however, made me smile. Those exhibited the spark of genius that caught at my heartstrings and reminded me why I did what I did and why I loved it.

I hung the photos up to dry and glanced over them again.

A light knock on the door was followed by the announcement, "Dana, time for supper."

"I'll be right there," I answered and glanced again at the last few photos I hung to dry. Something about one of them caught my attention. Peering closer at it, I frowned. I shook my head and made sure no negatives were exposed to light before leaving the small room—closet, really—to wash my hands and join Dad and Sam for supper.

We made smalltalk. Dad and Sam debated the merits of the football teams they thought would play in the Super Bowl. I mentioned a few of the better photographs I'd developed that day.

"Are you going to put together another calendar?" Dad asked.

"Yeah, I'm going to call it *Chicago Wilderness*," I replied. Sam raised his eyebrows in silent query, so I elaborated. "People think of Chicago as just one big, congested city. There are a lot of parks and wilderness areas in and around Chicago that most people don't realize are there. I've been taking photos of them and will pick out the best twelve for a picture calendar showcasing what I think are the best wilderness spots."

"My girl did an urban-focused calendar for the Chicago Chamber of Commerce last year," Dad added. "They liked it so well, they hired her to do another one."

I basked in his pride.

"You did that?" Sam asked. "I saw it in the gift shop at the Art Institute."

I nodded.

"I hadn't realized you were the photographer," he said. "You do really good work."

"Thank you," I replied, finding that his praise warmed the cockles of my heart. I couldn't have said why, but his approval meant a lot to me when it never had before.

"I think Dana's going to be this generation's Ansel Adams," Dad boasted.

"If only," I said, rolling my eyes. I thought Dad vastly overestimated my talent, but it was nice to have his support.

"Have you thought of being shown in an art gallery?" Sam asked.

My warm fuzzy feeling soured. I sighed and shook my head. "I've not been that lucky yet."

"Have you approached any galleries?" he asked.

I rattled off the six I'd approached in the last eight months without engaging any owner's or manager's interest, then said, "Macro-photography is big right now. That's what's selling and it's not really what I do best. I prefer doing landscapes, but that's seldom considered 'art.' Landscapes usually get relegated to off-the-shelf interior decorating."

He nodded, although I wasn't sure if he truly understood or was merely placating me. Then, he cocked his head to the left and asked, "Would having prints of your work in tens or even hundreds of thousands of homes be so bad? I'd guess it's a lucrative niche."

I shrugged. Because I wanted to make my mark as an *artist*, not some hack who just took pretty pictures, I said, "That's what the calendar is for."

"Ah."

Dad changed the subject and supper soon concluded without rancor. A familiar noise filtered through the windows and walls. We all perked up and stared through the passageway from the kitchen to the living room and out the front window. In the darkness of early evening, amber lights flashed.

"That's the snowplow," Dad said. He looked at Sam. "I'll fire up the snow blower and you'll be able to head home tomorrow."

"Dad, you can't shovel the drive at night," I protested.

"I've got to be at work early in the morning, pumpkin, so I've no other choice."

"Dad, if you get the damned thing running, I'll shovel the driveway."

"If I'm going to get it running, then I might as well use it."

I sighed. "Dad, you know that pull-start gets the better of me every time. But once it's running, I can push it."

Sam snorted. "Show me where the machine is and I'll do it."

"We can't let you do that," Dad protested. "You're our guest."

"I hadn't intended on staying here, so I'm an unwanted guest."

"But you helped out my little girl and brought her home. We already owe you."

I blushed, but didn't contradict him.

"There's no debt, Larry. No one owes anybody anything."

Dad pushed away from the table and stood. "No, no, I won't hear of it. Pumpkin, get your coveralls."

"You still have those old things?" I asked in mild horror.

"Sure do. You can still wear 'em. They're in the coat closet with your hat, gloves, and those old boots you used to wear to Sonya's."

With a sigh, I helped clear the table and trudged to the closet while Sam looked on. I wanted to cringe in embarrassment as I pulled on the worn, old Carhartts, fuzzy alpaca wool hat, and pink "barn" gloves. As Dad said, my old boots, dusty and musty with disuse, were in the back of the closet. I pulled them on, tucking the pant legs of my coveralls into them. The boots and coveralls still carried the lingering odor of livestock and dirt, familiar smells long since embedded into the materials.

"I'll start the snow blower," Sam offered as I straightened up and turned to head to the garage.

"Thanks." I tried to ignore the gleam of amusement in his eyes. I was glad he made no snide comments about my attire until he said, "You look better in my shirt."

The heat in his gaze ignited my libido. I took a breath and forced myself to ignore the flutter in my belly and the moist warmth gathering between my legs.

Sam followed me to the garage where I pointed out the snowblower. I found the gas can and made sure the fuel tank was filled.

"Think you can get it running?"

"I'll give it a shot." He gripped the handle, set the choke, and yanked on the cord. Nothing. He tried three more times before the spark caught and the loud motor blared.

"Thanks!" I shouted over the noise, punched the button on the wall to open the garage door, and guided the machine outside into the bitter cold. The frigid wind hit me with an icy blast that took my breath away.

An hour later I returned. The uneven old sidewalk that no one used was mostly cleared. The driveway was cleared. The neighbor's driveway was cleared. Hearing the noise, old Mrs. Patterson parted the old-fashioned lace curtains at her front window and waved at me. I didn't doubt she'd return the favor as soon as she could totter from her yard to ours with a plastic container of fresh baked goods. I hoped she'd make scones. My mouth watered at the thought. No one made scones like Mrs. Delia Patterson who'd moved from Cornwall to Ohio with her ex-military husband sixty-plus years ago.

Stamping my feet to clear my boots of snow after parking the snowblower in its assigned spot, I stepped back inside the house.

"Hot chocolate's on the stove, pumpkin!"

"Thanks, Dad!"

I stripped off the old, still serviceable outerwear and headed for the kitchen where, sure enough, a stainless steel pot gently steamed on the stovetop. Grabbing a mug from the cupboard, I poured myself a serving of hot chocolate. If no one made scones like Mrs. Patterson, then no one made hot chocolate like Lawrence Secrest. I knew he used milk and melted semi-sweet chocolate chips, but he always added something else. Sometimes it was a pinch of cinnamon, other times a dash of vanilla extract or amaretto. Whatever he decided to use to enliven our favorite winter beverage, it was always good.

I sighed with pleasure as the first slightly spicy drops hit my tongue. Carrying the mug into the living room, I said, "I taste orange, nutmeg, and ... what else?"

"Chili oil," he answered. "Just a drop to add a touch of heat."

"Trying out a new recipe?" I grinned and took another sip.

"Yep. You were always my best taste tester."

I glanced at Sam, who sat on the loveseat and sipped at his own mug of Dad's special hot chocolate with an expression that was both bemused and a little melancholy. I sat beside him and tucked my feet under me.

"Something wrong?" I asked, keeping my voice low.

He gave me a small smile. "Just admiring the relationship you have with your dad. It's a joy to see."

"I couldn't have asked for a better father," I agreed. "He adopted me right after he married Mom and never once made me feel as though I was anything but his daughter."

"You're lucky."

I blinked at the wistful note in his voice and whispered, "Yeah, I am."

I wanted to ask, to pry, but sensed Sam wouldn't welcome the intrusion into his personal life. The hint of envy I saw in him made my heart ache for what he'd apparently never had.

Chapter 20

Sam

I envied Dana the loving, supportive relationship she had with her stepfather, and I knew that she knew. Concern and curiosity flashed across her face, but she kindly said nothing.

I said nothing when she finished her hot chocolate and squirmed into a more comfortable position that had her leaning against me as we watched the sappy Christmas themed romcom Larry turned on. It surprised me that a man like him watched such programming, but I made no comment. Wrapping one arm around Dana's shoulders to snuggle her against my side, I lifted the mug of Larry's fabulous hot chocolate to my mouth and took a swallow. The rural folks of St. Paris had no idea what culinary genius lived among them.

A commercial break interrupted the program. Inserted among the televised advertisements was a 30-second broadcast news update. Flashing an empty, professional smile rimmed by gleaming red lipstick, the journalist glanced at the teleprompter and announced, "Authorities have identified a man found stabbed to death in Palmisano Park on December twenty-fourth as Omar Harimadi, a regionally prominent, fifty-three year old financier and venture capitalist responsible for underwriting the start-up costs of several prominent Chicago entrepreneurs and two Midwest restaurant chains, McGinty's Irish Pub and Zorro Rojo Tacos. Harimadi earned both acclaim and censure for his community support and his strong-arm negotiating tactics. Law enforcement has no leads as yet in the murder case and asks that anyone with information about this crime call the Chicago Police Department."

Taking a breath, the television journalist invited anyone with information to call the number displayed at the bottom of their television screens. I wondered why the television station broke into a broadcast with breaking news related to a city hundreds of miles away, then decided that the victim's Midwest prominence made the murder of interest to the entire middle section of the country.

I made a mental note to call the office and see if Harimadi's family had expressed interest in hiring personal security in the wake of the family patriarch's demise. If they were looking locally, only a couple other firms posed any competition for the contract; however, I believed we had the edge. Harimadi had previously hired my firm to provide security for the more public of his corporate events and once to guard a grandchild whose safety had been threatened in an attempt to extort money.

Dana shifted against me, nuzzling my shirt where her cheek rested. My body reacted with utter predictability that I hoped her father did not notice. I shifted, too, angling my crotch away from the woman cuddled beneath my arm and her father's perceptive gaze, as well as to ease the tightness of the fabric confining me. With the knowledge that I'd be returning home the next day, I contemplated the idea of calling upon a female companion for tomorrow evening. My erection wilted immediately, indicating a definite lack of enthusiasm. I wanted more than an empty fuck and, apparently, so did my dick. Dana nuzzled me again with a sleepy sigh. *I want her. Her and no one else.*

The warm scent of Dana's hair and body tickled my nose, a strangely appealing mixture redolent of furniture polish, gasoline, livestock, sweat, and her own feminine scent. Without being blatant about it, I inhaled deeply, taking in the fragrance of her deep into my lungs. It warmed my blood. I looked down at her glossy, dark chocolate curls and the creamy curve of her cheek and felt something within me settle, become centered and grounded. It felt comfortable and *right*. Of average height and slender with subtle curves, she wasn't my normal type. Of course, my normal type embodied a typical voluptuous phenotype as well as a certain personality that viewed sex as a recreational activity and tool for manipulation. Dana's old-fashioned attitude toward sex both charmed and frustrated me.

Her chest rose on a long, deep breath, then slowly descended on a slumbrous exhale. I smoothed a lock of hair away from her face, then looked at Larry who was watching me.

"You treat her right," he said in a low, nearly inaudible voice. "I see the way you look at her."

I glanced down, worried that she'd overhear her father's words and treat us to an explosion of temper.

"She's a sound sleeper, always has been," the older man said. His gaze flickered to her face, then back to mine. "I raised my girl right and she deserves respect. If you can't do right by her, then leave her alone. She doesn't deserve to be hurt because you're just playing around."

"I'm not playing," I replied, my tone quiet and intense. The raw honesty of my response startled me. The cynical part of my brain wondered how this diner cook in a small rural town dared confront me. He was no threat to me. I could do what I liked to him and his daughter, more or less with impunity. I blinked at the arrogance and callousness that spoke in my father's tobacco-roughened voice.

I looked up again and met the older man's unflinching gaze. He held my stare with the force of a loving father protecting his family, an emotional force I heretofore had never dreamed of wanting to feel for myself. I broke the connection and bent my head to inhale the scent of her hair again, warm, musky, a little sweet from the shampoo she'd used that morning, a little astringent from the photographic chemicals clinging to her, uniquely hers, complex and undefinable. I quelled the irrational urge to jiggle her awake just so I could see her pretty hazel eyes.

"Lay her down and I'll fetch a blanket," Larry whispered.

Instead, I lowered her to the loveseat while I maneuvered into position to slide her into my arms and cradle her against my chest.

"I'll put her to bed."

I carried her to her bedroom, her father following. He drew back the covers and I laid her upon the narrow bed. He pulled the covers over her and gestured at me to precede him from the room. Glancing back at her, I complied, even though I wanted nothing more than to crawl in beside her and hold her while she slept.

Larry closed the door behind us. I headed for the guest bedroom to make sure everything was packed so I'd leave nothing behind.

Chapter 21

Dana

I yawned and rubbed my eyes before enough self-awareness crept in to let me know that I'd slept in my clothes. Someone had put me to bed. Cuddled against my hip, Sly grumbled. My moving about disturbed his 22-hour nap. After a moment's squirming embarrassment, I decided it really didn't matter which of the two men had carried me into my room and put me to bed. After all, it wasn't like Sam or Dad had seen anything he shouldn't or done something perverted. Instead, I'd dropped off to sleep like a child and they'd put me to bed like they would a child. I decided their actions were caring and sweet, not creepy.

After a quick shower, I got dressed and headed to the kitchen where Dad left the coffeemaker switched on. I poured a cup and added liberal amounts of cream and sugar, then trekked back through the house and looked into the guest room. Sam left the door open. He'd made the bed. It was kind of him, but I knew that it was my duty to strip the sheets and wash them so they were fresh and clean for the next visitor. Wandering back to the kitchen, I finally noticed the general air of emptiness inside the quiet house.

Dad had gone to the diner.

Sam had gone home. Back to Chicago.

Contemplating the solitude facing me, I made myself a quick breakfast of toast and a banana. I read the *Springfield News-Sun*—St. Paris not having its own newspaper—while I ate. Emblazoned above the fold was the headline "CHICAGO VC MURDERED." I read the article and felt my stomach churn, realizing that I had been in Palmisano Park the same day Omar Harimadi was killed there. I finished my coffee, and tidied the kitchen. I fed the cat, refreshed his water, and cleaned the litter box.

Now what?

Feeling restless, I retreated to my dark room and ignored the scratch of claws on the door frame. Dad was going to flip his lid when he eventually saw the gouges in the wood. I'd have to find the money to pay for a handyman to fix it. Dad was many things, but a skilled carpenter was not one of them.

I did not keep track of time as I worked on developing the final roll of film and stopped when my stomach rumbled. I took a break for lunch—leftovers—and afterward spent a bit of time cuddling my cat.

"Poor guy, you've been through a rough few days," I crooned as I stroked underneath his fuzzy chin and down his neck. He loved that.

When he grew bored with me, he stalked toward the litter box, which was my cue to head back to the dark room and finish the day's work. By mid-afternoon, I had a stack of 8-by-10 photos, both black and white and color prints. I carried them to the bed where I sat and began sorting through them. First, I divided them into color and grayscale. Then I sorted them by subject matter: landscape, portraits, urbanscape. The very best photos, those that were particularly stunning, made a fourth and much smaller pile slated for my speculative calendar project.

Giving my brain a rest from that, I opened my new laptop computer, plugged the power cord into a wall outlet, and spent the next ninety minutes or so driving myself batty trying to configure it and recover my passwords and other settings to my favorite sites. After that, I logged-in to several sites and bid on a handful of freelance projects. More from habit than anything else, I checked Fiverr, Guru, and Upwork for potential projects. Not surprisingly, the buyer requests and budgets posted made me snort with contempt and incredulity. I placed no bids on any of those freelance platforms that day.

"Sure, I don't mind working for pennies per hour," I muttered under my breath as I clicked to LinkedIn with the goal of updating my profile.

Another hour passed. I updated my profile on LinkedIn, responded to several messages, and scanned through other subscribers' posts. Taking a methodical approach toward gig hunting and social media marketing, I managed to get almost everything updated by 5:00. I shut down the machine and moseyed back to the kitchen to start on supper. I called the diner from the house phone.

"Dad, you gonna be home for supper?" I asked.

"No, pumpkin, not today. I've been busier than a one-armed paper hanger," he replied.

"Okay. You're staying until closing then?"

"Yeah."

"Long day," I commented. He grunted. "I'll put a plate for you in the fridge, Dad."

"Thanks, pumpkin."

After hanging up, I filled a pot with water and put it on the stove to boil. While the water heated, I browned a pound of ground beef in a skillet, adding chopped onions, chopped bell peppers, sliced fresh portobello mushrooms, sliced green olives, some pickled artichoke hearts, and minced garlic. When the meat was brown and the onions translucent, I dumped in a can of diced tomatoes. I stirred in dried basil, a pinch of oregano, salt, and pepper. By that time, the water had come to a boil. I covered the skillet and dumped a box of penne into the pot of water. About fifteen minutes later I sat at the table with a book and a steaming plate of pasta.

After eating, I divvied up the leftovers, portioning them out for later consumption, and tidied the kitchen. Then I retreated to the living room to watch television and finish the glass of red wine poured to accompany my meal. Dad refused to pay for cable TV, so we made do with broad-cast television. I seldom minded, but that night nothing appealed. I opened my book, but couldn't concentrate on the printed words.

Muttering to myself, I returned to my room, turning off the lights as I went. Dad hated wasting electricity and having been on my own for a few years, I understood that. I made a quick detour in the kitchen to replenish my glass of wine. Looking at the label, I made a mental note of the brand so I could pick up another bottle the next time I went to the supermarket.

I set the goblet on my nightstand and retrieved the photos from where I'd stashed them in the nightstand drawer. Sly jumped onto the bed and sidled close, his green eyes gleaming with interest.

"Sorry, buddy, not for you," I said as I gently pushed him away and got back to evaluating the photos, either confirming my initial decisions or revising those deci-sions. I kept going back to one photo in particular. Some-thing about it disturbed me.

"Damn it," I muttered.

I once again stashed the photos where the cat couldn't ruin them. I took the photo that bothered me into the dark room, found the negative, and began the process of enlarging the print, thinking there must be some detail in the original that I just didn't recognize.

True to habit when working with my photographs, I paid no attention to time and heard nothing beyond my own mutterings. If the snowplows or any other vehicles passed by, I didn't hear them.

"Oh, shit. Oh, shit," I babbled as I stared at the latest enlargement of the photo of Palmisano Park. I looked at the negatives immediately preceding that picture and enlarged them, too. "Oh, *damn*."

The sound of glass shattering caught my distracted attention and I went still. Listening hard as I readied the dark room for my departure, I still heard nothing, especially not the expected cursing of my stepfather having to clean up broken glass. Disturbing prints rolled in one hand and negatives in the other, I emerged from the dark room. A waiting, silent dread made the fine hairs at the back of my neck prickle. Still listening hard, I heard the creak of old floors beneath the careful tread of heavy feet, but no light shone beneath the door.

"Bitch isn't in here," I heard a male voice say in low tones.

"Check that room," another man said.

The hinges of another door—the spare bedroom's door—quietly squeaked.

The realization that whoever had invaded Dad's house was looking for me galvanized me into action. I grabbed my phone, flung open the window, and climbed through. I slammed down the window from the outside just as the beam of flashlight aimed at the curtain.

"Oh, shit. Oh, shit," I muttered as I shivered in the bitter cold and trekked across the backyard to the neighbor's house. I hoped whoever it was wouldn't go looking behind the house for me, because there was no way I could hide my footprints in the snow.

I rapped on Mrs. Patterson's patio door. Peering through the glass, I saw her look up and frown, but she rose to her feet and slowly, so slowly, made her way to the door. Sliding it open, she let me inside.

"Why, Dana, why in the world are you outside without a coat?"

Teeth chattering, I said, "C-c-call police. S-s-someone's in th-the house."

Her eyes widened. Having known me since I was a child, she knew I wouldn't make something like that up. Without further ado, she picked up the old-fashioned corded phone and dialed 911.

"Yes, this is Alma Patterson. Is this Debbie Cummings? I thought I recognized your voice. Hello, dear, I hope you're doing well. Your mother's so proud that you found such a good job in this economy. Yes, I've called to report a problem. There's a disturbance next door. My neighbor says there are intruders," she explained. "No, I haven't seen or heard anything. But perhaps ... oh, really, your mother wouldn't like *that* at all. Don't take that tone with me, young lady. There's always time to be polite."

I wanted to make a rolling motion to hurry her up, but Mrs. Patterson did things in her own time and none could gainsay her. I mouthed that I was going to use her bathroom and she nodded as she conversed with the dispatcher who couldn't seem to keep the kindly old woman on track. She nodded and waved her hand at me in a shooing motion.

I headed for the bathroom where my stomach rejected its contents. Clammy and shaking, I rinsed out my mouth. As I emerged from the bathroom, I heard rapping on the patio door.

"Oh, shit," I muttered and headed for the door to the garage, on the way out lifting a set of car keys from the decorative ceramic bowl where she kept them. I slapped the button that activated the automatic garage door. I unlocked the car and crept into the back seat of Mrs. Patterson's car, pulling the door closed with agonizing care, then locking the doors using the key fob. The whine of the garage door motor covered the faint click of the car door's latch engaging. I hoped the noise would distract whoever was at Mrs. Patterson's back patio door and make them think I'd fled on foot down the shoveled driveway and up the road where my footprints wouldn't be so easily detected.

I crouched on the floor of the car and drew a dark blanket over me both for camouflage and warmth. Beneath the cover of the blanket, I pulled out my phone and dialed.

"Dana."

I nearly wept to hear Sam's voice and desperately wanted to feel his arms around me. I felt *safe* in his embrace. My own voice shaking, I said, "Sam, I know why they're after me."

"Why *who* is after you?"

"I don't know who," I replied, my voice a mere whisper, "but I know *why*. They broke into Dad's house and they came to Mrs. Patterson's. They're looking for me."

"Where are you?"

"I'm hiding in Mrs. Patterson's garage," I whispered.

He cursed under his breath. "Call the police, Dana. I'm already back in Chicago. It'll be hours before I can get to St. Paris."

"Mrs. Patterson's on the phone with the police now."

"Dana!" I heard Dad bellow. I heard the distress in his voice. Obviously, he'd come home to find the shattered glass—a broken window, perhaps?—and an empty house and was searching for me. I wondered if the intruders had trashed his house like they had my apartment.

The door to the garage began to descend.

"She's not here, I tell you!" Mrs. Patterson declared in a loud voice that trembled with fear.

"Look, lady, those are her footprints out back running from her house to yours. You *saw* her."

"Yes, I did," she confirmed as the garage door ground to a close. "But she's a flighty girl. And I didn't leave the garage door open. You heard it as well as I did. Obviously, she's run off!"

"It's dark," a second male voice griped. "We can't track her now. She'll keep to the cleared pavement."

Muffled by the now-closed garage door, Dad bellowed my name again.

"Fuck, you think he'll come over here?" the second voice rasped? "Maybe we should talk to him?"

"Dunno. She won't get far and we're not gonna screw with the old man—too risky," the first man rasped. "Everything's closing down for the night and the old bitch here says she didn't have a coat."

I heard Mrs. Patterson squeal in pain, but was too afraid to look up and reveal myself by seeing what they were doing to her.

"If you're lying to us, old lady, we'll come back and hurt you bad, real bad," the first thug threatened.

Sirens sounded.

"Shit, she called the cops," the second man said.

"Let's go."

After a moment, the garage door motor whined again, the automatic overhead light blinked on. Someone rapped on the car's window.

"Dana," I heard Mrs. Patterson's voice filter through the tempered glass. "You can come out now. I'd like my keys back."

Trembling, I eased from underneath the dark blanket and got out of the car. Mrs. Patterson held out her hand. I dropped the keys into her wrinkled palm. She led me back inside her house.

"I don't know what trouble you're in, girl, but you've brought it to my door and I'd just as soon as you take it right back out with you."

"Sorry, Mrs. Patterson."

"Go home, Dana. Your father's calling for you."

I went out the back way and entered through the back door, thinking that it was better to leave footprints than to expose myself by walking around the front. I made my way to the bedroom and groaned. The two intruders had destroyed my bedroom and dark room, everything except the creased prints and the negatives I didn't remember shoving into my pockets.

Sly growled from beneath my bed. I lifted the dust ruffle and peered at him, meeting his flat, accusing gaze.

With a sigh, I emerged from the bedroom and walked through the house and out the back door, looking for Dad. I found him in the garden shed, the porch light illuminating footprints showing that he'd been searching for me.

"Dana!" Dad exclaimed when he saw me. "What the hell happened?"

Overwhelmed, I burst into tears and fell into his arms. We headed back inside to the kitchen where Dad put on the kettle. A knock at the door startled us both.

"Hide," Dad said as he released me and headed to the front door.

I nodded and did as he bade me.

A minute later, he called out, "Dana, come here! The police need to take your statement."

I hugged myself as I obeyed him. The police took my statement. I showed them the wreckage of my room. Sly darted out as soon as the opportunity presented itself. Dad huffed in annoyance, but said nothing. I supposed he couldn't blame the cat for not wanting to remain in there. The police added more to the report.

"Do you know who they are?" one officer asked.

"No."

"Why would someone ..." Dad started to ask, but his voice faded as I gave my head a little shake.

"Why are these men after you?" one of the officers asked me. "What trouble are you in? Do you owe a debt?"

I gaped at the accusatory tone of his questions. "I-I think I might have witnessed a murder."

"You *think* you *might* have witnessed a murder?"

The other officer snorted in disbelief and asked, "What makes you think that? Where's your evidence?"

I sighed and glanced at the ruin of my bedroom and dark room. "I have a picture—"

"A picture? Did you photograph a murder?" the first officer barked.

"No, I didn't photograph a murder," I replied. "I—"

He harrumphed. "Then you've got nothing."

I opened my mouth to protest, then closed it. I had begun to learn about futility. The walkie-talkie hanging from his belt crackled with an announcement of an injury accident involving multiple vehicles on State Route 235 and a summons to assist.

The second officer looked at Dad and said, "Sir, we'll do what we can to catch whoever broke into your house and destroyed this room. I suggest you call your insurance agent."

After a few more platitudes that didn't help at all and promises to increase patrols on our street for the night and maybe the next day, they left.

"What the hell is going on, Dana?" Dad demanded.

Chapter 22

Sam

After Dana's call, I checked with the office to make sure business was being handled and told them I was heading for St. Paris, Ohio. I spent nearly two hours just trying to get through Chicago metropolian area's notorious rush hour traffic that lasted well into the night. Through the Bluetooth connection, the radio rang with another phone call as I sped down the highway at less than highway speed as road crews continued to work around the clock to clear the wintry mess Mother Nature recently dumped on the Midwest.

"What is it, Gordon?"

"I'm taking two weeks' vacation."

"This is not a good time, Gordon."

"Then I quit."

"Damn it, Gordon, you *can't* quit!"

"Which is it, boss: vacation or not?"

I wanted to roar, but remained coherent. "Take a vacation then. Is this related to Sonya Vermont?"

"Yes. Vermont sent some goons after her."

I sighed. "Damn it. All right, use the safe house."

"Thanks, boss."

"Keep her safe, Gordon."

"Yes, sir."

I wondered how I could have so misjudged Bradley Vermont.

Chapter 23

Sonya

"I'm sorry, Sonya, but I cannot jeopardize my wife and mother," Rev. Blankenship said as he comforted his wife while his mother looked at me with undisguised loathing as though I'd personally taken a baseball bat to the kitchen table.

No, Bradley's hired thugs did that. Suzanne sniffled and dabbed a cold, wet cloth at her swollen right cheek and split lip. Mother Blankenship, in turns, fussed over her daughter-in-law's injury and the splintered table that had been, she said, a family heirloom.

"Must be one magical pussy," one of the thugs sneered before leaving. "Maybe I'll sample it myself and see what's so wonderful about it."

Bradley's hired thugs gave the reverend a message that was actually directed at me: return to Bradley of my own free will or everyone I considered a friend would suffer. I cringed at the choice, but did not want to be the cause of anyone else's suffering. Vaguely, I wondered if Dana was safe. I shuddered and focused on the toes of my Keds sneakers. I owed my current small wardrobe to Gordon's generosity. It reminded me of the simple, comfortable clothing I'd worn as a teenager and then as a college student back in small town Ohio.

Gordon had somehow retrieved much of my wardrobe from Bradley's penthouse, but I refused to wear it. Instead, I donated it to the church. Rather than pass the expensive, designer clothing to the poor, Rev. Blankenship sold it and contributed the funds to help support the church's ministries. I could not find fault with his decision, especially since the proceeds from the sale of my clothing enabled the soup kitchen to purchase fresh fruits, vegetables, and meat for the many people it fed on a daily basis.

I didn't know how Gordon retrieved my clothing, and didn't want to. Sometimes it was enough to be grateful.

"Ready, Sonya?" Gordon asked, carrying a trash bag only half filled with the entirety of my vastly reduced wardrobe.

"Yes," I replied and bowed my head. I looked up for a second and whispered again, "I'm so sorry, Suzanne. I never imagined Bradley would do anything like this."

"You are not responsible for what evil men do," Rev. Blankenship intoned, although his voice did not throb with the usual passion of conviction. The lack of it informed me as nothing else could that he did blame me for the violence visited upon his home and his family. I was responsible.

"You're not responsible," Gordon said, his voice rasping.

I blinked. Had he read my thoughts?

"Come on, Sonya. Let's go."

I bade my hosts goodbye. They nodded at me and murmured something polite, but their expressions showed they were eager to see the last of me.

"I'll always be grateful," I said, my voice cracking.

"*Now*, Sonya," Gordon said.

I ducked my head and obediently followed him to his SUV. He tossed the bag into the back seat and boosted me into the front passenger seat. I'd finished buckling the seatbelt when he climbed into the driver's seat.

"Where are we going?" I asked, glancing at his stony profile.

"A safe house."

"Here in Chicago?"

"No." He started the engine.

"Where?"

"You don't need to know."

"But what if I need to meet with my attorney?"

"Your lawyer has the number to the parsonage and Rev. Blankenship has my phone number."

"But—"

"Let it go, Sonya. I'm going to keep you safe and that means no outside contact for you. If you need to meet with your lawyer, I'll bring you in and stay with you. You'll go nowhere without me, and you will never be out of my sight."

Gordon's peremptory command over my life probably should have annoyed me. It would have aggravated Dana to no end. But I could only feel gratitude, reassurance, and pleasure in knowing he would take care of me.

I supposed that made me a much weaker woman than Dana. I wanted to weep to think of how disappointed in me she would be.

Chapter 24

Dana

I warmed up leftovers for Dad, then cleaned up the destruction the two thugs left behind. He finished eating and helped finish the job. I told him what happened as I helped him cover the broken window.

"I'll call John's Handyman Service tomorrow," I offered as we trudged back inside.

Dad nodded, looking exhausted and old.

My lip trembled and I murmured, "I'm sorry, Dad."

He wrapped an arm around my shoulders and said, "It's not your fault, pumpkin."

I shook my head. "If I hadn't come home, then those guys wouldn't have been here."

I didn't want to mention that they would probably be back, sooner rather than later.

"Pumpkin, I've got to get to bed." He glanced at his watch. "The diner opens in six hours."

"Look, Dad, let me help. I'll open up the diner with you."

"Sweetheart, you hate working there."

"But—"

"But nothing. I can't keep you safe there, and I can't have your presence endangering the customers."

His words crushed me. I felt the wet heat of tears run down my face. "Daddy, what do I do?"

Strong beams of light penetrated an unbroken window. I glanced at the clock: 12:30 AM.

"That'll be Sam."

I gaped. How could he know that?

"You called him, right?" Dad reminded me.

"Yeah, but—"

"That man has feelings for you. When you told me you called him from Mrs. Patterson's car, I knew he'd come for you." He gave me a small, tired smile. "For what it's worth, pumpkin, I think you chose well. He's a good man."

I gaped again, confused.

The doorbell rang. Dad answered it. He greeted Sam, who looked tired, and then pulled out his wallet and counted off some bills. He pressed them into Sam's gloved hand, saying, "Keep track of your expenses. We'll repay you."

"What's going on, Dad?"

Dad turned to look at me and said in a voice as hard as I'd ever heard it, "Get your stuff. You're leaving with Sam; he knows how to protect you from whatever is going on. The damned cat can stay with me."

"But—"

"You're not safe here," Sam said and gave me a small, tired smile. "I'll keep you safe, Dana."

"But—"

"Make sure you take those negatives with you," Dad said.

"Negatives?" Sam echoed.

"Yeah, my girl's got a story to tell you, complete with pictures."

Not wanting to distress Dad further, I obeyed his orders to collect my meager belongings and stuff them into a bag. After a quick snuggle with Sly, I kissed his furry head and promised to return soon. He growled, still upset, then bolted under the bed. I slung the strap of a duffle over my shoulder and trudged outside to Sam's SUV.

"Allow me," he said, his tone quiet and brooking no objection as he took the duffle from my hands and tossed it into the back seat.

"Thanks," I murmured in reply, Midwestern manners taking charge.

"Get in, sweetheart. We've got a long drive."

I got in and stared out the passenger side window. After a good, long while, I realized we weren't on the highway to Chicago.

"Where are we going?"

"It's best you don't know," Sam answered.

"That's not helpful."

"It wasn't meant to be."

Again, I opened my mouth and closed it without saying anything, the lessons of futility again coming to bear. Instead, I leaned against the cold glass and stared at the passing scenery.

We stopped for breakfast and then again lunch at fast food restaurants. I chewed on a breakfast burrito and later a grilled chicken with lettuce, tomato, and pickle—no mayonnaise—and french fries with hunger, if not enthusiasm. I could have been eating cardboard for all that my tastebuds took notice. Immersed in my own worries, I took no notice of what Sam ordered. Grim determination suffused Sam's exhausted expression, so I doubted he paid much attention to what he ate either, beyond copious amounts of black coffee.

We were on our way again. Rolling hills gave way to the southern plains of Illinois. The landscape changed again, giving way to forested hills, pastures, and farm fields waiting for spring planting. I realized Sam was following a rural route to avoid urban areas. Three pit stops later—two of them included refueling the vehicle—and both of us were practically trembling with exhaustion.

"You should get some sleep," Sam's gritty voice advised.

"I can't sleep in a car," I replied, my own voice raspy, and resisted the temptation to comment on his own need for rest. "Never could."

I wanted to whine and ask if we were there yet, wherever there was. But I refused to be a caricature. Instead, I sighed and closed my eyes and listened to the constant hum of road noise punctuated by the occasional thump of the tires running over a pothole. I barely noticed when the vehicle pulled to a slow halt, the tires crunching over a gravel drive.

I blinked at the cozy cabin before us, my vision both bleary and blurry. We were surrounded by trees, many with dead, brown leaves still clinging to their branches.

"Where are we?"

"Missouri."

"Missouri?" I echoed. "What are we doing in Missouri?"

"My uncle has a place here. It's where we're going to stay until we figure this thing out and you're out of danger." He flashed me a weary grin. "You'll like the creek."

My jaw dropped. Finally, my dull wits made an attempt at collection. "And does your uncle know we're here? Is he okay with that?"

Sam shrugged. "He's in a nursing home and suffers from dementia."

I huffed, not knowing what to say to that or even what to ask next. I couldn't deny that we needed a hidey hole, but to take advantage of a man who'd lost touch with reality didn't seem right.

He must have seen the doubt on my face. "He'd not begrudge us the use of the cabin."

While my slow thoughts pondered this development, Sam exited the vehicle and retrieved my duffle. He walked around the front of the SUV and opened my door. "Let's get you situated, then I'll head out for some groceries to tide us over for a day or two."

I nodded and complied without protest, following him to the cabin's front door. He unlocked the door and led me inside. The cabin had the musty smell indicative of a space infrequently occupied, but not the rank odor of an un-kempt space allowed to go to ruin. Looking around, I saw a central fireplace made of stone. It divided the living room from a country kitchen. The western wall had two doors.

"Bedroom's through there," Sam said with a vague ges-ture toward the western wall.

I took my duffle from his hand and crossed smooth wooden planks to the first door and opened it. Bathroom. I opened the second door. Bedroom. Entering the room, I let the duffle fall from my hand to the floor and toppled onto the queen sized bed. I yawned, shut my eyes, and did not move until light streaming through the window woke me.

I lay there for a long moment, eyes open and brain slowly working its way back to functionality. I realized that I'd fallen asleep—collapsed was more like it—fully clothed. Heat, solid and delicious heat, pressed against my back from shoulders to ankles. It felt good. A band of heavy heat draped itself over my arm and across my front and surrounded one breast. Looking down, I saw a large hand loosely cupping my left breast and tried to drum up some outrage. It felt good. He was taking liberties I hadn't granted him. He was asleep and unaware of his actions. It felt good.

I gotta pee.

With exquisite care, I lifted Sam's hand from my breast and mourned the loss of that warmth. Where his body was not plastered to mine, I was cold. He sighed and shifted away, eyes remaining closed. His mouth opened, soft lips parting to emit a light snore. I eased away from him and rolled off the bed.

Tiptoeing across the room, I lifted the duffle and crept out the open door, closing it behind me. An immediate turn took me into the bathroom where a quick glance into the mirror revealed an atrocity of bed head and a face puffy from sleep and exhaustion. I relieved my full bladder, then stepped into the shower for a quick scrub. I hissed when cold water hit my skin. Minutes later, the water still hadn't warmed up, so my teeth chattered as I dried off with a threadbare towel and got dressed.

After massaging in some leave-in conditioner to tame my short, nearly black curls, I headed for the kitchen where I found a loaf of bread, a bottle of milk, and a carton of eggs in the small, apartment-sized refrigerator.

Doesn't he know that putting bread in the refrigerator will make it go stale faster?

I mentally slapped myself for the uncharitable thought and busied myself with searching for a skillet and utensils. In my search, I found a bottle of maple syrup and another nearly empty bottle of olive oil. I also found a can of Chock Full o'Nuts coffee and old percolator and put them to good use. Since I didn't see butter in the refrigerator, I used a few drops of the olive oil to grease the skillet. It didn't take much skill to whip up a batch of French toast. Soon the inviting fragrance of breakfast filled the rustic cabin.

Sam walked into the kitchen, hair still wet from his (cold) shower and jaw freshly shaved, as I flipped the last slice onto a chipped plate. I recognized the ancient Corelle® pattern. It hadn't improved with age.

"Have a seat," I bade him. "You want milk?"

"Coffee," he grunted.

I grabbed an ugly earthenware mug from the cupboard, rinsed out any dust, then filled it with the fragrant brew.

"Thanks," he murmured and lifted the cup to his mouth for an appreciative sip.

I loaded a plate for him and set it down. Without a word, he grabbed the bottle of maple syrup and drizzled the sweet, thick liquid over his stack of French toast. Carrying a mug of coffee and a plate with my stack of French toast to the table, I sat across from him.

"We need to talk," I said.

"Not now, Dana," he said.

I nodded. *After breakfast.* We ate. We polished off the coffee. Sam washed the dishes while I wiped down the table and kitchen counter. Then we adjourned to the living area. I sat in the armchair and he took the sofa. Before I could repeat my conversation opener, he spoke.

"Tell me what you found. Your dad mentioned you have a story to tell."

I pursed my lips while gathering my thoughts, then decided to go for broke. "The people who burgled my apartment and Dad's house were after pictures."

"Pictures?"

I took a deep breath. "Yeah. Hold on."

I rose from the chair and disappeared into the bedroom to dig into my duffle where I'd stashed the prints and negatives. I brought out the prints of the enlarged details, which made the images grainy.

"These," I said and placed the prints into his hands.

He looked at them, his expression at first puzzled, then turning grim as he realized what my film had captured. Finally, he lay the prints on his lap and muttered, "Shit."

"You know who those two men are?" I prompted, already knowing who one of them was: Omar Harimadi. In a sequence of three photos, Harimadi was speaking to one man, then lying on the ground with the second man standing over him, then the second man walking away. In the second photo, one could detect the dark shape of a large, military-style knife against his dark wool overcoat.

Looking at Sam's expression, I said, "You know the other man, don't you?"

Chapter 25

Sam

"I know him."

I pinched the bridge of my nose, because I wasn't sure if this safe location was actually all that safe. My work brought me into contact with a variety of wealthy and powerful men. I meant *men*, as few women commanded the kind of wealth, power, and influence that prompted them to hire my firm. More often, their husbands and fathers hired my firm to protect them.

"Who is he?" Dana asked.

"It's not important," I replied and shook my head, thinking that the less she knew, the safer she'd be.

Her expression needed no words to express her disagreement.

"Does he work for Bradley?"

That question put me on the spot, because I didn't know. The killer she'd inadvertently captured with her camera worked on contract. Bradley Vermont certainly had the funds to hire Avel Skliar, a Ukrainian assassin whose loyalty could be purchased, but lasted only until the next contract. I'd encountered his work more than once.

Avel Skliar enjoyed his work.

"Sam?"

"I don't know," I finally replied. "I'm not privy to all of Bradley's business."

She frowned. "I thought …"

"You thought that, as his bodyguard, I'd have that kind of information?"

She nodded.

"I was privy to a lot, but not everything. I did not accompany him to many of his private meetings."

"But … wouldn't you have seen the people he met with?"

"Not always," I admitted. "Sometimes he met with 'business associates' who entered through other doors."

"Huh," she huffed, dissatisfied with my ignorance. She sighed, then said, "I need to turn those pictures in. The police need them."

"They do," I agreed. "But we can't just hand them over."

"We could mail them," she suggested, hope lighting in her pretty eyes.

"No."

"Why not? It's not like this guy with the knife can monitor the Postal Service."

"No, he can't. But Bradley can easily find out who carries that route and convince them to divert anything that looks suspicious. I'd be surprised if he isn't already doing that." I'd heard rumors of more than one important package addressed to a business rival going amiss or being delayed until after an important deadline. Unfortunately, rumor did not equate to evidence.

"Convince them?"

I met her questioning gaze and marveled at her innocence. "Bribery. Threats. A possible combination of both."

"Oh." She frowned again, looking down at her lap. "Would he really do that?"

"Sweetheart, he's ruthless in business and he doesn't play fair. He plays to win every ... single ... deal."

A shudder rippled through her slender body, a delicate, delicious stretch of feminine flesh I'd enjoyed holding the night before as we slept. My palm tingled with the memory of her breast swelling to fill my palm. My cock twitched at the memory of her body cuddling against mine. I stifled a groan at another recent memory of our first night together, regardless of how chaste it had been. I reveled in the feel of her body soft and pliant within my embrace. I desperately wanted to sink into her flesh and awaken her to passion to claim and keep for myself. The idea of any other man taking her to his bed made fury burn in my gut, but the choice was hers. It was always hers. I wanted this woman to submit to me because she *wanted* to, not because she had no choice.

That was something Bradley Vermont never quite understood.

She met my gaze and asked, "What are we going to do?"

I couldn't help the small smile that tugged at my mouth at her use of the first person plural *we*. Reaching across the short distance separating us, I took her hand in mine, thumb stroking her soft skin. "We're going to help the police bring the killer to justice and, if we get lucky, he'll lead the police to whoever hired him."

She sighed and nodded and gave my hand a little squeeze, but her eyes held trepidation.

"I'll protect you."

She nodded again, accepting reassurance. "Do you think they'll find us here?"

"I give it two or three days. Bradley knows about this place, but the killer doesn't."

"How does he know about this place?"

I shrugged. "Sometimes even a billionaire needs a little time away, a quiet retreat."

"So," she said slowly, "if the killer shows up here, then we know that he's working for Bradley."

"That's a good assumption."

"What about the other guys?"

I raised an eyebrow in silent inquiry to prompt her to continue.

"The guys who broke into Dad's house."

"Did either of them look like the man in the photo?"

She shook her head. "I didn't get a good look at them, besides they were wearing ski masks."

I waited for her to continue when she paused. She didn't disappoint me.

"But I'm sure I'd recognize their voices."

"Good girl."

Dana flashed me a look of annoyance and in mild rebuke muttered, "Woof." I just smiled, and she looked both pleased and sheepish.

I leaned forward and brought her hand to my lips. Her eyes went wide when I pressed a soft kiss to her knuckles. My heart pounded at the soft hiss of her indrawn breath.

"Why did you do that?"

"Because if I kiss your lips, I don't think I'll have the strength to stop there," I answered with brutal honesty.

Her neck and face flushed with a mixture of embarrassment and excitement. The pulse at the base of her throat fluttered. Her respiration quickened. Her pupils expanded and her pretty hazel eyes flashed green. I liked knowing she thrilled to my touch, to my attention.

Aware that my control had already begun to fray, I released her hand and stood. I pulled my coat off the coat tree and shrugged it on, then grabbed a knit cap and leather gloves.

"I'm going to chop some wood."

Dana blinked.

"If you want to come out, feel free, but don't wander too far."

She nodded. "Um ... where's the creek?"

"About a hundred yards south-southwest."

She nodded again. Her fingers twitched. Her mouth pursed in a moue. "I don't have my camera."

"Use your cell phone."

She sighed with resignation. I didn't have a camera for her to use, so she'd have to make do or do without.

Chapter 26

Dana

After pouting for a few minutes, I put on my coat and followed Sam outside. I looked up at the sun's position and then figured out the direction for south-southwest. More or less. Regardless, I tromped through shin-deep snow and managed to find the creek, which burbled and babbled in cheerful, sunny ripples over a shallow gravel bed. The clear water looked deceptively shallow. It made a pretty scene, nothing awe-inspiring or spectacular. However, I'd long since realized that joy and wonder were made of small moments like that, small pieces of beauty and peace. I spied a boulder and brushed off the snow and took a seat, shuddering at the icy cold that seeped through the fabric of my jeans and panties.

I don't know how long I sat in the dappled sunlight of a sunny winter day and watched the water flow. I watched a flash of gray feathers, the diamond splash of water, and a shiny streak of silvery fish and thought, *kingfisher*. Further up the creek, a blue heron waded into the water and waited with patient stillness until it, too, dipped its long beak into the water and came up with its prey. Somewhere in the distance, I heard the yip of a coyote and the raucous cry of a blue jay. Elsewhere, snow plopped, falling from limbs to the ground. The *thwack* of an axe's blade against wood resounded through the forest with monotonous regularity until it fell silent.

Eventually, I realized I was cold, damned cold. With a groan, I rose and shook out my chilled limbs. Feeling more at peace with myself than I had in weeks, I followed my footprints back to the cabin. My stomach growled. I heard Sam's voice. As I neared, he caught sight of me, nodded, and ended his call with the words, "Nice talking to you, Mama. I'll call back soon."

"You hungry?" Sam asked as he slipped his cell phone into his pocket. He bent down to pick up the axe and another log. I paused to watch the precise aim and power he displayed when he split the log, the heavy muscle rippling beneath the plaid flannel of his shirt. He'd removed his coat and his forehead shined with perspiration. A splinter flew and a spot of blood welled dark red against his clean shaven skin. He blotted his jaw on his sleeve, then leveled a hard stroke at the wood, cleaved it with one stroke, and tossed the pieces onto the pile.

The Mountain Man at Work.

I chuckled softly as my imagination supplied the title to the portrait. *Didn't mountain men have full beards? They do on the covers of romance novels.*

"Something funny?" he asked, having paused in chopping wood.

"Yes," I replied to his first question, although the belated response could have answered the second one, too. "Do we have something besides bread, eggs, and milk?"

"There's some canned soup in the pantry."

"Pantry?" How had I missed a pantry in that tiny cabin?

"Next to the kitchen," he directed.

"Okay. Want some?"

"Sure."

"Any preference?"

He grinned. "You don't even know what's in there, so how can you ask if I have a preference?"

He had a point. I shrugged.

Sam chuckled and said, "Just make two cans of whatever you decide upon. I'll eat that."

I nodded and headed inside. I groaned at my obliviousness when I found the pantry, which was little more than a tall cupboard. I selected two cans of beef vegetable soup, found a pot, and began the heating process. Just as the soup began to simmer, Sam entered the cabin carrying a load of wood for the fireplace. Again, I berated myself for being oblivious, having not noticed that the cabin's interior was warm, practically cozy compared to that morning.

"Let me help," I offered.

"I got this, kitten. You dish up that soup. I'm starving."

I nodded and let him do his thing while I poured the soup into two bowls. As I set the bowls on the table, he washed his hands and rinsed off his face, drying them on a dish towel.

"It's nice here," I said when we sat down to eat. "Peaceful."

"You found the creek then."

I nodded. "Yeah. Pretty spot. I'm going to regret leaving." I looked around. "This was your uncle's hunting cabin, wasn't it?"

"It was," he admitted. "I didn't particularly like all the dead trophies staring at me, so one of the first things I did when Uncle Pete turned the place over to me was take them down."

"What do you use this place for?" I asked, prying because it didn't have the ambiance of a love nest.

"Vacation, usually." He leaned back in the chair. "When I need to get away, I come here, spend some time in nature, listen to the owls and the coyotes."

"Did you visit much when you were a kid?"

He chuckled again. "I wanted to live here when I was a kid. Every summer, every school break, my father turned me over to Uncle Pete and we came here."

His easy openness encouraged me to continue delving into his personal life. "This must be really different from Texas."

His expression closed.

"It is," he replied and rose to his feet.

Chagrined at my intrusiveness, I, too, stood and collected my bowl. Reaching out, I put a hand on his upper arm. He went still.

"I'm sorry, Sam. I don't mean to pry."

"Yes, you do."

I blushed. "Okay, I did. But I didn't mean to upset you."

He sighed. "I know." He took another breath. "It's ... it's not a pleasant topic."

"I'm sorry," I said, not knowing what else to say.

He wrapped his free hand around the back of my neck and drew me forward to press a kiss to my forehead. The sweet gesture of affection felt inadequate. I wanted more. The greed of my feelings surprised me and I found myself tilting my head back and looking into his blue eyes.

"Sam?" I exhaled in a breathy voice.

"I'm hanging on by a thread, Dana," he warned. "Tell me no. Tell me no, right now, or I'm going to take you to bed."

A thrill ran through me, setting my nerves aflame and my blood sizzling through my veins. Every sense felt heightened. Heat pooled low in my belly where excitement bubbled. Lower, moisture gathered and dampened my panties. It sounded like someone else's sultry voice that said, "Take me, Sam."

Chapter 27

Sam

Her nearly whispered acquiescence broke my control. My hand shook as I set the bowl on the counter and took hers to set it aside, too. I slid my hands through her short, dark curls and held her head steady as I lowered my mouth to hers. I tasted the rich flavor of the soup on her tongue, smelled the cold freshness of the winter forest on her skin and hair, and revelled in the press of her body against mine as she rose on tiptoe and wrapped her arms around me.

I savored her as we kissed, the heat between us building into an inferno. I moved her slowly, carefully backward, using the press of my body to guide her path so she avoided running into anything until the backs of her legs butted against the bed. Her hands clamped on my shoulders, relaxed enough to slide down my upper arms where they clamped my flesh again.

"Arms up," I murmured against her moist lips as I tugged on the hem of her shirt. She raised her arms and we separated just long enough for me to draw the shirt over her head and toss it aside. I looked down at the delicate bounty contained by simple cotton. "God, you're beautiful."

A red blush spread across her fair skin and she covered herself in modesty or embarrassment. Gently, I grasped her wrists and drew her arms away.

"No, don't hide from me," I rasped, my voice thick. "Never hide from me."

I released a wrist and skimmed my fingertips over the delicate sweep of her left collarbone and down the tender skin to pause over the hard thump of her heart.

"You're beautiful," I repeated, meaning it.

"I ... I want to see you, too," she whispered.

I couldn't help but chuckle. My woman was no shrinking violet when she knew what she wanted. Bending down to nuzzle the sensitive skin of her neck, I unbuttoned my flannel shirt and shrugged it off. Her hands stroked my upper arms.

"Undershirt, too," she whispered, the words ending on a soft, breathy moan.

I parted from her just long enough to whip off the cotton undershirt. Her hands flew to my pectorals and her eyes widened as she inhaled. From her expression, I knew she liked what she saw, the heavy muscle covered with a manly spread of curling blond hair. I gasped when her fingers stroked over my nipples and they tightened in response. Her boldness gave me leave to reciprocate. I unfastened her bra and bent her backward over my arm so I could more easily taste the puckered, coral colored tip.

Dana shuddered and cried out at the touch of my tongue and again when I sealed my lips around the generous aureole and suckled her. Her roving hands stilled and her fingers dug into my skin.

"Sam!"

"So responsive," I murmured against her sweet, sweet skin. "So lovely."

With one hand I unfastened her jeans and shoved them down to find plain cotton panties. I decided I liked her unpretentious undergarments chosen for comfort and practicality rather than to impress a potential lover. It meant she knew what she liked, she felt no need to impress a man with sexy accoutrements. That sweetly innocent confidence stoked my passion for her even further.

In moments, I'd toed off my boots and shoved down my own jeans. I lowered her to the bed, shoving the comforter aside. I drew off her panties and ignored the socks still on her feet as she writhed beneath me and her hands clutched and slid and stroked my body wherever she could reach. A moment later and my naked cock pressed at her opening, demanding to be allowed inside the heat of her body.

I ran a hand down her body to test her readiness. She gasped and moaned. I found gratifying moisture, but it wasn't enough. I wanted her sopping wet. I wanted her to enjoy the slide of my cock moving inside her, not wince from burning friction. Inserting a fingertip past the swollen labia, her body clamped down, resisting the intrusion. So, I stroked her, never allowing my finger to delve past the first knuckle. She moaned and her hips followed my touch in unconscious demand as I kissed, licked, and nipped her lips, neck, earlobes, and breasts.

My index finger tickled her clit and she jumped.

"Never touched yourself before?" I asked.

She shook her head. "Not like that."

"This is mine now," I growled and circled the sensitive bundle of nerves as her cream flowed freely to lubricate the source of stimulation. I felt her body stiffen, heard her breath grow shallow and rapid. Dana tilted her head back and tensed.

"Reach for it, kitten. Let it come."

I watched in awe as the orgasm swept over her. Her body convulsed beneath me, shuddering with tremors of her first experience with real passion. I slid a finger inside her. Ah, she was wonderfully wet and silky, but still too tight. Another orgasm was most definitely in order.

As she trembled with aftershocks, I slid down her body and spread her thighs further apart. The honeyed scent of her arousal filled my nose and made my mouth water. She yelped at the first stroke of my tongue, then moaned. Soon her fingers tangled in my hair as she ground her sex against my mouth. I speared her with my tongue, the tangy musk of her cream filling my mouth. I added a finger, slowly pumping it in and out. She shuddered and mewled. I added a second finger, scissored them to stretch her passage and prepare her for my entry, for my possession.

I added a third finger and her flesh clamped down as another orgasm roared through her body, making it spasm. Her fragrant wetness flowed with abandon, coating my hand and face as I drank her essence. My own dick felt ready to burst, my balls tight and painful with the need to unload their burden of seed. Dana gasped, keening my name as her body relaxed into boneless, post-orgasmic languor, the perfect state making her ready to be claimed. I surged back up her body and notched the weeping head of my swollen cock within the drenched flesh between her thighs.

"Tell me yes," I rasped, determined to give her the choice even if it killed me.

"Yes," she whispered, eyes shining, skin misted with perspiration, mouth slack.

I thanked God for her consent as I pushed forward and steadily sank into her body. Her channel squeezed me, the hot, wet silk of her both exquisite and painful. Dana's breath hitched as I breached her hymen and slid deeper, deeper until my aching balls felt squeezed between us. I held still to allow her body to accustom itself to my filling it. Perspiration trickled down my spine and face with the effort I exerted not to plunge in and out of her body, not to snap my hips like pistons, not to drill into her untried flesh as instinct demanded.

When her flesh softened around mine, I drew back, slowly, carefully. Dana gasped at the slow, wet glide and blinked. I eased back in. After a few slow strokes, I saw her expression change as discomfort melted into slick, hot pleasure. She tilted her hips to take me even more deeply and I surged into her, rolling like an ocean tide. She moaned, soft, breathy sounds that pleased me more than any previous lover's loud cries and dramatic screams. I heard my own low grunts, the harsh rasp of my own breathing with each coiled thrust. Soon, my hips lost the rhythm imposed upon them as biology overwhelmed control. At the last moment, I hissed and pulled out to spray my seed over her breasts and belly. The thick fluid spurted in long, white ropes that coated her skin with the pungence of my essence.

Muscles trembling, I crushed my mouth to Dana's as I rolled aside, one palm massaging my seed into her skin, marking and scenting her as mine, only mine. Then I skimmed my hand down between her splayed thighs and stroked. My fingers mimicked my tongue which mimicked the intimate dance of copulation. I felt her body stiffen, her channel ripple around my fingers, her cream pour anew from her body. She had one more climax to give me and it swept through her, a rolling tidal wave of pleasure she was helpless to resist.

Lifting my lips from hers, I gathered her to me, snuggling her sweaty skin against mine. I inhaled, filling my lungs with the heavy, distinctive scent of spent passion. With a long sigh, I felt Dana relax completely, content in the warm shelter of my embrace, and drift off to sleep.

I reached down and pulled the covers over us.

Chapter 28

Sonya

Seated across from the attorney recommended by Pastor Blankenship as one whose loyalties Bradley hadn't purchased, I listened to Rita Zorokowski rattle off the divorce terms and thought it more than I deserved. My hands clenched on my lap. Sitting beside me, Gordon noticed and covered one of my fists with the warmth of his own palm.

"I thought this would take a lot more time," I murmured.

"It typically does," the attorney replied, then flashed a tight smile that looked as if such expressions were foreign to her. I had the impression she ate razor wire for breakfast and found it mushy. "But the photos that Rev. Blankenship took and provided to me wouldn't go over well in court, especially if and when they were made public. Folks don't like to see evidence of physical abuse and they'll turn rabid at any reason to vilify a billionaire like your ex-husband."

I blinked and murmured, "I hadn't thought of it as abuse."

Gordon's hand tightened over mine.

"Mrs. Vermont, whether *you* think it's abuse is beside the point. The public will and they'll tear your ex-husband apart."

I shook my head. "I don't want to destroy him. I just … I just want to be free of him."

She nodded. "Mr. Vermont is no dummy. He doesn't want to relinquish you, but he's also aware of the ramifications of what will happen if those pictures go public. Therefore, he is not contesting the divorce."

I glanced at the copy of the papers she'd been reviewing with me. "It seems like more than the prenuptial agreement."

Again, that shark's smile flashed, accompanied by the glint of martial triumph. "That's because it is. Never underestimate the threat of bad publicity to gain additional concessions." She flipped the page and pointed to a line. "Now sign here … and here. Mr. Pasqualle and I will sign as witnesses."

I did as she instructed and Gordon did the same. With a crisp flourish, Rita added her scrawling signature.

"Once the judge signs off on this, you will no longer be married."

I sighed and felt the wet heat of tears spill from my eyes. My voice caught as I rasped, "I loved him, you know."

"I know," Gordon said, giving my hand a light squeeze. "But he shattered that love."

"I don't know what to do now."

"Ms. Vermont," Rita interjected, "you need not do anything. You're a wealthy woman and have no need to work."

Her words gave me pause. What would I do? Before, I visited friends, shopped, and participated in various charitable endeavors as the idle wife of a billionaire. Now I was an idle divorcée, and the future loomed uncertain and frightening.

"You could go back to school, get your degree," Gordon murmured. "You don't have to work, but that doesn't mean you can't get a job."

I sniffled, feeling sorry for myself. "I haven't any skills. I don't want to be a waitress or ... or ..."

"You don't need to make any decision like that right now," Rita said. "I'll check in on you every few days to make sure you're all right. Mr. Pasqualle has assured me that he'll keep watch over you, too, and ensure your safety as much as anyone can. Take some time to watch movies, eat ice cream—I personally recommend chocolate moose tracks—and maybe have a fling. Nothing like getting back on another horse to clear the cobwebs."

I blinked at her mixed metaphors. "I don't want to have a fling."

She shrugged. "All right. Some women can't handle casual sex, but you might want to give it serious thought."

I shook my head.

"Are we finished, Ms. Zorokowski?" Gordon asked as he rose to his feet and drew me up with him.

"Unless the judge throws an obstacle at us, yes, we're finished." She tilted her head to one side and fixed me with her gimlet stare. "Ms. Vermont, you might give thought to reclaiming your maiden name."

I nodded. "Yes. Yes, I want to do that."

She dipped her chin. "Excellent. As soon as the judge signs off on the divorce, I'll get the paperwork started to change your name."

She gathered the papers and gestured toward the copies nearest me. "Keep those for your reference. The originals will stay here. We've got a vault."

I nodded again and collected the papers as instructed.

Gordon escorted me out, his big hand resting in the small of my back in a gesture reminiscent of Bradley's possessive touch. I barely refrained from flinching.

"He used to touch you like that, didn't he?" Gordon asked, not missing my reaction.

I nodded. We walked into the elevator. The doors closed and he pushed the button to stop the carriage. Placing both hands on my shoulders, he turned me to face him and held me there.

"If you don't like something, tell me," he said, his dark eyes intense and focused upon my face, reading every flicker of expression. "I will not hurt you, nor will I have you hurt."

"I don't know what to do," I whined again, my voice a mere whisper. "Tell me what to do."

He cupped my cheek and I leaned into his touch.

"Sonya, I'm a dom, you know that."

I nodded, eyes closed.

"But I'm not a sadist."

My eyes flew open. "I don't understand."

"You're a submissive, a beautiful, responsive, sweet submissive, but you're not a masochist."

"But—" My voice faltered. I remembered the pain Bradley inflicted upon me, how it had led to screaming, burning pleasure.

"You enjoy a little bite of pain to heighten the pleasure," he said, "but you don't like being hurt. I don't like hurting a woman." He leaned forward and, tilting my face upward, pressed a feathery kiss on my lips. "I like control and a woman's obedience, not her pain."

I shivered. *Too soon.*

"I know it's too soon for you, but we'll get there, Sonya. And then you'll be mine to cherish."

I shivered again and revelled in the reassuring possessiveness of his tone and expression. This man would take care of me. He understood my needs, needs that I did not truly understand.

Gordon pressed the button and the carriage resumed its downward travel without interruption until we reached the ground level where he hailed a taxi.

"Where are you taking me?" I asked.

"My place," he answered. "You live with me now. As soon as you're ready, you'll take my name."

My jaw dropped.

"First, we'll stop at Winston's."

I blinked.

"You need an engagement ring."

"But—" My voice faltered again as my mind and body relaxed into the familiar comfort of obedience. My fingers pressed against my throat, feeling for the thin leather collar that no longer circled it.

"No collar," he said, his voice pitched low. "You're not a dog. You're a woman, a smart, beautiful woman."

"Do you mean it?" I blurted.

"I never say what I don't mean."

I nodded, because I'd never heard him say anything he didn't mean.

"What ... what about Dana?"

"What about her?"

"I—I can't give up my friendship with her."

He sighed and muttered something about our engagement lasting longer than he anticipated before responding to my remark. "Sonya, you are free to have whomever you want as your friends. You may hold down a job and work or go back to school. If you do something I disapprove of, then I'll tell you about it."

Distress made me tremble. "But if I don't know the rules, then I won't know why you're punishing me."

He wrapped an arm around me and held me close while I sniffled. "Sweetheart, if there's a rule about something, I'll let you know. I'll be very clear about it. In the meantime, I expect you to live with me, to sleep in my guest room, and to heal."

"Sleep in the guest room?" I parroted without understanding.

"You're not ready for intimacy," he whispered and kissed my hair. "I'll wait until you are."

The driver stopped the car in front of a building where a small brass placard indicated the upscale jeweler on the fifth floor. Gordon paid the driver and we took an elevator to the fifth floor.

"I never knew this place was here," I commented in a hushed tone as we walked into the understated showroom.

Jewels glittered against midnight velvet under bright lights. A clerk approached and offered to assist and gave advice only when asked. We walked out of there an hour later with a modest diamond adorning the third finger of my left hand. Its light weight felt reassuring, reminding me that I once again belonged to someone, someone who wouldn't hurt me. I found that knowledge comforting.

I didn't think Dana would understand.

Chapter 29

Dana

"Time to go," Sam announced.

"Huh?" I looked up from an old copy of *Reader's Digest*. The true story portion had captured my attention.

"We're headed to Chicago. Now."

I set the magazine aside and rose, my body deliciously sore. Now that I'd discovered just what the hullabaloo about sex was, I welcomed it with nary a flinch of regret for not having waited for my wedding night. Looking at the 2-day scruff on his jaw and the sparkle in his blue eyes, I licked my lips and felt my body heat up.

He grinned. "Don't look at me like that. We've got to go, kitten."

Puzzled, I asked, "Like what?"

"Like you're trying to distract me with more time between the sheets." He held out my coat and I took it with a quick glance at the bedroom door. "Where are we going?"

"I just told you—Chicago."

"No, *where* in Chicago?" I buttoned my coat. "Because I don't think the city's very safe for me right now."

"My place. Det. Olsen will meet us there this afternoon."

"Who's Det. Olsen?"

"He's our contact with the Chicago Police Department. We'll turn over your photos to him and let him pursue the case."

"Why are we leaving now? I mean—"

He sighed. "Because your father called."

"What? Is Dad okay? Did something happen?"

Sam opened the door, letting a whoosh of cold air gust inside the cabin. I narrowed my eyes at him.

"I'm not going anywhere until you tell me."

He sighed. "Your Dad's fine. Someone came into the diner and asked him about your whereabouts. He told whoever it was that you'd left. When he got home, the house had been broken into and searched. It's my guess that the burglar was verifying that you really had left."

I put my hands on my hips and glared at him. "And why do you think 'whoever it was' can find us here?"

"Because he identified himself as representing Bradley Vermont."

I shuddered. "And Bradley knows about this place."

Sam nodded. "He does."

With a sigh, I cast a longing glance at the cozy cabin where we'd had nearly three days of peace and almost two days of amazing sex. At least I thought it was amazing, having nothing to compare the experience to other than the overblown descriptions found in romance novels. When I looked back at Sam, I saw that he held out his hand. I placed my palm against his and shivered with foreboding.

Within minutes we'd left the back roads and were rolling down a 2-lane rural highway. It soon exited onto a 4-lane interstate. We stopped for lunch and once for gasoline. Neither stop was particularly memorable. Neither of us much felt like carrying on a conversation.

"Mind if I turn on the radio?" I asked when the monotonous, ceaseless hum of road noise mimicked the thoughts racing in circles inside my skull.

"Go ahead."

"Anything you prefer not to listen to?" Since it was his vehicle and his radio, I figured I could at least be considerate enough not to turn to something he detested.

"Rap."

"Gotcha." I pushed the button and adjusted the volume and scanned through the stations until a familiar country tune streamed through the speakers. "This okay?"

"It's fine."

I glanced at him and sighed. "Did I do something wrong, Sam?"

"What? No, why do you ask?"

"Because you seem angry," I ventured, although he didn't just *seem* angry, he *was* angry.

The small muscle at the base of his jaw bulged. When he unclenched his teeth long enough to respond, he said, "I'm not angry with you, Dana."

"But you *are* angry."

He sighed. "Yes."

"What—"

"Drop it, Dana. Just drop it."

I lapsed into silence and sulked.

We entered the south end of Chicago and navigated the busy streets until we reached Sam's apartment building. He parked in the underground garage and escorted me to the elevator. Tension hummed between us as the carriage ascended and disgorged us on the eighteenth floor of the highrise building.

"This isn't your place," I observed aloud, shifting the weight of my duffle more comfortably on my shoulder.

"I own it," he said, his voice tight.

A nasty suspicion entered my mind. "Is this where you bring your floozies?"

He paused, nearly stumbling, and gaped at me. "Floozies?"

"Yeah, the women you have sex with but won't allow to sully your home?"

His expression darkened. "What the hell, Dana? Is that the kind of man you think I am?"

Oops, now he really was angry with me. I tried to back-pedal.

"Well, it's just that—"

"Never mind," he snapped. "Det. Olsen will meet us here in—" he glanced at his watch "—about fifteen minutes. Take your stuff into the bedroom and leave it there."

I swallowed a lump of regret and obeyed. The apartment was small, so the bedroom wasn't difficult to find. I made use of the adjoining bathroom to freshen up and returned to the small living area, knowing I owed Sam an apology.

"Sam, I'm—"

"I don't want to hear it, Dana."

"—sorry. If this isn't your *pied-à-terre*, then what is it?"

He turned to look at me, his expression stony. "You're not going to let this go, are you?"

I ventured a smile. "Nope?"

He wasn't amused. With another small sigh, he explained, "I use this for short-term clients—"

My temper ignited and I interrupted him. "That's what I am to you—a *client*? Do you fuck all your female clients or just the ones who can't afford your exorbitant fees, so you take it out in trade?"

Sam's complexion whitened with rage at my accusation. "What ... the ... *hell*?"

"No! No, you don't get to blame all this on me!" I shouted as angry tears made my vision swim before trickling down my cheeks. How could I have been such a fool? "I thought I meant something to you, something important. God, if only I'd known you were playing me for a sucker."

Sam grabbed my upper arms in a tight grip and shook me. "Shut up, Dana. You don't know what you're talking about."

"Oh, really?" I sneered. "When I was pure, untouchable Dana, your client's wife's friend, I was worthy of being in your home. But now that *you've fucked me*, I'm not!"

"Stop saying that!" he shouted.

I wrenched myself from his grip and rubbed my arms, wondering if there would be bruises. I turned on my heel to head back to the bedroom and fetch my duffle. I'd learned the first time in making a hasty exit not to leave my possessions behind. He lunged after me and grasped my right arm.

"Where do you think you're going?"

"Out," I spat. "Away from *you*."

"The hell you are," he growled and yanked me against him.

His other hand clamped to the back of my skull and held my head where he wanted it as his mouth crashed down to mine and plundered it. I struggled against the brutal kiss, which wasn't nearly as romantic as those old movies made such dominance seem. I certainly didn't melt against him.

When he released me, I took a step back and wiped my mouth on the back of my sleeve. "You overbearing, arrogant swine!"

His eyes glittered as he returned my insult. "Temperamental shrew."

Stunned by the old-fashioned insult, I gaped at him. "Shrew?"

He took a step toward me. I stepped backward to maintain distance. "Harridan."

"Harridan," I repeated.

"Termagant," he added, taking another step toward me.

"Have you been reading a thesaurus?" I demanded as I took another step backward.

"Virago." He stepped forward.

A grin tugged at my lips. "I like that one better."

I stepped backward and hit the wall. He stepped forward and pressed his heavy, muscled body against mine, pinning me to the wall.

"Vixen," he whispered, lowering his head. His moist breath wafted over my lips.

My voice took on a breathy quality as I responded, "I liked virago better."

Sam wedged a leg between mine and kissed me again. I felt the hard ridge of his cock pressed against my belly through the layers of our clothes. That time I melted and moaned.

A knock on the door put an abrupt halt to the volcanic surge of passion. Muttering a curt profanity, Sam tore himself away from me and answered the door. Breathing heavily and heart pounding, I hastened to the leather sofa and sat down, tucking a curly lock of hair behind my ear.

Sam turned around to introduce the man at the door, "Dana, this is Det. Olsen. You're going to tell him everything you know about the murder in Palmisano Park."

I gulped and nodded, watching the fit, middle-aged man hike up his gray trousers and take a seat in the armchair. He pulled a cell phone from the interior pocket of his overcoat and set it on the table.

"This conversation will be recorded. Please verbally indicate that you understand."

"I understand," I replied.

"Now tell me what you saw and did on December twenty-fourth of this year."

I explained about the calendar projects, my own and the one I'd been hired to do for the city's chamber of commerce. I told him that I'd gone to Palmisano Park on a whim to capture some sunny winter scenes. I spoke of my apartment being invaded, trashed, and robbed, how Sam had driven me back to Ohio where I'd barely escaped harm. I told him about developing my photos in the old closet-cum-dark room and how one of those pictures captured my attention. I explained that I'd enlarged the details to get a better idea of what it was about that picture that fascinated me, and that I took a closer look at the pictures immediately preceding it.

"Do you still have those photos, Miss Secrest?" the detective inquired.

"Yes, I'll fetch them for you."

He nodded his consent and I retrieved them from my duffle bag. He thanked me as I handed them over, then asked, "Do you still have the negatives?"

With reluctance, I admitted I did.

"May I have those, too?"

"I'd rather keep them," I replied. "There were some good pictures on those strips."

What I didn't say was that I feared the negatives would go missing from the evidence file, because someone who had the money to hire an assassin to take out Omar Harimadi had more than enough money to corrupt the city's police department.

Det. Olsen tucked the pictures into the interior breast pocket of his overcoat and replied, "I may return for those."

I nodded, grateful for the reprieve.

"You may be called in as a witness for the prosecution," he added. "Don't leave town."

"She's staying with me," Sam said. "There have been threats against her well being and she's under my firm's protection."

I clamped my mouth shut against the protest that threatened to burst forth.

"And your company is?" the detective prompted as though he didn't know.

"White Knight Security."

"Thank you, Mr. Galdicar. Does either of you have anything else to add?"

Both Sam and I denied having any additional information to pass along. I suspected Sam might have been lying, but I felt utterly drained and couldn't think of anything else. The detective stood, thanked us again, and headed for the door. Sam saw him out. Not two minutes after the door closed, Sam hustled me up another two flights to the apartment I recalled from my first visit.

"Why didn't we just have the detective come here?" I asked as he deposited our bags in his bedroom.

"Because I like to keep my personal and professional lives separate."

I opened my mouth to point out the obvious, then shut it without saying anything. After a moment, I headed to the kitchen where I found a kettle and filled it with water from the tap. I set it on the stovetop and asked, "Do you have any tea bags?"

"Third cupboard left of the sink."

I found a small canister of tea bags and a mug and waited for the water to boil. Tea sounded much more soothing than coffee.

The doorbell buzzed.

"I'll get that," Sam said, giving me a hard look that clearly meant *you stay put*.

Chapter 30

Sam

Bradley Vermont burst through the doorway and demanded, "Where is she?"

"Where is who?" I shot back.

His sharp eyes noticed Dana's presence in my kitchen; the apartment's open floor plan did nothing to conceal her. His expression soured and he took a step toward her. I counter-moved, putting myself between the angry billionaire and his prey.

"My *wife*," he snarled.

"Last I heard," Dana called from the kitchen, "she was divorcing your ass."

"Why you—" he growled and surged toward her.

I grabbed him and halted his progress.

"—little bitch!"

"Get out, Bradley," I ordered.

"That stupid bitch knows where my Sonya is."

"No, she doesn't," I replied.

He turned his head to face me, understanding dawning. "*You* know where she is."

"I know where she's supposed to be," I prevaricated. "But if she doesn't want to see you, then I certainly won't interfere."

"That's *my wife* you're keeping from me."

"Search the apartment," I invited him. "She's not here."

His eyes narrowed. "Tell me where she's supposed to be."

"No."

"Sam, don't defy me in this. I'll ruin you."

"Brad, I can't help you win her back."

"There is no *winning*," he sneered. "She's fucking mine and I ... *own* ... her."

"Sonya's not a possession," Dana shouted, her eyes flashing green as they did when her emotions ran high. "She's a thinking, feeling human being with *rights*, and you *don't own human beings*."

"I'll ruin you, too, you meddling bitch," he snarled.

I bristled and put myself between them, sweeping Dana behind me. "Don't threaten her."

"Well, your goons probably already did that when they trashed my apartment and destroyed my equipment!" she shouted from behind me.

"What?" He looked genuinely taken aback by the accusation even as his eyes narrowed at me.

"I said—"

"I heard what you said, Dana. I had nothing to do with destroying your equipment. I have better ways to grind a guttersnipe like you into the dirt."

I looked between the two of them. *Shit, Dana's got more than one enemy.* I saw the fear in her eyes as she realized the same thing.

"Then who?" she whispered as the kettle began to whistle.

Bradley smiled with vicious glee. "Pissed off someone else, too, didn't you, you stupid twat?"

Dana turned her back to him and poured hot water into the mug.

"Leave, Brad," I said softly. "You have no friends here."

He leveled a cold glare at me and his upper lip lifted in a sneer. "I haven't begun to—"

"Go away, Brad," I interrupted. "I'm—"

"That little bitch means something to you," he hissed, interrupting me. His lip curled. "You *care* for her."

"I'm not interested in your threats, and you can't hurt me as much as you think."

"I'll—"

I interrupted him again. "One word, just *one* word to Samuel Macintyre Galdicar, III, and you'll see how little I fear your threats."

Brad never knew how bitter my own threat tasted. I held down the gorge long enough for him to remember who my father was and to know that the old man tolerated no threat toward his family. Dear old Dad had the political, social, and financial power to ensure anyone who did was summarily removed, even tech billionaires like Bradley Vermont. The man who insulted and threatened the woman I loved—dear God, I *loved* her?—could not know that I'd not used my father's name to my advantage since Tommy Ramirez beat the snot out of me in the sixth grade.

For what it was worth, Tommy had been two years older than my uppity little ass, big for his age, and meaner than Jim Croce's famed junkyard dog of "Bad Bad Leroy Brown" fame.

The door clicked behind Brad as he stalked from the condo, a quiet pronouncement of his control. This was not the sign of an out-of-control man falling victim to ungoverned fury. Brad was many things, but uncontrolled was not one of them. He'd always struck me as calculating and ruthless, which initially made him appeal to me as suitable for training as a dom. But I had erred. A good dom incorporated a high degree of sensitivity as well as cunning and control. A good dom carefully watched his submissive and never went beyond what she could honestly handle. A good dom didn't abuse his submissive, but took her to her sexual limits to experience the most exquisite pleasure a woman could endure.

Brad, I had realized all too late, cared mostly for his own pleasure.

Of the handful of doms I'd trained, he was the only one I regretted introducing to the discipline. He'd learned the techniques, but not the heart. I found myself grateful that Dana resisted the lifestyle, resisted the total abandonment of will required of a good submissive. She liked an alpha male's command and would follow his lead, but I respected her nature to make her own decisions, to decide whether to follow or or not, whether to acquiesce or not.

I'd grown disenchanted with the subculture, seen it for the flimsy excuse it was to abuse those who didn't really know what they wanted. However, I preferred control, I needed to dominate, I relished the command.

Glancing at Dana's back, I wondered if she'd always go where I led, or what compromises I'd have to make to keep her with me, because I abruptly realized that I wanted to keep her with me always. I admired her spunk, her moxie, her intelligence, and her determination to succeed in a notoriously difficult profession. Few submissives exhibited that kind of determination and courage. Dana often led the charge and wrestled destiny with both hands, she did not submit to fate.

"I made you a cup," Dana's voice broke into my reverie.

I blinked and accepted the mug she held out to me. I lifted it to my mouth, tasted honeyed tea. "Thanks, kitten."

"Who's Samuel Macintyre Galdicar III? Your father?"

"Yeah."

"Your expression hints at some problems there," she commented, looking at me over the brim of the mug as she took a swallow.

"Dad and I don't get along all that well," I admitted with a sigh and made a mental note to call my father at the earliest opportunity. I'd dropped his name and now needed to let him know. I shuddered at the concessions he'd demand from me.

"Why not?"

"Is it really any of your business?" I shot back, annoyed at what felt like the beginning of an interrogation.

She blinked in surprise at my hostility. "No, but you met my dad and you seemed to get along with him." She snorted and a small smile curved her lips. "It was hard to have a boyfriend when I lived at home. Dad scared all the boys away."

I chuckled, because I'd seen the protective eye Larry Secrest cast over his stepdaughter. Yeah, I believed that he made a point of shooing away those teenage boys with one-track minds interested in only one thing from his beloved little girl.

"You wouldn't believe the flak I caught when Tim Zimmerman was assigned as my study partner in biology," she commented. "Not that I was interested in boys at that time. I was horse-crazy. Thank goodness for Sonya and her family."

"Oh?" I prompted.

Her eyes took on that dreamy distance of fond memory. "Yeah. Sonya got a new horse, a nutty, off-the-track thoroughbred. His registered name was Total Deduction. We called him Total Destruction." She chuckled. "God, he was a handful. Anyway, her parents let me lease Jitterbug, the older Arabian mare she'd been riding." She sighed and smiled wistfully. "I miss those days when all I truly worried about was being able to ride Jitterbug."

"I miss the ranch," I volunteered, surprising myself. "And the horses."

"Really?" Her eyes brightened with curiosity and interest, not avarice. Her lack of greed warmed my heart.

"Really. My sister Elaine pretty much runs the ranch now. It's her passion," I replied, giving her a smidgen of the information she craved. "My brother Tobias is interested in taking over the family business."

Dana frowned as she swallowed another mouthful of sweetened tea, then commented, "You've got that sour look again."

I felt my lips twist into a wry smile. "My brother's a chip off the old block. He eats, breathes, and sleeps CenterTex Holdings. My sister's the rancher, he's the businessman."

"Never heard of it." She tilted her head. "And you're quite the businessman yourself." With her free hand, she made a vague, sweeping gesture. "This is not the home of a failed businessman."

I looked around, seeing the monochromatic décor with sleek, modern furnishings with a fresh perspective, and shrugged. "It's a place to live."

Dana snorted again. "Granted, it doesn't have cranky plumbing or century-old linoleum in the bathroom, but it's cold, sterile, and imposing—perfect for a high-powered security consultant."

Her assessment surprised me. "You really think it's cold and sterile?"

"It's all black and white and gray," she explained with a small sigh as though she pitied me my impersonal luxury. "There's no color, no personality, no *hominess*. Where are the family portraits? Pictures of friends and pets and fabulous vacation memories?"

Again, I looked around the space from an habitual perspective and said somewhat defensively, "It's clean and uncluttered."

"A little clutter is necessary for a home," she opined. "This place is all sharp edges and sterile planes. There's no warmth, nothing to invite one to come in and visit. It's not cozy."

"Cozy is just another term for cramped, like your apartment," I countered, finding that I was vastly enjoying this mild debate on the dubious wisdom of my interior décor which had been created by a highly recommended, cutting-edge interior designer. "I'll have you know my condo's interior designer has received accolades from *Metropolitan Home* and *Livingetc.*"

Dana wrinkled her nose. "I did a few photo shoots of Chicago residences for *Metropolitan Home* and, honestly, didn't think much of their décor. They were a lot like this: cold, made for looking at, not living in."

Curious, I asked, "Well, then, what would you do with my condo?"

She began to slowly wander through the space, moving from the kitchen into the living and dining area, trailing the fingertips of one hand over hard, shiny, granite countertops and thick glass tabletops.

"Since this is basically a big square with a few half-walls to divide the kitchen from the rest of the main living space, I'd install hardwood floors. Wood is always warmer and less forbidding than marble." She tapped her short fingernails on a glass tabletop. "I'd put colorful rugs, probably Persian rugs, on the floor to soften the hard surface of the wood. I'd paint or wallpaper the walls in something other than white or gray, add more color with throw pillows and paintings—maybe some art glass or pottery and fresh flowers—and invest in furniture upholstered in something less automotive than leather. All the chrome, leather, and glass makes a body feel like it's inside a vehicle, not a home."

"Wallpaper?" I parroted in mild horror.

"Wallpaper is quite chic," she informed me with a smirk. "I can see something in a floral patterned silk, maybe in a muted green on that wall. Your home could use some potted plants, too, but only if you don't have cats. Cats and houseplants don't get along very well. You wouldn't believe what happened to the Boston fern Sonya gave me as a housewarming gift. Sly had great fun pretending to be 'jungle kitty.' That fern didn't last a week."

She threw a quick grin in my direction at the memory of her oversized cat's destructive antics and pointed toward a long wall where large format, black-and-white, framed photos were displayed. With narrowed eyes, she approached one of the smaller photos, a dramatic landscape showing clouds scuttling over barren mountains that loomed over a desert plain. She gasped and said, "That's a *genuine* Ansel Adams!"

"Yes, it is," I confirmed, not mentioning that the photograph had come up for sale at auction a few years ago when I acquired it as a birthday present to myself. I also didn't mention the price I paid for it. "Follow me."

"Those things sell for tens of thousands of dollars," she murmured under her breath, not going so far as to ask me to divulge the price. Either she knew it wasn't any of her business, or she understood the question was vulgar and had better manners than to ask. It didn't matter; I appreciated that she controlled her curiosity.

Eyes wide, she obeyed and followed me into my home office. I flipped the switch and the overhead lights came on. She immediately saw what I intended her to see—the newest acquisition which my housekeeper had kindly picked up from the gallery and hung on the wall during my absence—and gasped.

"That's one of mine!"

I nodded. "I attended an art gallery showing a few weeks ago, and one of the patrons enthused about an up-

and-coming young photographer. I liked the picture, so I bought it."

Her eyes glistened, suspiciously wet. "I never knew who bought that photo."

"Well, now you know."

She sniffled. "It was the only one I sold that night. The gallery said I wasn't a good enough bet for them to include in another show."

"Sweetheart, you have a magnificent talent," I assured her. "Few people see what you see until you *make* them see it in one of your pictures. You're wonderful at sharing what you see with us lesser mortals."

She chuckled, a watery sound. "Oh, that means *so* much to me." She raised glistening eyes wet with tears to mine and smiled. "I'll stop criticizing your décor."

"Even though it has no heart?"

"Your décor has no heart, but that doesn't mean you don't."

Chapter 31

Dana

At my unguarded words, Sam's expression quickly changed from a certain supercilious amusement to raw vulnerability. He concealed it by leaving his home office and heading for the kitchen in the condo's mostly open floor plan. I followed him, switching off the lights and gently closing the office door behind me. He finished his tea and set the empty mug in the sink. I'd already drained my mug, so I rinsed it out and set it in the sink alongside his.

"Dana," he said, his voice low and thick.

"Sam."

"I want you."

I felt my cheeks flame at his bald statement of desire, which ignited an answering surge of lust within my own body. I gaped at the heady candor and realized that he held his hand out. I placed my palm to his and a shudder rippled through my body when his fingers closed over my hand. I met his gaze and understood that I had given consent to whatever would happen next.

Without a word, he led me to his bedroom. Rather than lower me to the bed, he let go of my hand and cupped my face, his touch light and, dared I say, reverent. By the barest of touch, he held me where he wanted me as his mouth descended to brush mine, his lips delicately nibbling and softly caressing wherever they touched: my lips, my cheeks, my chin, my eyes. I shivered as he tended the fragile spark of my desire, his hands tracing the line of my jaw and the column of my neck to feather along the sweep of my collarbone.

He seduced me with butterfly kisses and murmured words of praise for my beauty and talent that found a welcome home in my needy heart. My skin soon pebbled in the cool air of the condominium without my knowing exactly how or when he had divested me of my clothes. Sam eased me back and kissed up and down my legs before settling between my thighs where he teased and stroked me until I gasped and begged for completion. He chuckled softly, the sound mixing with the magic of his tongue as he explored my most delicate flesh.

His hands clamped my hips with a firm hold when I leaped over the precipice of glory and shattered into a gazillion shards of brilliant light. The gentle lap of his tongue soothed as I drifted back to lucid passion. With an almost chaste kiss to my swollen and sopping lower lips, he sat back and pulled off his shirt. I heaved deep breaths of cool air as he stripped, my eyes inexorably drawn to the heavy, throbbing rod of rigid flesh that bobbed at the juncture of his legs. He wrapped his hand around his swollen cock and grated, "I want you to suck me."

Acknowledging the fair play of reciprocation, I whispered with trepidation, fearful of doing it wrong and disappointing my skilled lover, "I've never done that."

"I know," he said. A sly grin stretched his lips. "No time like the present to learn."

His comment drew a nervous giggle from me. I scrambled to my knees, trying to arrange my legs so that I didn't smear my wetness against his bedspread. I extended my hand, then drew it back.

"Touch me, Dana. I won't break," he encouraged.

Close up, his erection loomed larger than I remembered. *That* monstrosity had been inside me? I shuddered as my body remembered the incredible pleasure of his possession and wrapped my hand around him. My fingers did not touch my thumb. His hand settled over mine and he began to stroke himself using my hand.

"Like this," he whispered and squeezed just a little.

I added my other hand and tried to match his grip and pace. He groaned. I glanced up, only to see that his half-shuttered eyes burned with pleasure. Growing bold, I leaned forward and licked the weeping tip, tasting the warm, salty fluid he produced. I let it sit on my tongue, deciding whether I even liked it. I dipped my head again and inhaled the warm, masculine scent of him, felt the light tickle of his bushy pubic hair against my face, and wondered if tasting me was anything similar to what I experienced in tasting him.

"Take the crown into your mouth," Sam instructed.

Opening my mouth wide, I obeyed, determined to deliver pleasure for pleasure. He hissed as my lips closed over the spongy glans and he hissed again when the tip of my agile tongue tickled the sensitive frenulum. My mouth watered, saliva combining with semen to produce a slick slurry that had me making loud slurping sounds as my head bobbed over his cock. When my lips tingled and my jaw ached, I turned my attention to laving the long, thick stalk. I moved a hand down to his scrotum and marveled at the softness of the delicate skin covering his balls. He moaned as I massaged his testicles and licked his cock, burying his hands in my short, thick curls as though to command my performance.

However, his touch remained gentle, following my movement rather than directing it. Despite worry to the contrary, Sam did not fuck my mouth. He did not force his dick down my throat and make me gag.

"I'm going to come," he warned.

I felt my eyes widen and pulled back, not ready to accept his ejaculation in my mouth. I wondered if my reluctance to swallow disappointed him. He said nothing, but tipped my head back and pressed a sweet kiss to my tingling, swollen lips, and murmured, "Thank you, kitten. That was wonderful."

I wanted to purr.

He gently maneuvered me back to lying down and lay beside me. I watched as his hands skimmed over my body, quickly revving up my passion again. I closed my eyes when he fondled my breasts and plucked at my nipples. My thighs relaxed and opened at the slightest of touches, my hips tilting in a wordless search for the resumption of ecstasy. My bones melted beneath his heated touch and I reached back to reciprocate, absently contrasting the smoothness of my skin to his hair-roughened masculinity, the hard bulge of muscle, the latent power that he employed with such gentle, tender care.

I realized that I whimpered, begging him to come inside my aching, needy body. I sighed when he finally complied, easing in and out of my flesh in long, slow thrusts. The wet sound of our coupling made my cheeks burn, but he did not seem to notice it. I decided that the sound was normal and natural and nothing worthy of shame. With the release of that self-conscious worry, I found myself better able to participate rather than merely receive. I rocked my hips and stroked his body wherever I could reach.

I whined when Sam withdrew from my body, uncertain what he wanted until he whispered, "Roll over. Hands and knees, sweetheart."

A full body shudder shook me as I obeyed. Sam moved behind me and rubbed his palm up and down the length of my spine, a soothing touch accompanied by a whispered, guttural, "Good girl."

His warm hands gripped my buttocks, then clamped over my hips, holding me in place while he notched his cock between my lower lips and then slid inside, going deeper than I'd previously experienced. I grunted and blushed at the squeal that erupted from my lips. I felt the heat of his large body as he bent over me and whispered into my ear, "Like that, do you?"

His low chuckle smacked of triumph and was soon followed by the loud smacking of his hips against my ass. Each deep thrust expelled a grunt from me. My breathing quickened and deepened as my breasts swayed with each heavy smack. I heard him groan and grunt as his hips increased their pace.

Sam again bent low over my back, one brawny arm slamming down to the mattress to brace himself and the other wrapping around to strum my clit as his cock moved like a piston inside me. My body tensed as another orgasm built. I cried out as it burst over me, almost obscuring the rapid thrusts of the thickening cock that throbbed and pulsed inside me, filling me with Sam's seed as he bit down on the nape of my neck.

He withdrew from my body as his cock softened, and we both collapsed to the bed. I bit my lip at the feel of his seed dripping from my vagina, and closed my eyes in panicked realization that we might have just created a baby.

"Fuck," Sam muttered as he, too, came to the same understanding that our lack of caution might have serious consequences. He knew I wasn't on birth control and he'd neglected to put on a condom. To be fair, I hadn't reminded him nor insisted he wear one.

I turned my head away to hide my disappointment at his sudden attitude, realizing that somehow I'd fallen in love with this unexpectedly kind, generous, and good man who made my body sing and with whom I wanted to build a life and have a family.

"Dana."

I didn't look at him. My lip hurt from where I was gnawing on it.

"Dana." He settled his hand on my shoulder and rolled me over to face him. "I'm sorry."

I closed my eyes.

"If there's a baby, I won't abandon you, either of you."

I nodded, then levered myself upright and raced to the bathroom to take a hot shower. Although I knew that aggressive washing wouldn't prevent conception, I did it anyway.

Dad would be so ashamed of me.

Chapter 32

Sam

I draped a forearm over my eyes as I lay there in a pool of recriminations. I wanted to go to her, join her in the shower, but doubted she'd welcome my presence, much less my attention. I'd screwed up. Literally. The mental image of Dana growing round and heavy with my baby made my cock twitch and rise again with the intention of ensuring I impregnated her, but I knew she wasn't ready. She didn't yet want to become a mother. She wanted the whole dream: marriage, a house with a big yard and picket fence, and probably a sad-faced hound to torment her bad-tempered cat. She wanted to succeed in her career, to become the twenty-first century Ansel Adams of the female variety. She had ambitions and dreams that I feared did not include me.

I resolved that if she were pregnant, that neither she nor the child would lack for anything. Should I marry her, I wondered? Surprisingly, the concept of marriage—at least to Dana—didn't fill me with dread or horror. The idea of having her in my bed every night filled me with anticipation.

It's just infatuation. Lust. It won't last.

I winced at the rote, determined denial of anything genuine between us. I admitted I wanted Dana to be mine. I wanted to beat my chest like a gorilla and proclaim that this woman belonged to me. No other man had any right to touch her.

Mine!

I snorted at my own possessive nature and muttered aloud, "I'm a fucking Neanderthal."

Or a toddler.

I even recognized my hypocrisy in refusing to admit any reciprocation, that I belonged to her as surely as she belonged to me. But I disregarded that. *It's lust, incredibly potent lust, and I'll tire of her soon enough.* I wouldn't have called myself a manwhore or womanizer, but I was no monk either. I'd enjoyed several casually intimate relationships and a couple of serious ones since losing my own virginity at the tender age of 16, half a lifetime ago. Personal honor, morals, or perhaps just natural caution deterred any inclination to indulge in one night stands. That probably made me a hero to some women with low standards, but I knew better.

Dana would need assurance and understanding, and I wasn't sure that I was the right one to give it to her. Was I capable of offering meek apology and timid promises of support when what my caveman self wanted to do was haul her back home and hide her away so that no one else would have the pleasure of her company, her smiles, her conversation, or her sweet, luscious body?

Dear Lord, that gorgeous body! Soft, smooth skin. Wet, silken heat. Breathy moans and musky honey.

My hands crept down and pumped my cock, again hard and demanding release. As my balls tightened and the base of my spine tingled in warning, I reached with one hand to grab a wad of facial tissues from the cardboard box on the nightstand. Just in time, I caught the spurt of semen before spraying myself. With a groan, I crumpled the wad of soiled tissues and tossed them into the wastebasket on the other side of the nightstand.

The spigot shut off, my cue to get up. Naked, I opened the closet door and snatched two bathrobes off their hangers, one for me and one for her. I donned one and waited outside the bathroom door to hand her the other when she deigned to emerge all pink and moist and fresh and ... *oh, shit.* My cock tented the front of my bathrobe with renewed enthusiasm.

Well, if that wasn't a physical manifestation of undying devotion, then I didn't know what was. I'd never had such a potent physical reaction to any woman.

"Thank you," Dana murmured, carefully averting her gaze so she wouldn't have to meet mine as she took the bathrobe from my hand.

"Dana," I said, my voice hoarse.

She looked at me, her eyes blinking back tears.

Running the back of my knuckles down her smooth cheek, I whispered, "This is not a mistake. I won't abandon you, ever."

"This isn't what I wanted," she rasped and looked ashamed.

Her shame angered me. "Nothing we did was wrong, kitten. We're consenting adults."

"I feel like a sl—"

"No," I barked, cutting off the derogatory word she dared sully herself with. "No, you're *mine*. And if you're pregnant, then you're both mine."

She sniffled, then grew very cool and still.

"You sound like Bradley."

Chapter 33

Dana

I hated the comparison, didn't want to admit that I'd fallen for a dominant douchebag just like Sonya had. His eyes hardened, glinting like gunmetal at the accusation. All heat and softness in his expression vanished, leaving behind the cold-eyed warrior I recognized.

Without another word, I grabbed my bag and headed for the other bedroom to comb my hair and dress. Before I finished dressing, I heard the slam of the heavy door at the main entrance. Knees wobbly, I stood in front of the mirror and combed my wet hair before bending over to shake my head and separate the curly locks to air dry. With luck, my hair wouldn't turn into a frizzy mess. I pulled out my last change of clean clothes from the bag and dressed.

Glancing out the window, I saw fat, fluffy snowflakes swirl against the smudged gray sky and my fingers itched. I sighed and yearned for my camera. The monochromatic winter tableau of an overcast winter landscape could make for some subtly dramatic photographs.

My cheeks puffed out and I blew another explosive puff of breath, not a sigh, exactly, more of an expression of exasperation. Wandering through the spacious penthouse and admiring the original works of art displayed on the walls brought home as nothing else could how far apart Sam and I were on the socioeconomic spectrum. The comparisons kept coming. Bradley was rich, dominant, and controlling. Sam was rich, dominant, and controlling. I knew no other obscenely wealthy men, so I had to draw my conclusion from the small sample of data I had. What I didn't like was the conclusion that all handsome, wealthy men were also dominant and controlling assholes.

I was more like Sonya than I wanted to admit.

Bored with wandering and practicing a strict, hands-off policy that hearkened back to the days of "you break it, you buy it" and childhood admonitions of "don't touch that" and "no, you can't have it," I ended up in the kitchen where I found the makings for coffee and set the fancy percolator to brewing, fidgeting the entire time.

Oh, well, might as well do laundry. I gathered my pitiful wardrobe and carried it to the laundry room. It was easy to separate into three small piles: jeans, colors, lights and whites. I dumped the lights-and-whites into the washer first, poured in a measure of detergent, and set the machine to run, figuring I had about 45 minutes to fill before transferring the wet load to the dryer and washing the next load of dirty laundry. I wondered whether I ought to wash Sam's dirty laundry and decided against it. He'd probably consider that an intrusion into his privacy. Or maybe worse, he'd start *expecting* me to wash his clothes.

With 45 minutes to kill, I felt restless. I didn't do "cooped up" well and already felt the beginning of cabin fever. At least in the tiny hunting cabin in Missouri I'd had some room to roam outside. Here, it was too dangerous. There were bad guys after me, bad guys who knew I had incriminating photos ...

Wait.

How did they know I had those photos?

I hadn't known I had those photos until I developed them and noticed something unusual.

Pondering that made my head ache. I ran a hand through my damp curls and tucked the strands behind one ear.

How did they know?

Wandering back into the kitchen, I drummed my fingertips on the countertop.

Perhaps the bad guys weren't after me for that particular reason?

That, of course, led to another distressing thought.

Does that make three *villains now after me? Bradley for helping Sonya see the light and leave him? Whoever hired the assassin who killed Omar Harimadi? And who else? Who else counts himself as my enemy to the extent of hiring thugs to break into Dad's house and pursue me?*

Were the attacks not even related to my photography session in Palmisano Park on Christmas Eve?

What and why? *Why?*

At that point, the *why* mattered more than the *who*. I wracked my mind trying to come up with a feasible answer to either and got nothing. I hadn't yet attained the soaring level of success as a photographer or artist to inspire that kind of insane envy sufficient to motivate anyone to remove me.

I poured steaming coffee into a black ceramic mug and carefully carried it into the living room area. I sat on the sofa, sliding back on the slick leather, and picked up a remote control. Curious, I pushed a button. Nothing happened. I pushed another button and panel doors on the wall slid open to reveal a large black screen. I pushed another button. Nothing. Another button. The television winked on. The remote control had a donut-shaped button. I manipulated that and the channels advanced. With a bit of fiddling, I learned the toggle switch controlled the volume. Having mastered the basics of operating the television, I scrolled through a menu of too many channels, none offering anything I cared to watch. For once, I agreed with Dad's decision not to subscribe to cable TV.

I finished my coffee and refilled the mug.

The washer beeped and I tended to laundry.

I glanced at the time and decided that I might as well get started on cooking supper. Who knew when Sam intended to return and grace me with his exalted presence again? I was hungry.

Rummaging through his refrigerator and pantry yielded the fixings for a quick tomato sauce liberally doctored with vegetables and herbs. A package of high-end penne would complete the simple dish. I put a pot of water on to boil and found a wooden cutting board—Dad would have approved—and began slicing and chopping a slightly wilted green bell pepper, garlic cloves, an onion, and whole canned tomatoes while a pound of frozen ground sirloin sizzled in a skillet drizzled with a bit of olive oil. I skimmed off layers of browned beef and turned the meat as needed until the entire chunk was crumbled and cooked through. I added the chopped veggies and garlic and let them sauté with the beef for a few minutes. Then I poured in the liquid from the canned tomatoes and scraped the chopped tomatoes off the cutting board into the skillet. I sprinkled in dried basil and a pinch of dried oregano, salt, and freshly ground pepper.

Soon, the tantalizing aroma of a quick pasta dish filled the entire penthouse. My stomach growled. The water boiled and I added the pasta. It cooked quickly. I drained it and returned it to the pot, then dumped the sauce into the pot and stirred. Sam hadn't yet returned, so I dished a serving for myself and ate it in front of the television while watching an old rerun of *WKRP in Cincinnati*.

Screenwriters in the 1970s really had a good handle on humor.

Episode ended and my belly filled, I returned to the kitchen and cleaned. I portioned out meal-sized portions of the leftovers for later, covering them with plastic wrap and stashing them in the refrigerator. Sam came in as I filled the sink with hot water and suds.

"I made supper. There's leftovers in the fridge if you're hungry," I announced as he took off his overcoat and hung it on the coat rack.

He paused and directed his cold blue gaze at me. "That's it? You're not going to demand we talk?"

I shrugged, meeting his gaze. Apparently pasta gave me moxie. "What's there to talk about? You're an asshole."

He didn't flinch, although I wanted him to. I wanted my words to hurt him.

"I, however," I continued in a cool tone, "can be civil."

He pressed his lips together, but said nothing. I washed, rinsed, and dried the dishes and put them away while he availed himself of a plate of leftovers and a glass of cabernet sauvignon and retreated to the sofa. He turned on the television and paid no attention to the movie that played onscreen: *The Blues Brothers.*

"This is really good," he commented. "Thank you."

He doesn't have to sound so surprised. I swallowed the spiteful remark and simply thanked him.

"Mind if I have a glass?" I asked, gesturing toward the bottle of wine.

"No, go ahead."

I poured a glass of wine and joined him on the sofa, sitting at the other end. I made sure to keep plenty of distance between us.

Taking an appreciative sip of the dry, full-bodied vintage, I asked as though I had every right, "So, where were you?"

He raised an eyebrow in response. I answered by raising both my eyebrows in expectant silence. He broke the stalemate first.

"Out. I was out."

I maintained my silence and took another sip of wine. He sighed and took a bite of his supper.

"I *do* have a business to run," he added.

I took another small sip and waited.

"Fuck, Dana, what do you want from me?"

I blinked at his frustration, opened my mouth to respond. Onscreen, Aretha Franklin wearing pink slippers and a waitress uniform sang about deserving a little respect.

I couldn't have planned that any better.

Chapter 34

Sam

Dana couldn't have planned that any better.

I took the last bite of the flavorful pasta dinner she'd made and set the plate on the coffee table while Aretha Franklin's powerful voice filled the room. I picked up the remote control and turned off the television as the saxophone blared its iconic solo. Facing the woman who tangled me in knots, I opened my mouth and said, "Dana—"

"Sam—" she said at the same time. Then, with a small wave of her hand, she said, "No, you first."

After her expert interrogation through silence, I shook my head and grinned. "Oh, no, ladies first."

She shrugged and dropped a bombshell: "Whoever's after me isn't after me because of Omar Harimadi's murder."

"What?"

She explained her rationale and I found no fault with it.

"Well, shit." I rubbed my chin. Dana leaned forward to pick up my plate. "Don't, I'll get it."

She nodded, but didn't lean back. Staring at her fidgeting hands, she said, "I'm really confused, Sam. My phone was bugged, but I assume that's so Bradley—" she spat the name "—could keep tabs on me to ensure nothing I said or did affected his control over Sonya. The incriminating photo I took at Palmisano Park wasn't on my phone, so he couldn't have accessed it. Hell, the camera wasn't even internet-compatible. It used film. Even if he did hire the thug who killed Omar Harimadi, he couldn't have known I took that picture."

She glanced at me. I nodded to show I was listening and let her continue thinking aloud. I kept my thoughts silent: *Except we knew you were taking photos at Palmisano Park that day. Bradley leaves nothing to chance and he might have suspected you witnessed and photographed what you weren't supposed to see.*

She continued, "Bradley seemed genuinely surprised about my apartment being destroyed, so I'm prepared to give him the benefit of the doubt there. I've always known he didn't like me, but I don't think he'd resort to having me killed. I'm just not that big or powerful."

Again, I nodded, but not because I entirely agreed with her. "You're not that influential in the general sense, Dana, but you have tremendous influence over Sonya."

She huffed. "Hah. If I had that much influence, she wouldn't have married the jerk in the first place."

"She loved him," I reminded her.

Dana sighed. "Yeah, she did." She shook her head and rubbed her temples. "I never understood ..."

The words faded on another sigh.

"What did you not understand?"

She shook her head again, although I could tell the gesture was not one of denial, more of confusion. She sighed again. "Bradley's a popular romance archetype, you know:

smart, handsome, ruthless, kinky, alpha billionaire. He's not supposed to be real, but he is and I guess I shouldn't fault Sonya or any woman for falling for him."

I kept my mouth shut, because that archetype described me, too.

She turned to face me, her bright hazel eyes shining with candor and courage. "As least I didn't fall for a billionaire."

"Oh, honey," I murmured and drew her to me.

She rested her forehead on the top of my shoulder and let herself settle into my embrace. Predictably, my dick thickened and swelled, but I ignored it. Her honesty and bravery shamed me though, because I could not yet quite admit that I loved her, too. Sure, I'd acknowledged my feelings before in fleeting moments of honest introspection, but I always drew back, always attempted to convince myself that what I felt for her did not—could not—match that ultimate expression of affection and devotion and admiration.

Dana drew back and I released her.

.

Chapter 35

Dana

I averted my gaze, refusing to meet Sam's eyes. I wasn't sure whether that reluctance stemmed from not wanting him to see the sincerity of what I'd just admitted in decidedly lukewarm language, or from my not wanting to see his pity for poor, deluded me. I clasped my hands tightly and leaned forward, bracing my forearms on my thighs. I felt my shoulder hunch in what I knew was a defensive posture.

"Well, as much as I dislike the highly esteemed and powerful Bradley Vermont, I can't accuse him of trying to have me killed," I said, forcing strength and confidence into every syllable.

"No," he agreed, his tone subdued. "If he truly feared your influence over Sonya, he would have simply cut off all access to you."

"He very nearly cut off all her social access entirely," I pointed out. "That's what abusers do."

He said nothing. Since I wasn't looking at him, I didn't know whether he made any gesture or facial expression to indicate his own opinion. A ringtone emanated from Sam's pocket. He grunted, pulled the device out, and put it to his ear.

"Thanks for calling back, Dad."

He stood and stepped a few paces away. Heeding his unspoken request for privacy, I collected his dirty dishes and my empty wine glass and carried them into the kitchen to wash while he spoke to his father. Although my ears caught only the occasional quietly spoken word, I understood the tense tone of voice as I watched him from the corner of my eye.

"All right, Dad," he said. "Let me talk to Mama?"

After a moment, I overheard, "Hey, Mama, did Dad tell you ... oh, good. You'll be ready then. Yes, she's still with me. No, I didn't see the news, you know I don't read the social gossip columns. Yes, I know Bradley's getting a divorce."

He paused in his slow pacing, lips pressed together in a thin line as though he were biting back words. Finally, he spoke again, his volume increasing.

"Yeah, Mama, see you soon. Tell Elaine ... no, Mama, I will not speak with her about that bull rider. Yes, I checked. He's clean: no rap sheet, no paternity suits, no egregious debt beyond a fancy truck and trailer."

I raised my eyebrows, gleaning from my eavesdropping that his mother disapproved of his sister seeing a professional bull rider. Remembering my ephemeral, teenaged fascination with the rodeo and the handful I'd attended as a photographer trying to find my niche and earn enough to keep body and soul together, I thought I could understand that. Sure, the cowboys spoke nicely and respectfully *to* women, but I'd heard some of the conversations they conducted among themselves *about* women, especially the buckle bunnies: manwhores, the lot of 'em, except for the few who were happily married.

Of course, the buckle bunnies used the cowboys as much as they were used. An old friend of mine who'd joined the Navy and occasionally kept in touch once remarked upon the women who made a game or challenge of racking up the most "slept with a sailor" points and the many sailors who were only too happy to participate. I supposed it was the same concept just transferred from naval bases to rodeos.

My thoughts returned to the cowboys. Those few who loved their girls *really* loved them, as I knew Dad—so *not* a cowboy—had loved my mother. I reckoned a woman who received that love could do a lot worse. A woman could endure a lot of hardship if she had the love and support of a good man like that. I wondered what I could do, how far I could go, with Sam's love to support me. But I wasn't sure he loved me. I knew he wanted me, desired me, and felt possessive of my body. I wondered if some of that interest stemmed from being the man to take my virginity.

Those thoughts led to a weird longing to watch *The Phantom of the Opera* again, a favorite tale of love and obsession. I snorted at my own silliness and drained the sink for the second time that evening.

"You know, I have a dishwasher," Sam murmured in my ear.

I gasped, startled by his sudden presence. For such a big man, he moved very quietly.

"Washing by hand does a more thorough job," I replied in echo of Dad's oft-spoken answer to my childhood complaint when he assigned me dishwashing duties at the diner. By the time I'd graduated from college, I'd realized he was right. Some things really were better done the old-fashioned way.

"Well, anyway, thank you. You didn't have to cook supper or wash the dishes."

"I'm not really used to being idle."

"Tell me."

I shrugged. "I took over most of the household chores when Mom got sick. That, plus school, kept me busy. Then she died and Dad had funeral expenses and medical bills to pay off, so he was always at the diner. I replaced caring for Mom with 4-H activities to fill my time. When I got to college, I had to work to pay tuition. After graduation, I still had to work."

I shrugged again.

"Tell me about your cat."

"Sly?" I smiled, because I missed the big, squishy furball. "He's company and entertainment all in one cute package."

"That cat is not cute."

I couldn't let him have the last word on that. "Sure, he is. You've only seen him when he's stressed."

We argued amicably about the merits of my cat and cats in general as opposed to dogs and tropical fish for a few minutes before Sam dropped a bombshell.

"I'm taking you home."

I blinked in confusion. "Home isn't safe, remember?"

"*My* home."

I looked around. "*This* is your home."

"Texas, Dana. I live here, but Texas is home."

My eyes narrowed in suspicion. "Why?"

He sighed. "Because my family needs me and I can't protect you if you remain here."

I chewed on my lip, wanting to argue that his firm could protect me; however, that would place undue obligation on paid security that I couldn't afford. Being part of the gig economy, I knew well the annoyance of being asked—or expected—to work for free or insultingly paltry wages. I refused to do that to anyone else.

"Don't do that."

"Huh? Do what?"

"Abuse that pretty lip." He cupped my chin and swept his thumb over my lower lip. He leaned in and brushed a barely-there kiss over my mouth and said, "Because then I'll have to kiss it until it feels better."

I inhaled, the scents of his skin and cologne filling my nose. *Delicious.* My body reacted with immediate arousal.

"Sam," I whispered on a soft exhale. The washer and dryer both beeped, recalling me to domestic duty. "Hold that thought."

He followed me to the laundry room as I scooped out dry clothes from the machine and replaced them with a wet, freshly washed load. "I'll have Elaine take you shopping when we get home."

Heat crept up my neck and spread across my face. I knew my current wardrobe left much to be desired, but I hadn't asked to have the entire contents of my apartment destroyed. Instead of addressing the issue of my dependence upon his money to replace the clothes on my back, I asked, "Have you heard from the cleaners?"

No dummy, he knew exactly what I meant. "Not much could be salvaged, I'm afraid. You're lucky the cat survived."

Carrying the armful of warm, dry clothes to the spare bedroom, I sighed. "Yeah. Sly means a lot, he's more important than mere things. I hope he's doing okay at Dad's."

"I'm sure he's fine. And why are we in here?"

"I thought—"

"You thought wrong."

Looking up from the clothes I was folding, I narrowed my eyes and glared at him. "Sam, I am not a booty call."

He met my gaze with eyes that blazed. "No, you're not. But you'll sleep in my bed."

"Sam," I warned, breath and pulse quickening. My need to assert my autonomy battled with my need for him.

He leaned close and whispered in my ear, "If you don't want me to fuck you, then tell me no and I'll stop."

And just like that, my libido revved into high gear. Honesty compelled me to admit that I couldn't tell him no. Nor did I want to.

Chapter 36

Sonya

The New Year had come and gone, and Rita Zorokowski pushed through the divorce proceedings with a speed unprecedented in the history of law. Bradley contested the terms of the divorce before the judge could sign off on the earlier agreement. I didn't know why: my estranged husband seldom changed his mind. He prided himself on decisiveness. I wondered if, perhaps, he was yanking me around just to prove he could, that he still had control.

Now I faced Bradley across an expansive tabletop. Gordon sat at my left and Rita at my right. I didn't recognize the lawyers Bradley brought with him and knew he probably didn't really need them. I tried to listen and pay attention to the wrangling between Rita and the opposition, but the thud of my heart filled my ears and dread filled my mind.

"Breathe," Gordon whispered as his hand found mine under the table. He gave a little squeeze of reassurance. "You're going to be all right, Sonya. Breathe."

"How long have you been cheating on me, Sonya?" Bradley's voice cut through my mental fog.

I blinked and almost met his eyes, but training truncated that action. Bradley punished direct eye contact, taking it as a challenge to his authority. I felt both Gordon and Rita stiffen to either side of me, although my eyes were anchored to the polished tabletop.

"Whether or not Mrs. Vermont indulged in any extramarital activity has no basis in these proceedings," Rita said, every syllable clipped.

"On the contrary, it does matter," Bradley countered. "According to the prenuptial agreement Sonya willingly signed, her infidelity is grounds for divorce without any remuneration whatsoever."

"And what about your infidelity?" Rita shot back.

"I have never been unfaithful to my wife."

I couldn't help but shake my head. I knew Bradley didn't dally with other women. If there was anything he prided himself upon, it was his word. Bradley never broke a vow. Never.

Gathering the last drops of what courage still remained to me, I lifted my gaze and met his. I winced, but forced myself not to look down again. Taking a deep breath, I said, "I never cheated on you, Bradley."

My voice quivered, but the words came out clearly.

"You're living with *him*." There was no accusation in his voice. He made a flat, factual statement and let human imagination fill in the rest. "And I didn't buy that ring you're wearing, either."

Rita didn't suggest that, perhaps, I'd purchased the ring myself. She knew better than anyone that I had no money.

"I have not been unfaithful to you," I said, the glimmerings of anger lending strength to my voice. "I have not had sex with any man other than you since the day we met."

"Do you really expect me to believe that?" Bradley sneered. "He's a dom. I've seen him at the sex clubs."

Gordon gave my hand another small squeeze.

"Regardless of where you may or may not have seen Mr. Pasquale has no bearing," Rita stated. "Now as to the concessions for your divorce—"

"Nothing," Bradley said. He glared at me, his formerly heated gaze now frigid with contempt. "I loved you, Sonya. I gave you everything you wanted, everything you *needed*. And this is how you repay me? You even aborted our baby. No. No, you get *nothing* from me, not any more. I owe you nothing."

"I miscarried!" My wail filled the room. "You hurt me so badly that I miscarried our baby!"

"You can't prove that, Sonya, and you can't deny that you *loved* what I did to you in the playroom."

My cheeks flooded red with shame, because I had enjoyed both the pain and the pleasure, too much for any one body to withstand.

Bradley stood. His lawyers got to their feet, too.

"Nothing. Not a damned penny," he growled. "And don't think I'll take you back, either."

"We'll see you in court, Mr. Vermont," Rita replied as they exited the conference room. The door closed behind them and she turned to me. "Mrs. Vermont ... Sonya ... this is going to get ugly."

I nodded, felt hot tears drip.

"Would you be willing to speak to the press?" Rita inquired.

"What?"

"Speak to the press about—"

"No!" I broke into sobs. "No, I can't humiliate myself that way. It's private."

"It's a good way to discredit your husband."

"Ex-husband."

"Not quite yet."

"I just want to end this."

"Sonya, you deserve recompense for what you endured, for your tenure as Bradley Vermont's wife."

I shook my head and wept. "I don't want anything from him, not anymore."

She sighed. "You're upset. We'll discuss this at a later time."

Chapter 37

Dana

I could not help but marvel at the preferential treatment, the luxurious interior of the private jet, and the ease with which we flew to the hot, humid oil fields of northeastern Texas. The change in climate shocked me, too. *Summer here must be brutal.*

A long, black limousine sans tacky grille decoration of bull horns greeted us at a small, municipal airfield and carried us across and through a lush, green landscape where thick pine forests alternated with vast pastures populated with herds of cattle, horses, and oil derricks.

Almost too soon, the limousine turned onto a long gravel drive and drove to an immense plantation house built on the backs of slaves and maintained in stately elegance. Columns graced the imposing front entrance, making those who approached feel small and insignificant, like serfs petitioning the king.

"You grew up here?" My voice squeaked. I tried not to feel ashamed of the modest country home where I'd grown up.

"Yeah," Sam answered as the front portal—the word *door* seemed too plebeian—opened to reveal a tall, elderly Black man with gray hair and an equally tall, slender woman wearing a tailored dress and sensible black heels.

"That's our butler Conrad and my mother," Sam identified the two people.

I held out my hand to the butler and he merely inclined his head in a stiff, formal manner that made me wonder if he were practicing for a part in a *Downton Abbey* remake.

"Miss Secrest," he greeted me.

I squashed the urge to curtsey or bow and swung my hand toward Sam's mother, tall and regal in her tailored dress, discreet diamond earrings, and upswept blonde hair. "Mrs. Galdicar, it's a pleasure to meet you. I'm sorry for dropping in on you like this."

Yvette Galdicar née Hardy favored me with a tight-lipped smile and accepted my hand with a limp, cool grip. It was like shaking hands with a dead jellyfish. She withdrew her hand from mine before I could think to release it.

"Any guest of my dearest Sam is welcome here," she replied in a near whisper that exuded only civility, no warmth whatsoever.

Sam stepped forward to press a light kiss to his mother's smooth, unlined cheek. "You're looking as lovely as ever, Mama. Have you lost weight?"

Her chilly eyes softened at the compliment and made me wonder about what weird family dynamics were going on and whether I even wanted to find out.

"I have," she replied. Her lilting southern accent would have been pleasant to listen to if not for the icy temperature of her tone. "You know your father appreciates a trim figure on a woman."

Her gaze raked me over as if to discern whether I met Mr. Galdicar's stringent requirements for the female form. Sam slid an arm around my waist, resting his hand lightly on the flare of my hip. I wasn't sure if the gesture was supportive or possessive.

"Is Elaine around?" he asked.

Mrs. Galdicar's lips pursed. If she were trying to frown, it didn't work. I wondered if she was addicted to Botox®, because nothing except her lips moved.

"She'll be in the stables, Sam."

Sam nodded and turned his attention to the butler. "I'll bring in our bags just as soon as I get Dana settled."

"You'll do no such thing, Samuel," his mother said in that syrupy Southern accent, not Texan, but definitely reminiscent of Scarlet O'Hara. "Why, Conrad would just be insulted if you did."

From the corner of my eye, I caught the butler roll his eyes and had to repress a giggle. I liked that the stuffy butler wasn't so stuffy after all. Perhaps that stiff formality was an act he put on for Mrs. Galdicar's sake.

Sam grinned and said, "Thank you, Conrad. I wouldn't want to cause offense."

"Of course not, sir," the butler murmured.

"There's not much luggage." He grasped my hand and tugged. "The stables are this way. Let's see if we can catch Eileen."

"Nice to meet you!" I called back as Sam pulled me away.

"Two down, three to go," he muttered as we headed toward a long, open-air building that reminded me of the horse barns at the county fairgrounds.

As we approached, I noticed most of the stalls were empty and assumed that the horses were grazing in pastures. With my free hand, I wiped the perspiration off my forehead when we entered the shady environs of the long barn. Sam took a hard left and rapped on a closed door.

"Elaine!"

There was a clatter from behind the door, followed by a muttered oath and a feminine giggle. Sam looked at me, one eyebrow raised. I bit my lips and held my tongue. We knew what those sounds meant and neither of us was going to mention it. It wouldn't be polite. After a moment, the door opened and a woman around my age appeared. Her lips were moist and rosy, her color was high, and her eyes sparkled. Lurking behind her was a male figure who, I assumed, was responsible for the woman's appearance. He was buttoning his jeans.

"Sam!" she cried and launched herself at him. "You're home!"

He kissed the top of her head and wrapped his free arm around her. "Yeah, sis, I'm home." He focused his gaze at the man standing behind her. "And this must be Peter Redclaw."

A young man with coppery skin, long black hair pulled into a low ponytail, and exotic good looks filled the doorway. His shirt was unbuttoned, displaying a smooth-skinned, muscled chest and rippling abs. He nodded and said, "And you're Sam."

Giggling, Elaine took a step back and noticed my presence. "And who's this?"

"Dana Secrest," I introduced myself and held out my hand, determined to be polite regardless of what the other woman's hand had been doing a minute earlier.

Shaking my hand, Elaine looked at her brother and said, "She's a pretty one, Sam, and no pedigreed debutante. Mama's gonna be pissed if you marry her."

Everyone went still.

"Shit," Elaine muttered. "I'm always putting my big boot into my mouth."

Sam swallowed audibly. "Elaine, Dana is here as my guest. We had to leave rather suddenly and we don't know how long she'll need to stay."

"Sam, you haven't brought a client here since—"

"Elaine," he said, his tone filled with warning.

His sister huffed. "Well, she's bound to find out anyway, doofus." She looked at me. "Sam once brought Delaney Holmes here. It was a *disaster*."

She looked gleeful at Sam's discomfiture as only a sister could.

"Not only did she think we were her servants at her beck and call, but she thought *bodyguard* meant *gigolo*." She chuckled. "Boy, was she mad when she found out differently."

It didn't surprise me that Sam had served as security for an A-list movie star, only that he'd resisted her allure. Few men would have. I grinned. "Well, I'm pretty certain I know the difference. And I've never had servants, so I wouldn't know how to treat anybody like one."

Elaine's eyebrows shot upward. "You tried to shake hands with Conrad, didn't you?"

Was she psychic? I nodded.

"Yeah, all Sam's blue collar acquaintances make that mistake."

I felt something sour and curdle inside me.

"Really, Elaine? Could you be any more snobbish?" Sam muttered.

"Oh, was I being a snob?" She blinked in confusion, then favored me with a tight smile all too reminiscent of her mother's. "Sorry. Old, ingrained habits I can't quite kick."

She returned her focus to her brother.

"So, why bring Dana down here instead of waiting until suppertime to introduce her?"

"Because I have a favor to ask of you."

"Oh?"

He summarized my situation quickly, "Dana's home was burgled, just about everything destroyed. She needs a wardrobe: unmentionables, shoes, socks, shirts, pants, dresses, pajamas, everything. Anyway, I'd be grateful if you'd take her shopping, get her enough to wear for a week."

Elaine's expression shifted from interested to bewildered. "Pajamas? I guess she really is your client."

"I didn't say she was going to wear them."

The heat of embarrassment flooded me.

Elaine chuckled at my discomfiture and winked. "Ah, keeping up appearances for Mama's sake."

"And Dad's."

She shrugged and held out her hand, open palm facing up. "Give me your credit card, Sam."

Sam dug out his wallet and extracted a black credit card. I'd never seen one before, but I knew what it meant.

"Don't go too hog wild, sis."

She sniffed. "Well, we won't be rummaging through the clearance racks."

"Um, I'm all right with clearance racks," I interjected, thinking of what I'd have to repay.

Sam, apparently, read my thoughts. "Dana, it's my gift to you. No reimbursement needed."

"Just make sure he doesn't take it out in trade," Elaine quipped.

"Elaine!"

She huffed again. "Come on, Sam. She's hardly your type; her boobs aren't nearly big enough. Besides, the 'rents already have a bride picked out for you."

"Dear God," he groaned.

Elaine's eyes gleamed with unholy glee. "Yeah, Deborah Baker-Cunningham."

"No. Not only no, but hell no."

"Yeah, well, you'll have to clear things up tonight. Mama invited her over for supper."

"You gotta distract her."

"Who? Mama or Debbie the debutante?"

"Either. Both."

Elaine's expressive face took on a crafty look. "Favor for a favor."

"This is gonna get me in hot water, isn't it?"

"Boiling."

He sighed. "What is it?"

"You cover for me," she reached back and took Peter Redclaw's hand in hers, twining their fingers together, "while we go to Vegas."

"You sure about this, Elaine?"

She nodded and her expression turned serious. "I love him, Sam. We love each other."

I glanced at the other man, but his dark-eyed expression remained inscrutable.

"If this is truly what you want ..."

"It is."

"Let me know when and I'll pull out all the stalling tactics."

She grinned. "Don't tell Toby."

"No, of course not. Is he home? I didn't see his car."

"Nah, he's at the office making gazillion dollar deals. He thrives on that boring stuff."

I noticed that Sam didn't mention "that boring stuff" kept her in a lifestyle to which she was accustomed. Tactful of him.

Sam and his sister made small talk, bringing each other up to date while Peter and I exchanged the glances of mutual tolerance. Bored, I gestured and we adjourned to a park bench placed against the wall of the stable office. I inhaled and smelled the faint, familiar odors of sawdust, horses, and male sweat.

"So, you're the other person who has Yvette Galdicar's knickers in a twist," Peter remarked in a quiet tone.

"Huh?" I blurted.

He leaned back and stretched out one arm along the back of the bench. He looked at ease, although I thought it nothing more than a pose. Not one muscle in that long, lean body was relaxed.

"I asked Elaine to marry me, but her mother doesn't approve." He snorted, upper lip lifting in an elegant sneer. "Of course, that might be because I'm a bull rider or because I'm an Indian, rather than because I'm not the man she handpicked for a son-in-law."

I shrugged with a nonchalance I didn't feel. *Perhaps being a successful bull rider gave one the supreme confidence to stare down an uppity society matron.* "Well, I'm not an Indian or a bull rider, but she doesn't approve of me either if that chilly reception I got was any indication."

Peter's teeth flashed in a quick, humorless smile. "Don't take it personally. She has plans and her children aren't towing that line."

"You're mixing your metaphors."

He shrugged again. I sighed and felt the need to explain.

"Look, Sam's not going to marry me. He's not even sure he likes me, I think."

Peter raised an eyebrow. *What is it with men who do that?*

"He looks at you like he means to keep you."

"I'm just new and the shine hasn't worn off yet."

"I don't think so, curly-girl."

Self-conscious, I ran my fingers through my hair and tucked a stray lock behind my ear. "So, tell me what to expect in the big house."

"I've never been inside," he replied with a one-shouldered shrug. "Not good enough, I suppose. I can ride anything on this property and fix damned near everything else. I'm at the top of my profession, and all Yvette sees is a dirty Indian."

I didn't know what to say to that, so I kept my mouth shut.

"And you," Peter continued, "you're not a society debutante from the right family."

"No, I'm not." I shrugged. Having met a couple of those debutante types in college and not being impressed by them, I didn't regret not being counted among their rarified numbers. "I'm a photographer."

"Family and kiddie portraits?"

"Sometimes," I admitted. "I particularly like doing landscapes, Ansel Adams type of stuff."

"I like Michel Kenna's stuff better. The stark emptiness of his landscapes speaks to my spirit. Adams is all romance and melodrama."

"What about Brett Weston and Franco Fontana?" I asked, pouncing on the topic with pathetic eagerness.

"I prefer Weston. Fontana's too commercial for my tastes, like a graphic artist who gets his inspiration from a Cheerios box."

I snorted, never having imagined I'd be discussing the world's greatest photographers with a bull rider.

"Surprised you, didn't I?" he quipped.

I sighed and gave him honesty. "Yeah, you did. Most people know who Ansel Adams is, but the rest? Not so much."

"Peter have heap big brain."

I snorted again and chuckled, glad he had the kindness to put me at ease. "You're a nice man, Peter."

He grinned at me, but his eyes were serious. "It's you and me, kid, against Yvette Galdicar. Don't underestimate her."

I wondered why he said that, but didn't ask because Sam and Elaine had stopped talking and were looking at us.

"Nice chat?" she asked, her eyes narrowing with the beginning of suspicion.

Peter removed his arm from behind me and rose to his booted feet. "Sugar, your jealousy feels nice, but I've no designs on the curly-haired girl there."

"You better not," she growled.

"Damn straight," Sam added, darting a glare at him that heated when he focused on me. "The curly-haired girl is *mine.*"

A tingle ran down my spine and settled in my groin.

Chapter 38

Sam

Elaine's words reverberated in my mind as I analyzed our conversation while paying half of my attention to Dana as we walked to the house. I noticed the black Audi R8 parked near the house and realized that Toby was home. Either he'd taken off work early, or the hour was later than I realized. Conrad met us at the door with a warm welcome and a smile. Dana blinked in surprise at his change in demeanor.

"Mama's not there to rain on his parade," I whispered into her ear.

"Mrs. Galdicar is serving cocktails in the east parlor," he informed us.

"Cocktails?" Elaine groaned. "Damn, that means we're expected to dress for dinner."

"I didn't bring my monkey suit, darlin'," Peter said.

"You're built about the same as Toby," Sam said. "I could ask if he'd lend you some duds for the evening."

Peter slapped his dusty cowboy hat on his head. With a small shake, he replied, "No, I don't need to borrow another man's clothes." He took Elaine's shoulders in his hands and turned her to face him. "You'll be ready for me?"

Her eyes sparkled. "You know I will."

He pulled her in for a quick, hard kiss and took his leave, leaving my sister breathless.

"You're sure you want this?" I murmured.

"More than anything, Sam. More than anything."

"All right, then. Do you think you might have something that Dana can wear?"

She looked Dana over with a critical eye trained by the best—our mother—and answered, "I've got a couple of things in mind. Nothing for it but to try them on. Come on, Dana, let's get ourselves gussied up."

With a look of reluctance, my curly-haired girl followed my sister inside and up the grand staircase. I climbed the other side of the staircase and headed to my old bedroom. A maid had already unpacked my bag and put away my clothes. I pulled a suit from the closet and fresh underwear and socks from their respective drawers. Sometimes having more money than God came in handy, as it allowed me to keep a ready wardrobe here as well as in Chicago.

After a quick shower and shave—Mama didn't tolerate scruff—I was dressed and waiting with my parents and brother in the east parlor. Toby greeted me with polite coolness before turning to talk business with Dad. His eyes flickered with resentment, and his shoulders were stiff beneath the fine fabric of his jacket. Looking like someone stuffed her plump curves into a pink, 1950s prom dress, Deborah Baker-Cunningham stood with Toby and Dad and looked bored. Mama commandeered my attention, drawing me away to stand beside the bay window at a polite distance that did not risk eavesdropping on their quiet conversation.

"Now that Bradley Vermont is casting off that totally unsuitable woman, I have petitioned your father into seeing what he can do to convince him to court Eileen," Mama chattered, flitting from one topic to another, none of them really capturing my attention until she said that.

"Elaine is not going to marry Bradley Vermont," I said as she lifted a crystal highball to her lips. I smelled the sweetness of her favorite cocktail, a Manhattan.

"Rubbish," she said, her eyes hardening with unreasonable determination. "He's exactly what she needs, a firm hand to control her wilder impulses. I'm afraid I indulged her too much when she was a child."

"Mama, Bradley's not looking for another wife."

"He's divorcing that tramp, so he's free to remarry. He'll not do better than my Eileen."

I sighed. "No, he couldn't do better. Eileen's a wonderful woman and any man would be grateful for her affection. But she's an adult, Mama, and she's made her choice and that choice isn't a man who until very recently was married to someone whom he treated quite poorly."

"Pshaw. Women like that deserve what they get, they *like* it."

"Women like what, Mama?"

"She's trash, Sam. We—people like us—have *standards*." She glanced upward and over in the direction of Eileen's quarters. "Females like the one you sullied our doorstep with are good for fun, good for a fling, but one doesn't *marry* them. Why, who knows how many men have used her?"

"One," I growled through gritted teeth. "Dana's a fine girl, smart, honest, and hardworking."

"Dear," she patted my arm, "that's how you describe a horse, not a woman you intend to marry."

Giggles cut into the unpleasant conversation and we turned to greet the two young women who entered the east parlor. Toby's eyes brightened with interest and my father's with speculation. Mama's face lost all expression, then adopted a polite facsimile of courteous welcome. Not for all the tea in China would my mother abandon her role as consummate hostess.

I felt my jaw drop and forced it to close before I began drooling. Elaine had somehow managed to find a 1920s style evening gown that beautifully displayed Dana's slender curves and pale skin to their best advantage without revealing more than a tasteful hint of cleavage and the delicate turn of her ankle. Her bare arms looked indecently naked against the midnight blue silk. I glanced at Dana's feet which were bare in silver sandals a size too big.

"You look *magnificent*," I complimented her as I darted forward to claim her hand and tuck it into my elbow before Toby or my father could beat me to it or Mama could attach Deborah to my arm. I looked at Elaine who also looked elegant in a beaded ivory dress with a floating skirt that looked to be made of layers of chiffon. "Thank you. You're my favorite sister."

She grinned. "I'm your only sister, doofus. Yeah, she cleans up well, doesn't she?"

Blushing, Dana smoothed a palm over the slippery fabric and said, "I've never worn anything so fine. I'm terrified I'll spill or dribble something on it."

Elaine shrugged. "I bought it a while back for a Roaring Twenties gala, some fundraiser or other such event I had to attend as a family representative. It's not really my style, but I thought it would work for you." She waved her hand. "Keep it, it's yours. I'll certainly never wear that thing again."

Dana's eyes grew wide. "Oh, no, I couldn't!"

"Of course, you couldn't," Mama interjected smoothly with a tight smile. "Wherever would someone like you wear haute couture? Certainly not waiting tables."

"That was unkind, Mama," I hissed as all the color drained from Dana's face.

"Nonsense, dearest. Girls like her appreciate plain speaking."

Deborah on his arm, Toby approached and inserted himself between Mama and Dana. He smiled his predatory, charming smile, the same one our father used to snag his many mistresses over the years. Taking her free hand, he bowed over it and raised it to his mouth with feigned Old World courtliness. I watched every practiced move, having seen them performed to perfection by my father.

After lightly kissing the back of her knuckles, he said, "Sam has utterly outdone himself and weaseled his way back into the family's good graces by bringing you here." He glanced at me, then back at her to gauge her reaction as he added, "Brother, where did you find this goddess?"

"Knock it off, Toby," I grunted as jealousy surged through me. If it wasn't enough that Peter liked her—even though he showed no romantic interest in Dana—I had to somehow keep my brother from working his panty-melting magic on the woman I wanted to keep for myself.

He raised his eyebrows and chuckled. "Don't believe him, you gorgeous thing. However much he may deny your divinity, we know he's lying."

She blinked, totally out of her element in this shark-infested pool, and pulled her hand free. "Um ... thank you?"

A heavy hand clamped down on my shoulder, and my father captured the hand Toby formerly held. "Son, you didn't tell me you were guarding a movie star."

He brought Dana's hand to his own lips for a courtly kiss while his eyes glittered with avarice. I dared not look at my mother; the expression in her eyes would have surely broken my heart.

"Uh, nice to meet you, Mr. Galdicar," Dana said and pulled her hand from his with a sharp tug.

"Would you like a drink, Dana?" I asked.

"Yes, thank you," she replied, the hand tucked into my elbow clutching my arm with desperate strength. Under her breath, she whispered as we crossed the room to the wet bar where Dad's valet, pressed into double duty, waited to mix and pour, "Are they always like that?"

"Yes." I met Oliver's dull gaze and said, "Whiskey neat for me and a sauvignon blanc for the lady, please."

"I can see why you moved to Chicago."

Oliver poured and handed over the drinks. Dana took a sip of her wine and murmured, "Very nice."

"Don't guzzle it," I warned. "You need to keep your wits about you."

Her eyes flashed. "I'm not stupid, Sam."

She withdrew her hand from my arm and left me to stand near Conrad who apparently was the only member of the household who hadn't yet offended her. A quick glance around the room showed smooth, unobtrusive movement: Deborah, Elaine, and Mama gossiped in a tight little group. As I stood there watching her, my father sidled up next to me.

"If you haven't tapped that yet, son, I'll be sorely disappointed in you," he remarked in a low voice and lifted his single malt scotch to his mouth. The aroma of smoked peat floated in the air. "Of course, if you don't want her, I'll certainly take her. A sweet little apartment, a nice car, some jewelry ..."

"She's not like that, Dad."

He shrugged. "They're all like that for the right price. Some are just more expensive than others."

I wanted to grind my molars to powder.

Toby joined us. "Brother, if you're not fucking that sweet ass, I'll ask Dad to have you commited. Either that, or you're a fucking fag."

I wanted to pinch the bridge of my nose as a headache suddenly bloomed behind my skull and began to pound. Through gritted teeth I tried to dissuade my horndog brother and lecherous father, "Dana is a respectable woman and my *client.*"

"She's not your client any more, son," Dad said, clapping me on the back. "I think now you're *her* client. Or us."

"What do you mean, Dad, she's not his client any more?" Toby asked, eyes narrowing with suspicion and burgeoning rage.

"It means your brother has agreed to take his rightful place at the helm of the family business."

"What!" Toby hissed. "I thought—"

"You think too much, boy. You're not the businessman Sam is, the businessman Sam was destined to be."

"Dad, I have *worked*—"

Our father cut him off again. "I've set aside some of the companies for you, Tobias. They'll keep you busy. Now go talk to your mother. She's got a list of debutantes for you to consider. It's high time you married and gave us some grandchildren."

"Sam's not married."

"He will be soon," Dad promised. "I've about finished negotiations with Harold Baker-Cunningham. An alliance between his hospitality empire and CenterTex will add another fifty billion to the family coffers."

"I am not marrying Deborah Baker-Cunningham," I grated through clenched jaws, trying to keep my voice low enough so the poor woman wouldn't overhear and suffer the embarrassment of blatant rejection.

My father turned cold, hard eyes on me. "You asked a favor, boy. That's how you're going to repay it."

"Coming to work in the family business *is* repaying the favor."

"That's only part of it, son." He took a sip and waved his hand in a dismissive gesture. "Now, I'll look the other way if you want to keep that pretty, curly-haired piece on the side. Debbie Baker-Cunningham ain't much to look at, that's for damn sure, but she's the kind of girl you gotta marry to get what you want."

"Dad—"

"I bought that thug's loyalty, boy, because you asked. He won't divulge details of the last job, but he's agreed to take on nothing more while I'm paying him. He won't hurt a curly hair on that girl's head or pussy—or is she smooth down there? I'm also adding a few dollars to push Vermont's divorce through, because your mama wants him for Elaine—and I make sure your mama always gets what she wants."

While I appreciated my father's confirmation that he had purchased Avel Skliar's loyalty, gorge rose in my throat at the expectation of marrying Debbie the debutante. I swallowed it back down with a hasty gulp of whiskey. The liquid burned all the way down. *No, I can't—I won't—do that.*

"I'll do it," Toby volunteered, eager to win his way into our father's favor by any means necessary. I was the heir and he was the spare and Dad never let him forget it. "I'll marry Deborah."

"Now see, Sam," my father said. "Your brother's smart, willing to do what it takes to keep this family strong and prosperous. But I've got my eye on someone else for him."

"Oh? Who?"

"That Carmichael girl."

Toby frowned. "Dad, she's only twelve and wears glasses with Coke bottle lenses."

Dad shrugged, dismissing my brother's objection. "So, you'll have to wait a couple of years. I'm sure her daddy will get her eyes fixed. They've got surgery for that now, don't they? I'm sure she'll grow out of that big nose, too. If not, docs'll fix that."

Toby's expression soured with distaste. It pained me to admit I didn't know whether his distaste stemmed from being matched to a girl less than half his age or because she had a prominent nose and wore eyeglasses. I hoped it was the former.

"Everyone, dinner is served," Mama announced, her voice cool and brittle.

Dad stepped forward and took her arm. In the family hierarchy, I went next, escorting Dana. Toby followed with Deborah on his arm and Elaine took up the rear. We sat at a long table set with the finest china and crystal and silver money could buy. The tablecloth and napkins were made of the finest Irish linen. A fresh bouquet of flowers formed an impressive and obstructive centerpiece. I always wondered if Mama required such a bouquet so she didn't have to face the man she married at the other end of the table. As usual on such formal occasions, Conrad served all twelve courses.

"Good Lord, does this never end?" Dana murmured under her breath as a small serving of Dover sole was put on her plate for the fish course.

"Hors d'oeuvres, soup, bread or pasta, fish, chicken, red meat, salad, fruit, cheese, dessert, coffee, then *digestif*," I rattled off.

Having overheard me, Mama asked, "Oh, dear, does your little *client* not know the proper progression of a formal supper?"

"No, ma'am," Dana replied before I could swallow what was in my mouth and clear it for a response. "My humble background didn't include such extravagant indulgences."

Mama sniffed and glared. "Bless your heart, you are rustic. I'll have to make sure you get a taste of what you've been missing all your underprivileged life."

Dana again went pale and bowed her head. The rapid flutter of her eyelashes indicated that she was probably blinking back tears. I set down my fork with a hard *clink*. "Mama, that's enough. Dana is a guest in our home."

"My home, dearest. This is still *my* home and darling Deborah is here as *my* guest."

"Now, Yvette darlin', don't get your knickers in a twist," Dad called across the table. "Girl can't help being what she is. Just think of this as an opportunity to show her how the best of us live. Maybe she'll decide she likes it and want to earn a bit for herself."

Mama gasped at the inference that Dana earn such luxury and sophistication as his mistress. She clutched the thick rope of pearls at her neck. Elaine, who'd maintained her silence during supper, also gasped. Deborah focused her gaze upon her plate and pursed her lips. Toby's lips pressed together in a thin line of controlled fury and resentment, once again probably assuming our father was denying him something he wanted merely because Dad wanted it, too. I wondered how many of Toby's so-called girlfriends over the years were Dad's discarded mistresses.

Dana raised her head and met my gaze with eyes that shone wetly and said, "I take back every nasty thing I ever said or thought about you. It's a miracle you turned out as well as you did."

I rose from the table, kicking the chair back, and held out my hand toward her. "Come on, kitten, let's blow this popsicle stand. There's a hamburger somewhere with our names on it."

"Sam!" my mother snapped.

"Sam!" my father shouted.

I ignored them both and tucked Dana under my arm as we rushed out of the toxic environment that was my family home.

Chapter 39

Dana

Sam commandeered a Ferrari from the long garage with its magnificent collection of high-priced vehicles, all of which were utterly impractical for a ranch. I supposed the work trucks were kept somewhere else where they wouldn't degrade the value of the more pampered vehicles. With a high-pitched whine, the sports car left the ranch in a cloud of dust and sped along a rural, two-lane highway.

I said nothing, still reeling from the viciousness we'd just escaped and to which I'd have to return. Nothing in my life had prepared me for that.

"She's not always like that," Sam murmured.

"But your father and brother are?" I shot back, outrage and offense still boiling. "They all but called me a whore."

His hands clenched on the steering wheel, knuckles whitening.

"There was no call for that," he admitted in a quiet voice. I noticed he didn't deny that his father and brother normally treated women with such disrespect.

"No, there wasn't," I agreed and sniffed back tears. "Sam, I don't want to go back there."

"Just for tonight. I'll move us out first thing tomorrow."

"Just … just put me up in a hotel somewhere. I *really* don't ever want to step foot inside that house again."

The lights of a small town came into view. On the town's outskirts, Sam whipped the car into a sharp turn and drove into the parking lot of a honky tonk bar. Two big rigs were parked in the lot, plus a couple of dozen pickup trucks and a few passenger cars and motorcycles. Nothing there approached the level of the gleaming red Ferrari.

Trepidation filled me. "Uh, Sam, we're a little over-dressed for this place."

He shrugged. "The Howl has the best burgers in the county."

My stomach growled, making the decision for me.

"All right."

He opened the passenger side door like a gentleman and handed me up from the low-riding vehicle. Keeping my hand firmly tucked in his elbow, he escorted me into the tavern that reminded me all too much of *Roadhouse* before Patrick Swayze's character cleaned it up. A live band behind chickenwire fencing played loud country music. The wooden floor thumped from those dancing near the stage. Myriad pairs of eyes turned to stare at us.

"That you, Sam?" called someone whose face I couldn't see.

"Hey, it's Sam!" someone else shouted.

I guess I know where Sam spends his time when he visits home.

"Who's the fancy chick?"

"You gonna share?"

The comments and suggestions flew as Sam guided me to an empty booth. We sat across from each other. I set my palms on the tacky surface of the wooden table. Someone hadn't cleaned it properly.

A waitress appeared momentarily and slapped down two menus. "Get ya anything to drink?"

"Ice tea," I replied.

"Sweet?"

"Unsweetened with lemon, please."

"Y'all want a shot of bourbon in that? It's just a dollar extra."

I shook my head. "No, thank you."

"Your loss." She turned her attention to Sam. "Somethin' to drink, sugar?"

Sam ordered a bottle of Modelo Negro.

"Whiskey chaser? Just a dollar extra."

"No, thanks."

The waitress shrugged and left us to peruse the menus.

A large man approached the table and loomed over us. "Sam, good to see ya back. Y'all mind if I dance with this little lady?"

"Hey, Rock," Sam replied. "You'd have to ask the little lady."

The big man's eyes glittered as he looked me over. I wanted to squirm.

"Well? Folks here like a friendly lady."

"Thank you, but—"

"He won't molest you, Dana," Sam urged me. "Rock won't let anything happen to you and he won't even notice when you step on his toes."

The big, bearded man guffawed. "That's why I wear them steel-toed boots. C'mon, I'll teach you how to two-step. It's simple and my hands won't go nowhere they ain't supposed to."

"You'll have fun," Sam urged.

With reluctance, I nodded and let the Rock draw me to the dance floor. Looking back, I saw Sam pull out his cell phone and knew why he encouraged me to dance with a man I didn't know. He wanted a private conversation.

Fuck him.

I gave Rock a bright smile and said, "My name's Dana. Pleased to meet you. I really don't know how to do this."

He grinned and put his big hand over my left shoulder blade and took my right hand in his big paw. "I'm gonna start with my left foot. We'll take four steps backward, quick, quick, slow, slow. Keep it smooth. I'll guide you in a counterclockwise direction."

I nodded and looked down at our feet, noticing his were offset from mine.

"Look up at me, darlin'."

I raised my eyes. His twinkled.

"Y'all follow me and I'll follow the music."

I nodded and yielded to the light, steady pressure on my hand. Further guidance came from the big paw resting against my shoulder blade which he gently used as a rudder to direct me. Much to my delight, we soon fell into an easy rhythm.

"You ready to twirl?"

I grinned and nodded. He extended his arm and I twirled. He reeled me back in and his free hand went right back to my shoulder blade.

"That was fun," I exclaimed. "Thank you, Rock."

His eyes flickered over my head as the tune wound down. "Looks like Sam ordered for ya. I'd better get you back to the table so y'all can eat."

The gentle giant guided me through the dancing couples back to the booth. Sam had put away his cell phone and was watching us. I tugged Rock down and pressed a kiss to his bearded cheek and whispered again, "Thank you, Rock."

Face flushing, he straightened and muttered, "You're playin' a dangerous game, little lady."

I sat.

"You enjoyed that," Sam said in a flat, disgruntled tone.

Asshole. Affecting a look of utter innocence, I asked, "Wasn't I supposed to?"

His expression soured and he lifted an enormous burger to his mouth, probably to block any words he'd likely regret. I looked at my own plate and knew I'd never be able to eat the entire burger in one sitting. I spread a paper napkin over my lap and picked up the sandwich, hoping I wouldn't dribble grease, melted cheese, or mayonnaise on the fine satin of my borrowed evening gown.

We ate without speaking. As predicted, I could not finish the hamburger or the gigantic mound of french fries that accompanied it. Our waitress returned to ask if we wanted dessert. I shook my head and Sam asked for the check. She pulled it from the pocket of her apron and headed off to the next table.

"Why are you so angry with me, Sam?" I finally asked. "I danced with Rock because you practically forced me to. Granted, he seems a really nice guy and I did enjoy dancing, but you could have simply told me you needed to have a private phone conversation, no subterfuge necessary."

Color bloomed on his cheeks and I knew I'd scored a hit.

"You saw that?"

"Yeah."

He sighed. "You're not going to ask what it was about? You're not curious?"

"Of course, I'm curious," I replied. "But that doesn't mean I'm going to pry into what obviously isn't any of my business. Sam, I can respect your privacy."

He sighed again. "I'm sorry, Dana."

"Let's get out of here. I'm tired and it's been a long day."

"I'll take you home."

I immediately resisted. "I don't want to go back there, Sam. I told you that."

"Just for tonight," he reiterated. "We'll leave in the morning."

Without money, a phone, or even a drivers license on me, I had little choice but to bow to his decision. My begrudging acquiescence drew no triumphant grin from him, so I had to give him credit for that. He merely took my hand and walked me to the Ferrari. We drove, again without conversation. He pulled into the garage and handed me out of the vehicle.

Hand in hand, we entered the house through a side door that led directly into a spacious kitchen Dad would have envied. Leaning against a countertop with a glass in his hand, Toby raised his eyebrows at our entrance.

"The prodigal returns!" he announced, raising his glass in a mocking toast.

"Not now, Toby," Sam warned, his voice a low growl.

"What, you afraid your little *fling* might prefer someone else?"

I yanked my hand from Sam's, marched over to Toby, and jabbed a stiff finger in his chest. "Look, you prick, I've had it with the insults. Are *you* a virgin? I bet not. So, take your fucking double standard and shove it up your ass."

He grabbed my wrist and held it. I yanked my arm, but he refused to release me. He belched, fumes of boozy breath wafting over my face.

"Oh, you'll spread those pretty legs for me," he sneered. "All's I gotta do is show you enough cash. Lucky thing I got enough of that for someone like you."

Sam's hand clamped over his brother's wrist and he pried Toby's fingers off mine. He pulled Toby in close, their chests bumping.

"Don't you dare touch her again, Toby. I'll let it go tonight because you're hammered, but insult her one more time and I'll pound you into the ground."

Sam grabbed my upper arm and pulled me away. We ascended to the second story via a back staircase that I assumed was built as the servants' staircase. He marched me to a room that looked to be several doors down from his sister's. When the door closed behind us, he turned the lock and said in a low voice, "Toby's room is on this floor, too."

I nodded and wrapped my arms around myself, feeling the animosity that filled the big house as a pervasive chill. I watched as Sam removed his jacket and slung it over the back of a chair. I had no idea which room had been assigned to me and wondered where my few pitiful things had been stashed.

Probably in a stall with a horse.

At that moment, sleeping in a stall with a horse didn't sound like such an awful idea. I heard a sniffle and realized it came from me.

"Oh, kitten," Sam murmured and enveloped me in a warm hug. "I'm sorry."

And I wept.

Chapter 40

Sam

I listened to the soft, regular breathing of the sleeping woman cuddled next to me and felt a sense of contentment that made me want never to rise from that bed. With a delicate touch, I smoothed the soft tangle of near-black curls away from her face. I relished the soft, silky texture of those curls, complemented by the coarser texture of other curls lower on her body. Dana sighed and nuzzled the linen pillowcase as I lightly stroked her hair.

Early morning light streamed through the windows. Ranch hands would already be at work, taking care of livestock, mucking stalls, running tractors. The ranch grew more than cattle and horses: it served as home and breeding ground for chickens, hogs, goats, rabbits, turkeys, sheep, and even a small herd of llamas and alpacas. Elaine never ceased exploring species diversity for agricultural health and sustainability. She'd even broached the subject of agritourism with Dad, although both he and Mama shot that idea down. Too vulgar and bourgeois.

In the distance, the rumble of large diesel engines spoke of fields of cotton, corn, wheat, oats, barley, and flax. Some of those did better than others in the hot, humid climate of East Texas. The family had fields of produce—strawberries, celery, green beans, potatoes, peppers, and more that I didn't bother to keep track of—that an army of hired migrant workers mostly tended. Elaine provided plenty of opportunities for employment, but my parents kept wages low. It just wouldn't do for those migrant workers to get uppity and demand more, like health and dental insurance.

Since Dad sent me the monthly profit and loss statements, I realized that the ranch itself barely broke even. Profits from oil and the family's many other businesses sustained the ranch. Knowledge of Elaine's impending departure made me wonder who would run the business of the ranch.

A knock on the door was followed by the false cheer of my mother's voice, "Rise and shine, darling. We're *all* going to church this morning."

A devout Presbyterian, my mother's iron will ensured that no one in the family missed a Sunday morning service. Even my philandering father and brother would slide into the church pew while wearing pious expressions. Her announcement also reminded me that I'd entirely lost track of days.

Then I wondered if Dana were Presbyterian or even Christian and whether she'd want a church wedding. I supposed I'd have to ask her. Not being particularly devout myself, I didn't care and had no desire to evangelize her into my family's purported faith.

I leaned over and nuzzled the warm, soft skin of her neck, pressing a kiss just beneath her ear. "Time to get up, kitten."

"Hmm?"

She blinked and rolled over, the smooth sheets sliding over her skin to reveal delicate, rounded shoulders and the most beautiful breasts I'd ever seen. Morning wood which had begun to wilt, stiffened with immediate reaction. I moved down to kiss those pouting nipples, feeling them bead beneath my tongue.

"Mmmm."

Her hand moved, fingers threading through my hair. I skimmed one hand down her body, pushing the covers away to clear my access to her sweet, sweet flesh. She hummed again, one delicate hand reaching to stroke my erection. A few kisses later and I had rolled on top of her and was sinking into her wet heat, once again neglecting the safety of a condom.

Perhaps she'll stay with me forever if I get her pregnant.

After we'd both shuddered to completion, I sent her to the shower first while I rummaged through bureau drawers in an effort to find Dana's clothes. The maids, apparently, hadn't gotten the memo to unpack her clothes and put them away with mine. She emerged from the bathroom wrapped in one of my old bathrobes.

"Did you find my clothes?"

"No, I didn't, kitten. Give me ten minutes to shower and shave, and I'll hunt them down."

She nodded, eyes shuttering, and meekly did as I requested. I padded naked into the bathroom as someone else knocked on the door. I paused to listen.

"Hey, it's Elaine. I've got something for Dana to wear to church this morning."

"Church?" Dana mouthed.

I nodded and gestured at her to open the door. A fiery blush covered all visible skin, but she did as I bade her while I whipped a towel off the rack and wrapped it around my waist. My sister didn't need to see my junk.

"Thanks, Elaine," I said as Dana put panties, a bra, and a pretty cotton dress on the bed.

Elaine's nostrils flared at the unmistakable aroma of spent passion, but her expression remained neutral.

"You're welcome," she answered and turned her attention to Dana. "I hope you don't mind that I fished out your unmentionables from the guest room where Mama had them unpacked. She put you in the guest room across the hall from Toby's room."

"No, not at all."

Elaine smiled. "I'm glad. I heard you two come in last night."

I frowned, wondering if Toby had been so rude and creepy as to paw through Dana's meager possessions. From the way he'd behaved the night before, it wouldn't have surprised me.

"We'll go shopping after church," Elaine said.

Dana glanced at me, her expression clearly showing that she would hold me to my promise to vacate the premises that morning. I shrugged, feeling caught.

"Oh, are you going to Mass?" Dana inquired.

"Mass?" Elaine echoed.

Dana's mouth twitched in a thin smile. "I take it you're not Catholic."

Elaine's eyes danced with sudden merriment. "And you are?" She chuckled. "Oh, Mama's gonna have a cow."

"Either that or organize an intervention," I commented.

My sister snorted. "That could happen." She looked at Dana again and explained, "According to our parents, the Roman church is good only for uneducated migrant workers."

"Really?" Her tone could have freeze dried an entire cow.

"Yeah," Elaine replied on a sigh. "Look, let me run interference for you. I'll tell Mama that you're not Presbyterian and that Sam will take you to the worship service of your preference. As long as she thinks you're Christian—"

"I am Christian," Dana bit off.

"But you're Catholic."

"Catholic and Christian are not mutually exclusive. The Roman Catholic Church was the *first* Christian faith."

"Huh." Elaine waved her hands as though clearing away a swarm of gnats. "No matter. I'll make your excuses to Mama, so you won't be dragooned."

"Thank you for the clothes, Eileen."

"Sure," my sister replied.

She headed down the hall and Dana closed the door. Turning to look at me, my lover said, "I really dislike your family."

"I know," I said in a quiet voice. "I don't blame you."

"As soon as you're dressed, I want to leave and never return. You *promised* me we would leave here this morning."

"I did. Like I said, give me ten minutes."

She gave me fifteen.

Chapter 41

Dana

We didn't leave as soon as Sam showered, shaved, and dressed. Instead, he insisted we further abuse his family's grudging hospitality and have breakfast. I suspected he merely wanted to talk with Conrad before heading out.

"Mama, I didn't expect to see you here," Sam exclaimed with genuine surprise, even as he subtly moved to put himself between me and the older woman. Whether he meant *still home* or *in the kitchen* was up for interpretation.

Dressed in tailored pale blue, Yvonne Galdicar set a pitcher of orange juice on the counter and hesitated before turning around. I assumed she was dredging up her manners. She turned around and held out the tall glass.

"Dear Dana," she addressed me with a saccharine smile, "you *must* forgive my *appalling* manners from yesterday. That is *not* how I was raised nor how I raised my children. We are simply *ashamed* of our lack of welcome. I *do* hope you'll be *gracious* enough to allow me to make amends."

She walked closer and I accepted the glass of juice with a murmured thank-you. She watched, blue eyes glittering. I belatedly realized that Sam had inherited his piercing eyes from her, and wanted to shudder.

"It's fresh-squeezed," she said, painted pink lips peeling back from her whitened teeth in what was supposed to be a smile. "The oranges come from our groves in Florida."

I took a sip. It was indeed freshly squeezed juice, but had a bitter, metallic aftertaste.

"Now, go on, drink it up. It's healthful and there's plenty more," she urged. "It's obvious Sam's smitten and I must do my best to ensure your welcome ... and that includes seeing to your health and proper nutrition."

"That's kind of you, Mama," Sam murmured.

Her smile turned genuine as she refocused her attention on her elder son. "Now, what would you like for breakfast? I warned Letititia—" she gestured toward a tall, rounded black woman with short salt-and-pepper hair standing near the gas range "—that you were to be indulged in whatever you wanted for breakfast."

Brightening, Sam smiled and left my side to embrace the cook.

"Drink up, darling."

I took a sip.

"Is something wrong, dear?"

Not wishing to be rude, since my lover's mother was at least making the appearance of trying to welcome me, I murmured denial of anything being amiss and took another small sip.

Sam finished speaking to the cook, gave her another quick hug, and returned to my side.

"Sam, your sister tells me that our guest does not share our faith," Yvonne said, an expression of distaste flitting across her face. "So, I'll leave you to do whatever it is you do on Sunday mornings. We'll speak after the worship service."

She left, stiletto heels clicking on the hard tile. The cook moved into efficient, brisk action and within a few minutes slid in front of us plates piled high with fluffy pancakes. She noticed the mostly full glass of juice and asked, "Shall I get you something else, ma'am?"

"Oh, no, you don't need to bother," I protested.

"Very good, ma'am."

She retreated, poured a mug of coffee for Sam, then went to the sink and began to clean.

Sam explained as I doused my pancakes with maple syrup, "Letittia is Conrad's wife. She's the one we all ran to with our childhood scrapes and when we needed hugs and cookies. She and Conrad have eight children."

He shook his head at the idea of such a large brood.

"She managed Elaine, Toby, and me like she managed her own kids." He chuckled. "She swatted my rear end more than once."

I chuckled around a mouthful of pancake that rivaled anything Dad could make and washed it down with a slug of orange juice. I grimaced at the unpleasant aftertaste.

Sam frowned. "I thought you liked orange juice."

"I do, usually." I pushed the half-empty glass aside. "Maybe I'm just used to the stuff that comes in a carton."

He picked up the glass and sniffed it. "It smells all right." He took a tiny sip and let the liquid sit on his tongue, then spat it back into the glass. His frown deepened. "You're right, it tastes off. I'll get you some milk."

A moment later, he poured a tall glass of milk and placed it in front of me and ordered, "Drink it, all of it."

"Sam?"

"It'll be all right," he assured me, but didn't pick up his fork and resume eating.

"What's going o—?" A vicious cramp cut off the question, making me groan.

"Drink the milk, *now*."

I lifted the glass, hand trembling. "Sam?"

Another slice of pain whipped through me.

"Drink the milk, honey," he said, and rose to his feet.

Perspiration beaded on my skin as I watched him confer with the cook. She shook her head and spoke to him in low tones, too low for me to eavesdrop. I drank the milk, thinking that he wanted me to coat my stomach because ... *oh, shit* ... Yvonne Galdicar had poisoned me. I glowered at the half-empty glass of juice.

Sam pulled out his cell phone and spoke in terse words, then returned to my side.

"An ambulance will be here soon, kitten," he assured me as more pain twisted my gut and I groaned.

He wrapped an arm around me and helped me stand. My legs trembled, knees buckling as the waves of pain quickened and intensified. I had no desire to ever drink orange juice again.

Sam walked me into a screened-in porch connected to the kitchen and settled me on a divan. I shuddered and sweated and curled into the fetal position and tried to bite back moans of agony. Letititia brought out a large bowl of water and two washcloths. She eased down beside me, soaked a cloth, wrung it out, and began to pat my sweaty skin with it. I welcomed the coolness.

Sam pulled out his phone again and texted. A few minutes later, although it could have been days for all I knew, he lifted the device to his ear and hissed, "Elaine, you and Peter need to get the hell out *now*."

"What's going on?" I overheard her screech.

"I'll tell you later. Just get out and don't use the family credit cards or anything CenterTex Holdings can trace."

Apparently, she agreed, because Sam ended the call and took over for Letititia. "They need to hurry."

"Sam, the nearest hospital's half an hour from here. It will take time," the cook said.

He cursed, then looked at the cook. "Do you think we ought to make her vomit?"

"Not knowing what she ingested, that might make things worse."

"I'm willing to chance it. Whatever is in her stomach needs to come out."

Sam wrestled me around so that my head hung over the cushion. Letititia dumped the bowl outside and placed it under my face.

"I'm sorry, kitten," he whispered as he pried my jaw open with one hand and stuck two fingers from the other down my throat to trigger my gag reflex. My body convulsed as soured milk, chewed pancake, and the remnants of tainted juice spewed from my mouth. When my body went limp, he did it again, repeating the process until I could only dry heave.

Letititia brought a cup of water and handed it to him. He tilted me to the side and held the cup to my lips.

"Rinse."

Sobbing and weak as a newborn kitten, I let him dribble the cool liquid into my mouth. I swished it around and spat it out.

"Rinse."

I did it again.

"Rinse."

And again.

My throat burned. The vile taste of vomit lingered. My belly cramped. My clammy skin crawled with the knowledge that my lover's mother had tried to kill me. Weak as I was, I could not hold back the sudden pressure upon my sphincter.

"Oh, God, Sam," I wept in shame as I soiled myself.

My blurry vision swirled with darkness and I suddenly feared losing my sight. What good was a blind photographer? Then the darkness became complete, and oblivion rescued me from further humiliation.

Chapter 42

Sam

I watched with worried, frantic impatience as paramedics loaded Dana into the ambulance.

"You can't come in here, sir," they said when I tried to climb into the vehicle.

"I'm her fiancé," I protested.

"Sorry, sir, regulations. Follow us to the hospital."

I took the Ferrari.

Emergency room doctors and nurses swarmed the gurney as the paramedics unloaded Dana and reported vital statistics, action already taken, and the like. Not daring to interfere, I hung back and followed the emergency room team inside. One nurse noticed me.

"Who are you?"

"Sam Galdicar, her fiancé."

The nurse's eyebrows rose in recognition of the family name, then she frowned and muttered in disgust, "Poor woman."

I was too worried to wince at the censure which hinted at my brother's and father's less than savory reputations. I met her hard brown gaze and begged, "Please, save her. I can tell you don't like my family, but she's *everything* to me."

She held my gaze, then responded with a curt nod. The emergency room team rolled the gurney through large swinging doors emblazoned with HOSPITAL STAFF ONLY. A burly, armed guard standing at the doors barred my passage.

"You'll have to wait in the waiting room, sir."

I bowed my head and retreated.

I didn't keep track of time and was astonished when a familiar voice asked, "What's going on, Sam? What happened?"

Startled, I looked up. "Elaine? What are you doing here?"

She stood in front of me, Peter by her side. "Conrad said your girl was taken to the hospital in an ambulance, but didn't say why."

I shook my head. "Elaine, you can't be here. You and Peter need to get out of Texas."

She frowned. "I thought you wanted me to take Dana shopping and Peter and I would leave afterward. Obviously, that's not going to happen right now, but—"

"But nothing. Mom's gone off the deep end."

Her blue eyes, as familiar as my own, narrowed. "Explain."

I sighed and loathed to admit that our mother had attempted to kill the woman I loved. "Dana was poisoned."

My sister gasped. "You're sure?"

I nodded.

"Who would do such a thing?"

By asking that question, Elaine didn't want to admit the truth either. I held my silence.

"No, she couldn't have."

Peter met my bleak gaze with one of weary acknowledgement. He knew the truth, recognized it, and would not push my sister into that same hard reality until she was ready. I both admired his protective attitude toward her and wanted to shout at her to admit the horror that was our mother.

Then I wondered if Peter had somehow suspected Mama would attempt to rid Elaine of him by such underhanded means, which was why he never entered the house or took a meal with my family.

Wiping my face with my hands, I recalled Dana's burgled apartment, her possessions ruined. That suggested more than mere greed. That kind of systematic destruction indicated hatred and malice. Dana hadn't been personally harmed, but the focus of that attack was indeed personal. Dana and I hadn't been involved at that time, but I'd expressed my admiration for her and enthused about the photograph I purchased. Had Mama interpreted that as undue interest? I wondered if the destruction of Dana's apartment had been meant as a warning, rather than as bodily harm.

I wondered about the attack in the hotel parking lot. Was that intended for Dana, too? Had I just been in the way? Or had it really just been a particularly violent crime of opportunity?

I recalled the attack in St. Paris. That was personal and direct: someone wanted to hurt Dana.

Looking at Peter, I asked, "Has your home been burgled? Your property stolen or destroyed lately? Have you been attacked?"

His black eyes glinted. His voice was quiet so as not to be overheard. "Yes."

Elaine's eyes widened with horror.

"What happened?"

"I couldn't say."

"I won't be calling the law," I whispered and meant it.

"I left their bodies in the desert."

"*What?*" Elaine shrilled. We shushed her. Eyes blazing, she hissed in a dangerous undertone, "You were *attacked*? And you didn't tell me?"

"Nothin' you could've done about it, darlin'."

I mulled that over and recalled Dad's words: "*I make sure your mama always gets what she wants.*"

Mama wanted Dana out of the way.

Dear God, Dad's in on it.

My stomach churned. I met Peter's gaze and said, "Get her out of here, out of Texas."

"They've got a long reach, Sam."

"They can't force my sister to marry Bradley Vermont if she's already your wife."

"They probably can if I'm widowed," Elaine whispered, her eyes shining with tears. "I'm not as strong or as resourceful as you, Sam. I never was, never will be."

"What about Toby?" I asked.

She shook her head. "Toby does whatever Mama and Dad tell him. Hell, he's already offered to marry Deborah Baker-Cunningham in your stead, poor girl. She's a better match than the little Carmichael girl—at least Debbie's an adult."

Distaste churned in my gut, but I had to admit that Elaine was right. Debbie the debutante could accept or refuse my brother; the Carmichaels' 12-year-old daughter had no such option, especially since powerful, wealthy families like ours could easily purchase immunity from the law.

"Do you want us to wait here with you?" Elaine interrupted my thoughts.

I sighed. "No. No, leave. Don't go back to the house to get your stuff: just go."

"I'll keep her safe," Peter promised. He wrapped his arm around Elaine's shoulders and murmured, "Come on, honey, let's go."

She nodded and meekly let him take her away. The worried look in her eyes asked, *Who will keep Peter safe?*

I wished I had an answer.

Chapter 43

Dana

Black oblivion receded, leaving pain and nausea and weakness in its wake. Bright overhead light pummeled my eyes through the red glare of my eyelids. Antiseptic odors filled my nostrils. My ears caught irregular announcements and summons over a public address system, the quiet squeak of rubber-soled shoes, and occasional moans from the distance.

It didn't take a genius to realize I was in a hospital.

"Water," I rasped through a parched throat and dry, cracked lips.

A thick arm slid beneath my neck and lifted me while an unseen hand held cool plastic to my bottom lip.

"Just a sip, honey," a masculine voice urged.

Tepid, stale water trickled over my lip and into my mouth. I let it rest there a bit before swallowing. Swallowing hurt.

"More."

Another small mouthful dribbled in. Then a third.

"That's enough for now," another voice said. "We'll see if that little bit stays down before giving her more."

"When will she be able to go home?" the first voice asked.

"Probably in a day or two. It depends on how rapidly she improves. She nearly died, you know."

"Yes, I know."

"You still haven't explained how she came to ingest whatever poison that was. It didn't show up on any of our standard tests."

"I'm more concerned that she recovers than with assigning blame."

The second voice turned stern. "Then you'll be extra careful to ensure no such thing happens again."

With diamond hardness, the first voice replied, "You can be sure of that."

"Pumpkin?" a third voice I recognized burst into the conversation.

My eyelids fluttered open, then snapped shut again.

"Dim the lights," the third voice snapped. "Can't you see it's too bright for her right now?"

The red glare through my eyelids darkened, soothed. With caution, I opened my eyes again and blinked against the blurred figures standing bedside. One wore a white and green. I assumed that one was the doctor: green scrubs and a white lab coat. Another appeared as a shadow, black, with a golden halo. The third in blue smelled familiar, of English Leather with an undertone of kitchen grease.

"Daddy?"

Warm hands enveloped one of mine, which brought to notice the cool tubing to which I was attached. *Ah, intravenous drip.* A bristled cheek bent close, dry lips surrounded by prickles brushing a kiss to my forehead.

"Oh, pumpkin, I came as soon as I could. Shirley's minding the diner."

"I wanna to go home, Daddy."

"I know, baby girl. And you will."

I sighed, thoughts in my cotton wool brain drifting and dissolving until one struck me.

"Sly? How's Sly?"

The big hands gave mine a light squeeze. "He's doing fine, Dana. I've been eating allergy meds like candy so he can have the run of the house."

A smile tugged at my mouth and something tight eased within my heart.

"He's a good kitty."

"Yeah, he is."

I yawned.

"You sleep now, pumpkin." A light touch of fingers brushed hair back from my forehead. "And as soon as you're ready, I'll take you home."

Chapter 44

Sam

Larry Secrest rose to his full height, which wasn't but an inch or two less than mine, and glared at me with all the fury of an outraged father.

"You said you'd keep her safe."

Every word hammered at me and I absorbed each blow. "I did."

"You failed."

"I did."

"Give me one reason why I shouldn't—"

"Gentlemen, this is not the place for such a discussion," the doctor whom we'd both forgotten about said. "Take it outside this hospital now, or I will call security to have you removed and barred from any further entry."

Larry and I both took deep breaths to calm ourselves and walked out of the stepdown unit. We sat in the lobby. It was time to level with Dana's stepfather and apologize.

"Larry, I truly am sorry—"

"You know who did this and why," the small town cook leveled a hard glare at me, reminding me that he'd once been in the military, too, and knew how to use a gun. "You're the one who put my little girl in harm's way."

I sighed and nodded and raised a hand, a gesture begging for patience, for forbearance. "Larry, please hear me out before you say anything further."

Upper lip curling in a sneer, he crossed his arms and leaned back. "Go on then."

I caught the unsaid epithet *punk* that he didn't say and said, "Yes, I do know why and who. I didn't before."

"And you're not going to do anything about it."

"I can't."

"Won't."

I bowed my head and took another breath. "All right then, won't—not because Dana doesn't deserve justice, but because some people are beyond its reach."

"No one is above the law, Sam. Just a couple months ago, two senators were convicted for insider trading," he pointed out.

"The people responsible for what happened to Dana *own* senators, as well as governors, judges, and other civil authorities. They wield immense financial, social, and political power and influence."

The older man's eyes narrowed. "Is Vermont responsible?"

"For the attacks on Dana? No. I suspect he was involved in Omar Harimadi's execution which Dana inadvertently photographed. Her pictures were turned over to the police."

"That doesn't address my concern."

"I'm working out a deal," I said. "I can't tell you more than that. If I'm successful, then Dana will be safe."

"And if not?"

"Then we're all screwed."

Larry wasn't satisfied with our discussion and I couldn't blame him. He returned to Dana's room to sit at her bedside and hold her hand and talk to her. I stepped outside into the facility's "contemplation garden" and called my former client.

"I spoke to Avel Skliar," I said, referring to a clipped, tense, and brief conversation I'd coerced my father into arranging when I confronted him with Mama's heinous act. His protestations of shock hadn't appeased me much at all, but his reaction to my threat to expose both him and her for their crimes did.

"Who?"

"Don't play stupid with me, Brad. Skliar admits you ordered the hit on Harimadi."

"What's this about, Sam?"

"Dad bought Skliar. Money's very persuasive, you know."

Brad hesitated, then demanded, "What do you want?"

"You leave Sonya, Dana, Gordon, and me alone. I'll give you the ammunition you need to rein in Samuel Macintyre Galdicar, III."

"And this ammunition has a name?"

"It does. But first, you agree to my terms."

"Fine, I wash my hands of you, Gordon, Sonya, and her bitchy little friend. Now, why would I care about your father?"

"You don't, but you do care about money and power."

I could almost hear his shrug.

"So?"

"What I want you to do is stage a hostile takeover of one of Dad's more profitable ventures."

"And how will I do that?"

"I have the information you need and I'll even help you by handing over my shares of that company."

"And in return?"

"You wait. I'll let you know if I need you to pounce again."

"What are you playing at, Sam?"

"Cat and mouse, only this time I'm the cat." I took a break. "I'll send you the information. Let me know as soon as the transaction is completed."

"Nice doing business with you, asshole."

As promised, I sent the information. A keen eye on the transaction showed a rapid transfer of majority interest to Bradley Vermont's control. I smiled and called my father: "Meet me in the contemplation garden. Bring Toby, too."

I waited an hour.

"Boy, you have a lot of gall summoning me here," Dad greeted me, a thunderous expression on his face. I noticed he didn't include Toby as a recipient of that offense.

Toby maintained a carefully neutral expression, but his eyes were sharp, calculating.

"Have a seat," I said and gestured toward a pair of park benches organized in a conversational grouping.

We sat.

"We're going to make a deal," I said without preamble. Dad opened his mouth, but I forestalled him with an up-raised hand. I showed him the corporate takeover on my phone. Toby's eyes widened, then narrowed. He pulled out his phone and checked with the corporate finance department to verify.

"We no longer control the Oklahoma oil fields," he confirmed. "Bradley Vermont owns the majority share, sixty percent."

"What's going on, Sam?" Dad growled.

I met his gaze and held it. "You know what Mama did. Worse, you don't care."

He shrugged again, not admitting to anything.

Toby's eyes widened again. "*Mama's* responsible for what happened to your—"

"Don't you dare insult her," I snarled.

"—girl?"

His surprise and horrified expression gave me hope that Toby could be redeemed, that he maintained a few moral standards.

"That's *murder*," he hissed, appalled.

"Mama is clearly unhinged and out of control," I murmured, holding my father's icy gaze with my own. "Beginning now, you will ensure Mama harms no one and that *you* act according to the highest moral standard, or I will *beggar* this family."

The muscle at the base of my father's jaw bulged, he clenched his teeth so hard.

I twisted the knife just a little more. "And you *will* keep me updated on *all* corporate holdings every month, just like always. Toby, I expect you to take over as CEO within the next two years. I know you'll keep the business thriving and I will expect to be informed of *everything*."

Toby asked a question I hadn't expected. "What about Debbie?"

"Debbie? You mean Deborah Baker-Cunningham?"

"Yeah."

I shrugged. "Toby, the best thing that will ever happen to you is to fall in love with a good woman. If you don't love Debbie, then don't marry her."

That reminded me. I focused again on my father. "Don't you *dare* make any agreement regarding the Carmichael girl."

Dad stood. He brushed off his pants and tugged on his jacket. "If you're finished making demands, I'll take my leave."

I waved my hand. "I trust I won't have to see you again, because there won't be any second chances."

"Don't flog a dead horse, boy."

I allowed myself a small smile at the analogy. Toby rose to follow our father. For the first time in years, he looked at me without bitter resentment and held out his hand. I shook it.

"Thanks, Sam."

"Do me proud, Toby."

Chapter 45

Dana

February winds blustered cold and strong off Lake Michigan. Small, puffy clouds skittered high in a pale blue sky. Snow sparkled like broken shards of glass where weak winter sunshine struck it. On the ice beyond, a temporary village of fishing shacks had sprouted, populated mostly by grizzled, beer guzzling men who found no greater joy than ice fishing. The scene charmed me. I raised my new camera and adjusted the focus. (Sam kindly purchased new equipment for me. The insurance check had come in, and I was determined to use it to reimburse him.) My fingers, red with cold, tingled a warning that I'd best get this shot quickly before frostbite took up residence.

Michigan's upper peninsula offered spectacular beauty regardless of the season, but its winter weather left much to be desired. I glanced back at the cozy cabin where Sam had sent me and Dad while I convalesced.

Who knew that many of the summer vacation cabins were so well insulated against winter weather?

I snapped the shot, capped the lens, and headed back to the cabin. The blast of frigid air announced my return.

Without turning around, Dad called out, "Put your gear away and wash your hands, pumpkin. Lunch is ready."

I wrinkled my nose, but didn't complain. A moment later, I sat at the small kitchen table and spooned Dad's renowned tomato bisque into my mouth. Sly twined his fat, sinuous body around the legs of the chair and my own legs, looking up at me with big eyes in silent pleading for table scraps. I reached down to scratch his head, then straightened and took another slurp of soup.

"You did something different to it," I commented and took a sip of water.

"A dash of Tabasco and a dollop of sour cream."

"Ah. It's good, really good."

He smiled, pleased at the genuine compliment. I seldom minded being his guinea pig.

"You gonna add it to the menu?"

He glanced at the calendar hanging on the wall and grinned. "Shirley's more than ready for me to come back."

"I'll bet."

"I'm leaving tomorrow."

"Tomorrow?" Dread filled me. I set down my spoon. I did not want to be alone. Sly nuzzled my ankle, reminding me that I wouldn't be alone: I had him. I reached down to pet him again.

"Don't worry, pumpkin. I stocked the fridge and the pantry."

"But—"

"But nothing. You've enjoyed being a little girl again for her daddy to take care of, but it's time for you to grow up and resume being an adult. And I have to get back to my own life."

"But—"

"Sam says renovation of the house is finished and he's settled the other details." Dad alluded to the arrangement

Sam negotiated with his family and Bradley Vermont. He hadn't divulged the specifics, but only assured me that I'd never have to fear his mother's evil scheming and machinations again, or his father's insults. He also assured me that Toby was reforming, but I had my doubts.

"Sam's sister called while you were outside," Dad said. "Peter placed second in the latest rodeo. Reno, I think."

"Didn't he crack a couple of ribs two weeks ago?" I asked.

"Yeah, but these bull riders are tough and stupid, been kicked or landed on their heads a few too many times."

I grinned. Peter hadn't struck me as stupid. Tough? Yes.

"Did she say how Sam's doing?" I hadn't heard from him since leaving the hospital. "Is he coming?"

"No, she didn't."

My heart sank.

"You know I'm not happy with him, don't you, pumpkin? I don't think he's good for you."

"What happened wasn't his fault, Dad."

"He promised to protect you, to keep you safe, and I trusted him to do so." He grimaced at his own bad judgment. "He failed and you almost died."

I shuddered. "No one could have expected him to assume his mother wanted to kill me. Besides, he did fix it, he's made sure I'm safe."

Dad muttered something profane under his breath. I paid little attention to it.

"You gonna be okay, pumpkin?" Dad's eyes brimmed with concern.

I nodded and exhaled and squared my shoulders. "Yeah. Yeah, I'll be okay as long as I don't eat anything too spicy." I glanced at the bowl of soup. "This is good, but probably pushing my limits."

"Baby steps."

"Yeah."

After lunch, I took a nap. When I awoke, Dad's bags were packed and sitting by the door. I wondered for a moment how I'd get around when he took the rented vehicle to the airport, then remembered that, since arriving, I hadn't gone anywhere I couldn't walk. The tiny Catholic church, the corner drugstore, and the small library in the tidy village clustered on the Great Lake's shore where I sometimes encountered the parish's elderly priest who lived out his so-called retirement thousands of miles from where he'd grown up. I loved listening to his lilting Irish accent.

The wind died down to a strong breeze and I headed outside again, wandering along the village's periphery and listening to wolves howl in the distance from within the enormous forest a few miles beyond the village. The forest stretched far across the Canadian border and housed wolves, cougars, bobcats, bears, moose, deer, and other wildlife that recognized no national boundaries. Locals advised against going out alone at night when the big predators were feeling peckish. I saw the flicker of a prowling shadow and ducked into the village's one coffee shop.

"Well, hello there, Dana," the barista hailed as warm air redolent with the rich fragrance of roasted coffee beans swirled around me like a friendly hug.

"Hey, Susan," I replied with a smile. "I think I saw a mountain lion out there."

"Probably," she acknowledged. "There have been reports of some big cat tracks around some of the houses. You know moose are probably more dangerous than either the cats or wolves? Anyway, you shouldn't be wandering alone this close to evening."

I shrugged and took off my coat, hanging it on the convenient coat tree near the front entrance. I slid into a tall chair at the bar. "Hot chocolate, please?"

She smiled and poured me a large mug and topped it with whipped cream. I fished out some cash and set it on the wooden countertop.

"Dad's leaving tomorrow," I blurted after taking a first appreciative sip.

She nodded with sage understanding, although she was younger than I. "He can't put his life on hold for you forever."

"That's pretty much what he said."

She nodded again. "I know you were pretty sick when you arrived, but you look like you've recovered."

I didn't correct the assumption that I'd been ill. I preferred the world at large thinking that instead of them knowing my lover's mother had tried to kill me because I didn't fit in with her plans for world domination.

"I've noticed you wandering about with a fancy looking camera," Susan remarked, changing the subject. "You a professional photographer?"

"Yeah."

"That's cool. One of my friends has a cousin who takes pictures for *National Geographic*. You do anything like that?"

"Not really my bailiwick," I admitted. "I prefer landscapes."

"Oh? Maybe I've seen your stuff somewhere?"

I pulled out my phone and located my website showing the latest calendar project completed and available for sale. I slid the device across the counter. "This is my stuff."

She scrolled through the pictures. "Wow, that's awesome."

"Thank you."

She slid the cell phone back to me and asked, "Have you ever thought of having a gallery showing?"

I chuckled and explained my one and only gallery showing in which I'd had three pieces among hundreds. I remembered Sam had purchased one of them.

"Well, I'm sure you'll have better luck next time."

"I hope so," I replied, her words making me think that maybe I really should negotiate a second gallery showing. My spirits brightened and I felt the surge of energy that accompanies a new goal.

It felt *good* to have purpose and direction again.

Chapter 46

Sam

I shivered as the cold wind cut through my coat and layers of clothing beneath that. A quick peek through the window showed Dana snuggled in an overstuffed arm-chair, the cat on her lap while she read a book. A mug gently wafted steam on the end table beside her. She looked calm, content, and healthy. I sighed, breath puffing from my lungs like tobacco smoke, and rapped gloved knuckles on the door. A few seconds later she opened the door.

"Sam?" Her hazel eyes looked bright. "Sam!"

Dana threw her arms around me. I staggered back a step at the force of her body launching into mine, one arm wrapping around her and the other clamping onto the door jamb.

"Sam, you're here!"

I walked us inside and closed the door behind. Without removing my gloves, I cupped her face and held her where I wanted. With searching eyes, I examined her for any lingering signs of illness and saw only a face and form a little gaunt for my preference, but Dana glowed with life and vitality. As inexorably drawn to her as though magnetized, I lowered my mouth to hers and devoured her.

"Rusticating looks good on you," I complimented when I had to draw back to breathe.

She grinned. "That and Dad's cooking. Oh, Sam, I'm so glad to see you again."

"You've been well?" I needed her verbal reassurance.

"I take a long walk every day. I've made some friends in the village. I even went ice fishing last week." She took a breath and added, "And I've been taking photos."

"That's good news, kitten."

She withdrew from my embrace. "I'm being remiss. Here, let me take your coat. Would you like some hot tea? The kettle's still steaming. Or I could get you a soda. I'm sorry, but I don't have any alcohol here. Or coffee."

"Tea would be great, thank you." I divested myself of hat, gloves, and coat and hung them on the coat rack. Seeing her in winter weight leggings and an oversized, tunic-length sweater made my dick twitch and begin to swell. I headed to the sofa and sat before the bulge became noticeable.

The cat hopped onto the sofa and crawled into my lap, settling himself with a decisive plop. I ran a hand over the soft pelt. "Yeah, I missed you, too, buddy."

The cat stretched out a paw, claws extended, and pricked one sharp claw through the layers of cloth. I quelled a hiss of pain. My erection withered. The cat retracted the claw and tucked its paw away and purred, as though content in having accomplished its mission.

Damned cat.

Dana returned shortly with a steaming mug. She placed it in my hand and went back to the armchair. She met my gaze with brave candor and said, "I owe you gratitude."

"I don't want your gratitude, Dana."

"Perhaps not," she said softly. "But you have it anyway."

I took a sip of tea.

"You look tired. Perhaps you could use some rusticating as well?"

I was tired. Instead of explaining that, I changed the subject. "I have news from Sonya."

"How is she? Is she okay?"

"The divorce is finalized," I said. "She didn't fight the prenuptial agreement, but Bradley settled a few million on her anyway. He'll never miss it, and she'll never need to work if she doesn't want to and doesn't squander the money."

"Oh, that's good. I worried."

"She's engaged."

"Engaged?" Dana's eyebrows nearly hit her hairline. "That was fast. To whom?"

"Gordon Pasquale."

She frowned, searching her memory. "Wasn't he one of her bodyguards? Older guy, graying at the temples?"

I winced, because Gordon wasn't all that much older than I. "Yes, but he's not her bodyguard anymore."

"Is he ... is he ... you know ... weird?"

I knew what she meant. "Sonya's happy with him and he'll never harm her."

Dana frowned.

"You won't have to worry about seeing bruises on your friend."

She relaxed. "Oh, good." She tensed again. "And ... your family?"

I gave her a reassuring smile. "Elaine and Peter are fine. Happy. Mama and Dad are ... contained. There'll be no more shenanigans from them. And Toby's improving, no longer having to dance to their tune."

Her expression revealed doubt as to that last statement, but without them interacting, I couldn't prove my brother's onset of redemption. I doubted I'd ever get her consent to tolerate his presence and understood that, even if it hurt. She had no reason to think well of him.

Conversation stuttered to an awkward halt.

"I called a gallery," she announced, her voice sounding hesitant.

"Oh?"

A tentative smile illuminated her face. "Well, actually, I called nine galleries. Um, yeah. I had them look at my online portfolio." Her smile stretched wide and her eyes gleamed with pride and enthusiasm. "One of them really likes my stuff. They've agreed to host a show in May. Isn't that fabulous?"

"It's wonderful," I agreed. "I'm proud of you, kitten. You have an amazing eye, and your photographs ought to be celebrated around the world."

A cloud of doubt dimmed her smile. "Do you really think so?"

"Yes."

Conversation again lagged. I said nothing about having picked up two new clients, one of whom was an A-list celebrity in Hollywood. I offered no details about the deal I hammered out with Bradley Vermont and Samuel Macintyre Galdicar III. I made no mention of having secured the services of Rita Zorokowski and the other razor-toothed sharks in her firm to write and administer the water-tight contracts that would enforce their compliance and obedience. I did not speak of how my father had hired a small army of medical personnel to manage Mama and keep her confined to the property. Their vigilance would render her harmless and ensure she stayed that way.

All Dana needed to know was that she was safe. I did not want to dim her bright spirit with unnecessary worry or fear. I wanted her attention focused on me, at least for now. After having neither seen or spoken with her in over four weeks, I ached to touch her and to be touched by her. I yearned to taste her, to feel her mouth on me. I missed her breathy sighs and soft moans of exquisite pleasure, the high, keening cry she made when she climaxed. I longed to return to heaven, to slide inside her body until I could not distinguish between her flesh and mine.

Beneath the cat lounging on my lap, my groin thickened again. Sly again extended one front leg and flexed his claws.

"Don't do it," I warned under my breath.

"I got a call from Dad yesterday," Dana volunteered, picking up our paused conversation. "He says the house looks great."

I nodded, pleased that he approved of the renovation. Without changing the building's footprint, the crew I hired had fast-tracked a completely new house for him. No physical memory remained to remind him of the night my mother's hired thugs had broken into his home and tried to kill his beloved stepdaughter. I thought it the least I could do.

"He doesn't want me to come home." She sounded forlorn.

"He wants you to realize how strong and capable you are. You can stand on your own two feet, kitten. He'll always welcome your visits."

She blinked, then averted her gaze. Her chin trembled.

So much, lately, had been out of her control. I understood that it was difficult to take charge of her own life again. As much as I wanted to coddle her, I knew she needed more. She needed the offer of shelter, not enforced confinement. Otherwise her spirit would suffer and she'd wilt like a neglected plant denied water and sunlight.

"I had some remodeling done in my condo," I announced.

"Oh?" Her interest was polite, nothing more.

"I had a dark room built."

"Oh?" Her interest piqued as did her suspicion.

"I was thinking you would come back to Chicago with me."

Something flickered in her eyes. Pain? Disappointment? "You want a roommate?"

"No."

She frowned. "I can't just live with you as your girlfriend, and I can't yet afford to pay the kind of rent worthy of your condo."

I smiled at her assertion of self-respect, glad that hadn't dimmed. "I'm sure you won't."

"Building a dark room sounds like you're pretty sure I will."

"Hopeful," I admitted. I shoved the cat off my lap and shifted to my knees. Kneeling in front of her, I dug into a pocket and pulled out a small box, flipping the lid open. Diamonds sparkled against gleaming gold. "I'm hoping you'll live with me forever. We'll buy or build a house with a nice, big yard for our children and maybe a couple of dogs. And Sly, too. Maybe we'll get a kitten he can torture. And we'll grow old together."

She blinked shining eyes, wet with unspilled tears.

"Dana, will you marry me?"

Her jaw worked. "I ... I ..."

"I love you, kitten. I've loved you for so much longer than I ever wanted to admit."

Warm tears dripped down her cheeks. "Oh, Sam, I love you, too."

My hands trembled as I removed the diamond ring from its box and slid it over the third finger of her left hand. Sly tried to crawl onto my thighs. I pushed the cat away. I cupped her cheek and wiped the tears away with my thumb.

"It's beautiful," she breathed, blinking at the fiery shards of light refracting from the small, clear stones adorning her slender finger.

"You're beautiful," I stated.

She seemed to realize she hadn't answered my question. "I don't know what to say."

"Say yes," I urged, clasping her hands. "Say you'll marry me and be mine. Let me love you forever."

"Yes."

I kissed her. She kissed me back. And one thing led to another until the cat scratched at the closed bedroom door, demanding to be let into the room while I made Dana cry out over and over again with each orgasm in an effort to make sure her body never forgot she belonged to me as much as I belonged to her.

Thank you!

Thank you for reading *Focus*. As an "indie" author, I realize you have an overwhelming number of choices in reading material and am conscious of the honor you do me in choosing to read this book.

Like every other author in this digital age, I depend upon reader reviews. Not only does your review help to bring this book to the attention of other readers, but your comments help me to improve forthcoming stories. I take reader comments seriously and consider reader insights when writing.

Please leave a review!

I deeply appreciate your willingness to purchase this book and spend your valuable time reading it. I hope you enjoyed the story as much as I enjoyed writing it.

Books by Holly Bargo

Since 2015, I have published over 20 titles spanning fantasy, romance, and westerns. All my books, listed on the following pages, are available for purchase from Amazon, except where noted with an asterisk. Check my author page on Amazon:

https://www.amazon.com/Holly-Bargo/e/ B00JRK6VGQ.

All books within each series are written as complete, standalone novels. For my readers' peace of mind and my own, I don't write cliffhangers.

Tree of Life Series

Rowan
Cassia
Willow

Immortal Shifters Series

The Barbary Lion*
Tiger in the Snow
Bear of the Midnight Sun
The Eagle at Dawn

Twin Moons Saga

Daughter of the Twin Moons
Daughter of the Deepwood
Daughter of the Dark Moon

Russian Love Series

Russian Lullaby

Russian Gold
Russian Dawn
Russian Pride

Other Novels

The Diamond Gate
The Dragon Wore a Kilt
The Falcon of Imenotash
Hogtied
The Mighty Finn
Pure Iron
Triple Burn
Ulfbehrt's Legacy

Short Story Collections

Satin Boots: Six Short Romances of the Old West

Shot from the Hip: 12 Tales of the Old West

Six Shots Each Gun: 12 Tales of the Old West
co-written with Russ Towne

Individual Short Stories

By Water Reborn*
Skeins of Gold: Rumpelstiltskin Retold*

Available for free download from the Hen House Publishing website (www.henhousepublishing.com).

About the Author

Holly Bargo is a pseudonym and really did exist as a temperamental Appaloosa mare fondly remembered for watching over the author's toddler children and crushing the author's husband's pager. (If your electronics device manufacturer no longer warrants destruction by livestock, blame it on us.)

Holly works full-time as a freelance writer and editor, applying 30 years of professional writing and editing experience. Her project experience encompasses books, newsletters, brochures, blogs, and other documents for a wide range of clients.

Married for over 30 years, Holly lives on a hobby farm in southwest Ohio with, yes, horses. Morgans, mainly. She blames her mother and Laura Ingalls Wilder for that particular preference. Holly and her husband also have two adult children, several cats, and one very big, yellow-bellied coward of a dog.

Made in the USA
Monee, IL
13 March 2025

13624280R00187